BACK TO MOSCOW

BACK TO MOSCOW

GUILLERMO ERADES

FARRAR, STRAUS AND GIROUX   NEW YORK

Farrar, Straus and Giroux
18 West 18th Street, New York 10011

Printed in the United States of America
Originally published in 2016 by Scribner, Great Britain
Published in the United States by Farrar, Straus and Giroux
First American edition, 2016

Chapters 4 and 11 were originally published in *American Literary Review*.

Library of Congress Cataloging-in-Publication Data
Names: Erades, Guillermo, 1975–
Title: Back to Moscow / Guillermo Erades.
Description: First American edition. | New York : Farrar, Straus and Giroux, 2016.
Identifiers: LCCN 2015036471 | ISBN 9780865478374 (hardcover) |
ISBN 9780374714307 (e-book)
Subjects: LCSH: Doctoral students—Fiction. | Moscow (Russia)—Social life
and customs—Fiction. | GSAFD: Love stories
Classification: LCC PS3605.R325 B33 2016 | DDC 813/.6—dc23
LC record available at http://lccn.loc.gov/2015036471

Our books may be purchased in bulk for promotional, educational, or business use.
Please contact your local bookseller or the Macmillan Corporate and
Premium Sales Department at 1-800-221-7945, extension 5442,
or by e-mail at MacmillanSpecialMarkets@macmillan.com.

www.fsgbooks.com
www.twitter.com/fsgbooks • www.facebook.com/fsgbooks

1   3   5   7   9   10   8   6   4   2

Ольга: (. . .) я чувствую, как из меня выходят каждый день по каплям и силы, и молодость. И только растет и крепнет одна мечта . . .

Ирина: Уехать в Москву. Продать дом, покончить все здесь и – в Москву . . .

Ольга: Да! Скорее в Москву.

Антон Чехов. *Три сестры*

Olga: (. . .) I feel how every day my strength and my youth are leaving me, drop by drop. Only one dream grows and gets stronger . . .

Irina: To go back to Moscow. To sell the house, to finish everything here, and – to Moscow . . .

Olga: Yes! As soon as possible, to Moscow.

Anton Chekhov, *Three Sisters*

BACK TO MOSCOW

FIRST I NOTICED THE cockroaches. Smaller, quicker. Every time the lights went on, I glimpsed their glossy mahogany shells darting across the floor. They were called tarakany and, perhaps because I liked the word, I felt no hostility towards them. They roamed freely around my room, enjoying the darkness beneath the rusty cot, crawling up the cracked walls, onto the desk – totally unconcerned by my presence.

Other than the cockroaches, Sektor E was deserted. On my first night I'd ventured into the maze of corridors hoping to bump into other international students. To my disappointment, I'd heard nothing but the creaking of the wooden floors under my feet. I'd located the communal kitchen, strewn with empty vodka bottles and crushed beer cans. The fridges were stocked with a wide selection of used ketchup

1

and rancid milk, courtesy of the language students who had fled the university at the end of summer, just before my arrival.

With nothing else to do, every night I would go for dinner at the sixth-floor bufet. The bufet was always empty and smelled, like the rest of the university building, of rotten wood and disinfectant. I would sit at the corner table, trying to read a bit of Chekhov, the greasy plastic tablecloth sticking to my elbows. On each table stood a glass bud vase with a single red flower. They were made of plastic, these flowers, but for some reason the vases always contained water.

As soon as I opened my book, a chubby lady with bleached hair and heavy make-up would storm in from the kitchen, slap the menu on the table and wait, hands on hips, for my order – her beefy body exuding a kind of impatience and irritation I was, in those early days, unaccustomed to.

The menu in front of me, a simple sheet of paper, bore a short list of dishes handwritten in Cyrillic. To my despair, I was unable to identify the different letters, let alone understand the meaning of the words. Nor could I rely on the lady's assistance – she had made it clear during our first encounter that it was not her job to make any particular effort to communicate with me, her only evening customer and yet a stupid nekulturniy foreigner.

Undeterred, I would stare for a few seconds at the menu, nodding slightly, as if to indicate that I somehow understood what was written on the paper, that I was indeed considering the different choices.

'Soup,' I would say, every night, but I'd pronounce the

word in a guttural way, making it sound, at least to my ears, more local.

So it was soup every night, with Chekhov as my dinner companion.

Now, when I look back at those uneventful nights, I feel a soft wave of nostalgia washing through my chest. So treacherous is the nature of memory that I can't fully evoke the boredom, sadness and disappointment I surely felt back then. What I recall when I picture my younger self reading the short stories of Anton Pavlovich in an empty canteen, is a sweet sense of tranquillity which, in truth, I might have not felt at the time. I'm aware that it's only from the vantage point of years passed that I now see those days as the calm prelude to the life I was sucked into — and to the tragic events that ended it.

One Tuesday night, two weeks after my arrival, I went for dinner later than usual and found two other international students at the bufet. They were chatting in English over the remains of dinner and cups of instant coffee. By their accents I guessed that the one who did most of the talking was American — the other one Latin American, perhaps Spanish. They wore well-ironed shirts, hair gel, cologne.

I pretended to read my Chekhov book, excited but unsure about how best to approach them, not wanting to look desperate or lonely. I waited patiently for a pause in their conversation and, adopting as casual a tone as I could muster, I jumped in.

'You guys going out tonight?'

'Sure,' the American said. 'Tuesday. Ladies' night at the Duck.'

'The Duck?'

'Man, you don't know the Hungry Duck?'

'I'm afraid not,' I said.

'How long have you been here?'

'Two weeks.'

And that's how I met Colin.

I put Chekhov aside and joined their table.

An hour later, the three of us were heading towards the city centre in a battered zhiguli we'd hailed outside the university. Colin sat in the front seat, chatting to the driver, giving directions. I couldn't understand what he was saying but I could see he knew his way around. Diego, who turned out to be Mexican, sat in the back, telling me how he had arrived in town, just a few months earlier, to study engineering. He had managed to score a little-known scholarship for Latin American students, he was saying, not too generous but enough to get by as long as he lived in the university residence. 'Awesome place,' Diego said, pointing to the dark city. 'You're going to love it.'

Following Colin's instructions, the driver pulled over by a small produkty shop where we bought a bottle of Stolichnaya and a few plastic glasses. Then the zhiguli drove through avenues five or six lanes wide, crossed the river, and passed beneath hanging traffic lights, which seemed to work but were largely ignored by the driver.

The zhiguli dropped us next to a metro stop. By foot we continued through a covered alley into a dark parking lot. We arrived at a poorly lit door and joined a group of young guys waiting in the cold.

4

'Vodka time!' Colin opened the Stolichnaya bottle and filled our plastic goblets. 'To the Duck,' he said, half smiling, 'best club on Earth.'

Colin's half-smile, I later learned, was a permanent facial feature, not meant to convey any particular emotion; every time he talked, the half-smile made him look as if he knew more than he was willing to share.

We drank up. The vodka warmed my throat. My stomach burned and shivered: the thirsty little Cossack inside me, expecting another quiet Chekhov night, had been caught by surprise.

More people arrived and joined the queue, bouncing on their feet to keep warm. As far as I could tell, they were all guys, all expats, all about our age.

After pouring more vodka into our plastic glasses, Colin grabbed my shoulder and said, 'Believe me, man, there is no better place to be young, foreign and male.' I couldn't tell if he was talking about the club or the city, but I agreed with a wide smile.

I glanced at other guys in the queue. They were drinking, smoking, chatting. I couldn't stop smiling and they returned the smile, with little nods. By the time we were done with the bottle of vodka, I felt an unspoken but strong connection among all of us in the queue – a sense of camaraderie and shared anticipation.

Suddenly I was no longer thinking about Katya or Amsterdam. The thirsty little Cossack was cheerful: up on his horse, rattling his sabre, ready for battle.

At eleven sharp the door of the club was opened from the

inside and I found myself carried through the entrance by an all-male stampede. I was pushed into a corridor lined with mirrors, where some of the guys hurriedly retouched their hair, and there was a booth where we paid the cover and a cloakroom where we dropped our jackets.

At the far end of the bright corridor, a black metal door throbbed with loud music. As we approached, my heart pumping fast, I was taken aback by the stench of spilt beer and vomit. I held my breath.

Colin pulled the door and beckoned me in. 'Welcome to the Duck.'

Stepping into the main room, I was slapped by a wave of wet heat. It was balmy and smoky and dark, and at first I saw only the colours of the disco lights – laser reds and greens and purples – but as my eyes adapted to darkness, I started to discern what, I later learned, *The Exile* was describing as the wildest clubbing scene in the Northern Hemisphere.

Hundreds of dyevs dancing under the strobe lights. On the chairs. On the tables. Singing, screaming, their eyes red and watery, their clothes drenched in sweat. A bunch of them danced topless on the bar, bouncing their shiny young breasts, waving their bras over the all-female crowd.

They had arrived at the Duck hours earlier, from all over the city, from the most remote metro stations and trashy suburbs, and by the time we guys were allowed to enter – Tuesday night, eleven sharp – they had drunk themselves into submission.

These were the same dyevs who just a few months later

would wear fake designer clothes with glittering logos to make it into Zeppelin or Shambala, and would only talk to us if we bought them overpriced cocktails and glasses of champagne; but back then, at the Hungry Duck, they gulped down tons of free beer, vomited on the carpets, stumbled among the tables and, when they were so wasted they could no longer stand on their cheap high heels, they threw themselves into the arms of those of us blessed with the chance to live, at such a turbulent moment of its history, in the wonderful city of Moscow.

PART ONE

Tatyana's Lesson

1

ON 8 JUNE 1880, shortly before he died, Fyodor Mikhailovich Dostoyevsky walked onto a stage in central Moscow and, in front of a cheering crowd, delivered a long and emotional speech to celebrate the unveiling of Pushkin's statue. According to several accounts of the event, which were captured in the diaries and journals of the time, the atmosphere was electrifying. Fyodor Mikhailovich himself wrote later that day that the crowd kept interrupting him, applauding enthusiastically every few sentences, standing up in ovation.

At the very end of the speech, the audience completely lost it when Dostoyevsky made his impassioned call to follow Pushkin's example and embrace both the uniqueness of Mother Russia and the oneness of humanity.

What came to be known as the Pushkin Speech had an enormous impact on Russia's intelligentsia at the time. It soon became one of the defining moments in the cultural history of the country – a new chapter in Russia's endless debate between those in favour of a Western course for their country and those, such as Fyodor Mikhailovich himself, who saw Russia as a unique nation with a crucial role to play in the history of humanity.

By the time he delivered the speech, Fyodor Mikhailovich was an old man in poor health. He felt this was his last opportunity to set the record straight on Pushkin, to prove that, to Russians, Pushkin was much more than 'just' the national poet. In a letter he wrote to his wife a few days before the speech, Dostoyevsky had said his participation in the event would be essential, as 'the others' were not only determined to downplay the importance of Pushkin in Russia's national identity, they were also ready to deny the very existence of this identity.

My voice will carry weight, Dostoyevsky wrote.

That day in June, Fyodor Mikhailovich talked about Pushkin's prophetic existence, and his role in understanding and defining the Russian character. Dostoyevsky made it clear that, without Pushkin's genius, there would be no Russian literature, at least not as the world knew it.

The speech was dedicated in great part to Pushkin's masterpiece, *Evgeny Onegin*. Dostoyevsky focused on the character of Tatyana, after whom, he said, Pushkin's verse novel should have been named. After all, Tatyana, not Onegin, is the central character of Russia's most famous love story.

Tatyana Larina, an innocent girl living in the provinces, has a crush on Onegin, a sophisticated dandy visiting from the capital. She writes him a rather tacky love letter, but Onegin, who had somehow misled Tatyana, doesn't write back as she'd expected. Instead, he rejects her in a cruel and condescending manner, causing her pain, humiliation and a lot of very Russian sorrow. There are some complications – and a duel, of course – and then Onegin splits.

The years go by and one day Onegin bumps into Tatyana in Peter, which back then was the capital of the empire and not the provincial backwater it is today. She's all pafosni and elitni, Tatyana, because she's managed to snag an aristocrat. Onegin now realises how hot Tatyana is and tells her he really really wants her. This time for real.

In spite of the years, Pushkin tells us, Tatyana remains in love with Onegin. Now, finally, she has a real chance to be with him. So, what does Tatyana do? Does she ditch her husband and elope with her true love?

Nyet, she doesn't. In the culminating scenes of Pushkin's long poem, Tatyana decides to stick with her husband and, in her own nineteenth-century way, tells Onegin to fuck off.

A simple love story which most Russians know by heart. Many are even able to recite entire chapters – 'ya k vam pishu', Tatyana's letter, being an especially popular passage.

The symbolism of the story should not be ignored. Tatyana, the pure girl from the countryside, embodies the essence of Russianness, while Onegin, the cosmopolitan *bon vivant*, is a cynical fucker corrupted by modern European values. Onegin's life is about superficial pleasures. Tatyana's is all about meaning.

Why does Tatyana reject Onegin? Dostoyevsky asks in his

speech. Pushkin had made Tatyana's feelings clear. Wouldn't she be happier if she dumped her husband and took off with her true love? Fyodor Mikhailovich pushes his case further. What would have happened, he asks his Moscow audience, if Tatyana had been free when Onegin finally made a pass at her? If she had been a widow? She would still have rejected him, Fyodor Mikhailovich says.

Russian as she is, Tatyana knows that there is more to life than happiness.

2

'TELL ME, MARTIN, WHAT impact has Aleksandr Sergeyevich had on your life?'

We were sitting in Lyudmila Aleksandrovna's office in the humanities faculty, a cramped room with ceiling-high bookshelves that lined every wall and partially covered the room's only window. It was a couple of days after my arrival in Moscow, and we were meeting to discuss my research project. With her fleecy moustache and thick glasses, Lyudmila Aleksandrovna matched the preconceptions I had of Russian professors.

For her, asking about Aleksandr Sergeyevich was not a simple icebreaker — it was her way of testing my commitment to the research project and, in a wider sense, my devotion to the world of Russian literature. But I was newly arrived and unaware that Lyudmila Aleksandrovna was on a first-name-patronymic basis with Russian authors, so it took me a while to realise she was not asking about a mutual acquaintance — she was talking about Pushkin.

You mean *that* Aleksandr Sergeyevich!

Once I understood the implications of Lyudmila Aleksandrovna's question I could not bring myself to tell her that I — a doctoral student in Russian literature, a scholarship laureate, a soon-to-be-called expert — had never read a single line by the national poet, the father of modern Russian language, the very incarnation of the Russian soul. She would be devastated and I would be uncovered as a fraud.

She stared at me across the books piled up on her desk, awaiting an answer, her smile revealing the sparkle of a gold tooth.

Of course I had read *about* Pushkin — he was all over the place when I drafted my project proposal. I just never got around to reading what the illustrious man himself had written.

Sitting on the wobbly visitor's chair, pondering what to say, I glanced around the office. The window, half-blocked by books, had been sealed around the frame with brown adhesive tape — a deliberate attempt, I imagined, to further isolate the academic space from the outside world.

'Pushkin,' I said. 'Of course.'

Then, looking into Lyudmila Aleksandrovna's magnified eyes, I launched into an improvised answer on the impact *Evgeny Onegin* had had on me. The greatest love story, I said, so much truth in it. I added that I'd read Nabokov's famous translation, and that it had so moved me that I'd resolved to learn Russian in order to absorb the poetry as originally written by Aleksandr Sergeyevich.

Lyudmila Aleksandrovna nodded slowly, visibly touched. She removed her glasses and wiped her teary eyes.

She believed me. How could she not believe in a foreigner who loved Pushkin?

3

'THIS IS FUCKING RIDICULOUS,' Colin says, his finger resting on an open page of *The Exile*. 'I can't believe they gave Propaganda two fuckies.'

Stepanov lifts his sunglasses, leans over Colin's shoulder, glances down at the newspaper. 'Propaganda is definitely no match for the likes of Cube or Papa Johns.'

'Papa Johns *deserves* its two fuckies.' Colin flips the page carelessly, ripping the edge. 'They pack the dance floor every Sunday night with dyevs from Samara and Tula and fuck knows where.'

'But there are very nice girls in Propaganda,' I say, not fully understanding Colin's point.

Colin looks at me, his Irish-blue eyes reddish from the night. 'Sure,' he says, half smiling, 'but when it comes to taking them home, man, they are uptight. Propaganda is full

18

of spoilt Muscovites. They've picked up stupid ideas from the West.'

The waitress is now refilling our coffee mugs.

'What do you mean, stupid ideas?' I ask.

Colin takes a sip of coffee, wipes his mouth. Then he takes a swig from his beer glass. 'You know, they got it into their heads that decent women must make themselves unavailable.'

My head is throbbing, I feel sick. I look around for the fastest path to the toilet and see that the place is empty, aside from a table at the back where three Russian men are drinking cocktails and laughing loudly. For a moment I can't tell where we are, or how we got here. My ears are buzzing. The lack of music fills me with sudden regret that we are no longer in a club. I see a buffalo head on the wall staring straight into my eyes, which scares the shit out of me, but then it makes me realise that we are at the American Bar and Grill, in Mayakovskaya.

'Man, you should take that shapka off,' Colin says, gripping Diego's shoulder. 'It's fucking hot in here.'

Diego grabs his hat by the earflaps and pulls it further down on his head, though it still doesn't cover his long hair at the sides. 'My shapka is part of my look,' he says, grinning. 'It gives me an edge.'

We all laugh. Diego has only recently switched his Latino image, which involved heavily gelled hair and unbuttoned black shirts, for the furry shapka look, anticipating – he would later claim – the style Pasha Face Control was to make popular during the elitni era. But, no matter what he wears,

Diego's large hairy body and clumsy moves give him the air of a big placid bear.

'This shapka makes you look like a tourist,' Colin says. 'Russians don't wear those hats any more.'

'Precisely,' Diego says, raising his thick dark eyebrows. 'The shapka gives me a foreign and exotic air. Besides, it's a great conversation piece. All the dyevs ask me about it.'

'That's not even real fur,' Stepanov says. 'Where did you get that piece of shit? On a matryoshka stand by Red Square?'

I look at my watch and realise it's six in the morning. My vodka-flooded brain is shutting down. The thirsty little Cossack is exhausted from battle, stumbling next to his horse, ready to crash in his tent. I can hardly keep my eyes open. I ponder whether to go to the toilet first or wait for my eggs and bacon.

This is two months into my stay.

In a way, Colin was right about Propaganda. It was at that time that Propaganda introduced a kind of face control. Not a strict door policy – that would come later – but they made an effort to keep the trashiest dyevs out on the street. Expats were always welcome, of course, all we had to do was say a few words in English to the bouncer and we were in. But Propaganda's face control – which heralded the arrival of the post-Duck elitni era – distorted the night's demographics, which had, up until then, played to our advantage. There were fewer dyevs inside the club now, and the ones who made it in somehow felt they could afford to be more demanding.

In any case, as *The Exile* famously wrote back then, Propaganda remained the best place in Moscow to meet dyevs who were out of your league.

It was in Propaganda that I met Lena.

Thursday night: Propaganda night. I'd been drinking with the brothers, vodka and whisky shots at Stepanov's place, then vodka shots and beer in Propaganda. After a piss run, I found myself standing by the bar, captivated by a pair of big blue eyes. Straight blonde hair falling over her forehead, stopping in a perfect line just above her eyelashes. Classic Propaganda haircut.

'I'm Helen,' Lena said.

The music was loud, so Lena and I had to talk into each other's ears. Lena's hair smelled of rose water and cotton candy. Her voice was soft and sensual.

I ordered two shots of vodka and we toasted za vstrechu, to our encounter. I held my breath, drained the vodka glass, bit the lemon slice, breathed again. The alcohol made a lovely burning pang in my stomach.

Lena took a small sip and left her glass, almost full, on the bar. 'I like the DJ,' she said.

I looked at the dance floor and saw Colin and the other brothers forming a circle around what I assumed were Lena's uglier friends. The music was a tedious techno beat I didn't really care for.

'I *love* the DJ,' I said.

Lena and I talked for two or three minutes, which, back then, was as long as I could go before my Russian started to fail.

She didn't smile, Lenushka, not even at the very moment when we first met, and, as I tried to make conversation, I couldn't help but think she was somehow distracted and absent. Lena was distracted and absent, I imagined, because she's a nice dyev and we're in Propaganda and, whatever *The Exile* said, nice dyevs come to Propaganda to listen to the DJ and dance with friends. Not to meet foreign men. In her eyes, I thought, I'm nothing but a shallow Westerner, a soulless pleasure-seeker looking for an easy fuck.

'So you're an expat,' she said.

Our cheeks touched accidentally. My entire body stiffened.

'Student,' I replied.

Lena was now fiddling with the lemon slice that came with her vodka. She looked towards her friends on the dance floor and for a moment I thought: she's about to walk away.

Then she turned to me and finally asked The Question.

'Why Russia?'

Now, I could tell Lena about my studies in Amsterdam. I could tell her about Katya and how she'd ripped my heart out and eaten it, leaving a hole in my chest. I could tell her how I'd had no choice but to leave the city. I could tell her how Moscow had not even been near the top of the list of universities I'd initially applied for. But that's not what I told her. That was not a good story for Propaganda.

Instead, I carefully placed my hand on Lena's shoulder, stared into her big blue eyes, and pronounced the magic word.

'Pushkin,' I said. To make sure she fully absorbed the

sweetness of the sound, I separated the two syllables. Push. Kin.

Lena was now intrigued. I carried on and delivered the Propaganda version of my coming-to-Moscow story, telling Lena how the poetry of Aleksandr Sergeyevich had changed my life. I'd practised most of the sentences at language class with Nadezhda Nikolaevna so I didn't find it too difficult to describe, in my simplified Russian, how I'd gone from discovering Pushkin to being interested in Russian literature to obtaining a research scholarship in Moscow. My story was a good story.

Colin said, with Moscow dyevs you just need a beautiful story that makes sense, it doesn't need to be true.

To my surprise, I found myself whispering some Pushkin verses in Lena's ears. Ya vas lyubil and so on.

Then, for a brief moment, Lena smiled. Lena smiled with her lips, with her big blue eyes, but also with her entire body. She pulled her shoulders back and I caught a glimpse of a small golden cross dangling above her cleavage, sheltered by the lovely curve of her breasts.

Lena smiled, I thought, because she now trusted me. How could she not trust a foreigner who loved Pushkin?

4

AS FAR AS I COULD tell, Nadezhda Nikolaevna was the oldest person I'd ever met. With ashy hair and deep wrinkles, she had reached that age where old people start to shrink and look pitiful. Yet, like most babushkas in Moscow, she radiated determination, a historical toughness visible in the way she pressed her lips together firmly and looked straight into your eyes.

I was meeting Nadezhda Nikolaevna four times a week in a small classroom at the humanities faculty. If I had been out the night before, which was often the case, I would spend our three academic hours – which each lasted forty minutes – struggling to keep my eyes open while she read bits from old soviet books and made me repeat words such as perpadavaltelnotsa, prepadavaltelnetsa, prepodavatelnitsa, which I couldn't quite pronounce but just meant teacher, for chrissake.

But, against my own expectations, the combination of lessons at university and chatting up dyevs in nightclubs seemed to be working — I was picking up the language. During our lessons, Nadezhda Nikolaevna, who had been teaching Russian to foreigners for decades, spoke simple Russian and mimed vividly, so, after a few weeks, I was able to figure out, if not exactly what she was saying, at least the general idea she was trying to convey.

Sometimes I got it badly wrong though. One day Nadezhda Nikolaevna walked into the classroom looking particularly morose and told me she was devastated because her cherepakha had just passed away. I'd been to the Duck the night before, so cherepakha day must have been a Wednesday. The remains of vodka in my blood had put me in a dark mood and Nadezhda Nikolaevna's tragic loss made a strong impression on me.

'I'm sorry,' I said, regretting my inability to express proper condolences in Russian.

I didn't know the word cherepakha. In my mind, I went through all family-related vocabulary I had learned so far, which at the time was limited: brat, brother; sestra, sister; syn, son; dochka, daughter. As far as I could tell, cherepakha had not entered my lexicon.

'Life goes on,' Nadezhda Nikolaevna said. 'Let's get to work.'

At that moment, confused by my unexpected encounter with death at such an early hour of the day, I couldn't help but admire what I identified as yet another example of Russian resilience. I found myself thinking of Ilyusha's death in *The Brothers Karamazov*, about *The Death of Ivan Illich*, about the natural and yet intimate relationship Russians have with mortality.

'Cherepakha?' Nadezhda Nikolaevna asked.

'I don't think I know the word.'

'Yes, Martin, you know, something that something slow and something hard.'

'I'm sorry, Nadezhda Nikolaevna, I don't understand.'

Then, in a gesture I will never forget, Nadezhda Nikolaevna raised her elbows and moved her arms in a slow crawling motion. She tilted her head, inflated her wrinkled cheeks, and stuck her tongue out. It made a gruesome sight.

'Cherepakha, cherepakha!' she repeated.

She took my notebook, started to draw. First she made a big circle. Then, with the precision of an architect, she drew two short perpendicular lines on each side, followed by a smaller pear-shaped figure on top, a head, I realised, and I gradually understood what she was trying to draw.

That's when I learned that cherepakha means turtle.

From then on, every time I encountered the word cherepakha, what came to my mind first was the image of Nadezhda Nikolaevna sticking her tongue out, and not the reptile she had mimicked for my understanding.

One day, at the end of our language class, Nadezhda Nikolaevna proposed that we go on an excursion into town later in the week. She thought that, as a prospective Russian literature expert, I'd be interested to see Gorky's house, a beautiful art nouveau building in central Moscow which had been turned into a museum. I wasn't wild about the idea of having to get up earlier to spend the morning in a museum, but Nadezhda Nikolaevna seemed really keen so we made plans to take our last lesson of the week to the city centre.

On Friday morning, I stood in the middle of the Arbatskaya station platform, among the rush of Muscovites, waiting for Nadezhda Nikolaevna. It was the day after I'd first met Lena in Propaganda and I'd had barely two hours' sleep. My head was aching and clouded; my throat dry. Yet, as I tried to identify Nadezhda Nikolaevna in the moving mass of people, I felt a cheerful tickle in my chest, an unusual feeling of excitement, provoked not so much by the prospect of visiting Gorky's house as of meeting Lena later in the day.

Nadezhda Nikolaevna emerged from the crowd wearing a babushka headscarf and carrying a plastic bag. Out in the street, we walked slowly along the frozen pavement of the Boulevard. The temperatures had dropped in the last few days and we were both tucked into our winter coats. Nadezhda Nikolaevna's gait was stooped and — in my head — turtle-like. For a brief moment, it crossed my mind to offer her my arm, but then I thought the gesture condescending, a bit ridiculous, and I continued walking at arm's length.

We turned left at Malaya Nikitskaya and soon reached Gorky's house. The babushkas taking care of the museum were almost as old as Nadezhda Nikolaevna. After paying for the tickets, we were ordered to wear giant felt slippers over our shoes so as not to damage the original parquet floors. Slippers strapped on, we glided carefully over the polished floors of the museum. I was particularly impressed by the large library, which, according to a laminated leaflet in faulty English, contained Gorky's own books, most of which were annotated in the margins by the great writer himself.

Despite my Propaganda hangover, I tried my best to follow Nadezhda Nikolaevna's enthusiastic explanations about the beautiful house and Gorky's life. The mansion, she was saying, had been commissioned in the early 1900s by a wealthy banker called Ryabushinsky. After 1917, the building had been expropriated by the Bolsheviks and used as headquarters for several soviet institutions. When, in the early 1930s, Gorky returned from Italy, he was bestowed with plenty of honours, including, Nadezhda Nikolaevna said, renaming both Tverskaya Street and the city of Nizhny Novgorod after him. Stalin awarded him the Ryabushinsky mansion, with the intention that it would become an intellectual hub for soviet writers.

As I listened to her talk, I pictured Gorky and his illustrious visitors – which, I was told, included Stalin himself – discussing literature and socialism beneath the stained-glass windows and carved wooden frames. Every now and then, my mind would temporarily drift from Gorky to Propaganda, as I was bombarded by flashes of the previous night. The big blue eyes. The goodbye kiss.

Nadezhda Nikolaevna seemed proud of the museum. I made sure that I looked impressed by everything she was telling me, even if I missed some of her explanations. When we were done with the first floor, we tackled the spectacular staircase, which had a wavy banister that ended in a bronze jellyfish-like lamp. I let her go first, and discreetly positioned myself behind, worried that, with the cumbersome slippers, she might trip and roll down this fine but slippery example of Russian art nouveau.

Half an hour later, as we walked back towards Arbatskaya, Nadezhda Nikolaevna suggested that we find a café and sit for some tea. 'The visit only took us one hour,' she said, 'we still have time left.'

I was hoping to stay around the centre, see if Stepanov was at home so that I could crash on his couch for a couple of hours before meeting Lena.

'It was a very interesting visit,' I said. 'I think we can consider it a full lesson. Let's stop here and meet next week.'

'Martin, I would prefer if we finish our lesson time. I'm paid for a three-hour lesson and it's my job to give it to you.'

She looked determined. Not wanting to offend her sense of duty or make her feel I didn't value her teaching, I agreed to continue our lesson.

We walked into the Old Arbat. A few stands stood in the middle of the pedestrian street, selling wares for tourists: soviet flags, matryoshka dolls, lacquered boxes, painted eggs. We walked into the first café we saw. It was warm and cosy inside. The wood-panelled decor imitated a traditional Russian country house and included, near the entrance, a real stuffed cow. We sat at a small table by the window, facing each other, and ordered a pot of black tea.

I was afraid we wouldn't have much to talk about, but Nadezhda Nikolaevna continued speaking about Gorky. To my surprise, in the intimacy of the café, she was giving me an entirely different spin on Gorky's story. As I understood it,

Nadezhda Nikolaevna was now telling me that Gorky was a sell-out. While he'd written very interesting stuff in his early years, after 1917 he'd become a puppet of the soviet regime, especially following his return from Italy. The house we'd just visited, I was being told, was unworthy of a writer who claimed to represent the proletariat. In exchange for supporting Stalin's increasingly totalitarian regime, Gorky had been granted plenty of favours, including a position as president of the Writers' Union.

'And for what?' Nadezhda Nikolaevna said. 'He didn't write a single good line after the revolution.'

I wondered why Nadezhda Nikolaevna hadn't told me this version of Gorky's story while we were inside the museum. Perhaps, I thought, she was afraid that the dezhurnayas following us across the rooms — to ensure that we didn't break or steal anything, I'd assumed — would intervene if she deviated from the official version of Gorky's story as presented by the museum.

When the tea arrived, Nadezhda Nikolaevna took a small foil-wrapped parcel from her plastic bag and placed it at the centre of the table. 'A little surprise,' she said, smiling. She unwrapped the parcel, uncovering a napkin with a few rolled-up blinis.

'I made them myself for our little excursion,' she said proudly, as she extended the napkin with the blinis next to the teapot. 'I hope you like blinis with tvorog.'

Noticing my hesitation, Nadezhda Nikolaevna explained that it was fine to bring your own food to cafés in Moscow. 'The food in these places is expensive and not very good,' she said.

I could see from the menu that it was possible to order an

entire meal for two for the price of a cocktail in Propaganda.

I took one of the blinis and had a bite. Buttery, sweet, delicious.

'They are lovely,' I said.

Over tea and blinis, Nadezhda Nikolaevna continued with Gorky's story, telling me how, in the end, the great soviet writer had fallen out of favour with Stalin and had probably been killed by the secret services.

'They painted the walls of his bedroom with poisonous paint,' she said. 'So Gorky fell ill and died.'

'Interesno,' I said, nodding. I wondered why Stalin's people, who had kidnapped, tortured and killed with pleasure, would resort to such creative methods to murder an ageing and not particularly dangerous writer. But I was getting accustomed to the myths and parables Russians used to explain their recent history. When the official version of historical events seemed artificial, the emergence of alternative narratives was only natural. These stories, some of which might have held a grain of truth, spread by word of mouth through Moscow's many shared kitchens.

The hot tea was bringing me back to life. I was really enjoying our excursion. The Gorky Museum, the stories, the chilly air outside. I was particularly touched by the home-made blinis.

As Nadezhda Nikolaevna was finishing the story of Gorky's death, the young waiter who had brought the teapot came over and planted himself next to our table.

'Woman,' he said, addressing Nadezhda Nikolaevna.

I had learned that, ever since the perestroika, Russians had had a problem addressing each other. The word tovarisch –

comrade — previously used to address any fellow soviet citizen, had become politically obsolete. But pre-revolutionary language was not really an option: during the seven decades of communism, the old words for sir and madam were deemed too bourgeois and had fallen into disuse. Now, when addressing a stranger, Russians were left with little choice but to say man, woman, boy, girl, or — to people around my age — young person.

Nadezhda Nikolaevna, wrapped up in telling Gorky's story, didn't seem to notice the waiter.

'Woman,' the waiter repeated, now louder, without the slightest trace of a smile. 'You can't bring outside food into this café.'

'Oh,' Nadezhda Nikolaevna said, looking up and smiling, 'but these are blinis that I made at home.'

'I don't care what they are,' he said. 'You need to order food from our menu.'

Nadezhda Nikolaevna blushed, embarrassed at having been talked down to — or perhaps, I thought, at having provided me with the wrong information about Moscow's customs. The cheerfulness she had shown all morning dissolved at once. She looked down, started to wrap the rest of the blinis.

'Woman,' the waiter said, not moving an inch from the table, 'if you can't afford the food in here, just stay home.'

'Go fuck yourself!' I found myself saying, in plain English, as I jumped up to face him, knocking over my chair.

The waiter, confused, stepped back and disappeared into the kitchen.

*

A few minutes later Nadezhda Nikolaevna and I were walking in silence along the Old Arbat. 'I'm sorry I snapped in the café,' I said. 'It wasn't my intention to make a scene.'

'Moscow is changing,' she murmured, gaze fixed on the pavement, a sad tone in her voice.

She seemed even older, more fragile – walking now with difficulty. As we moved along the pedestrian street, I offered Nadezhda Nikolaevna my arm. We made our way towards Smolenskaya, flanked by families and tourists. With one hand she clutched my elbow, with the other she carried the plastic bag with the unfinished blinis.

5

Leaving Nadezhda Nikolaevna at Smolenskaya, where she unexpectedly kissed me goodbye, I decided to avoid the metro and take a walk. I had some time to kill before meeting Lena.

The sky was brighter now, almost blue, but the sun didn't seem powerful enough to dissipate the late autumn chill. As I marched among the towering constructions of the New Arbat, I remembered how, on a previous stroll, I had been told that the large buildings on the southern side were meant to represent open books. Each structure was formed by two flat wings joined at a wide angle, but, as far as I could see, nothing else in their design suggested the shape of a book. Glancing at their plain façades, I now wondered if the architect's intention had really been to emulate books or if, more likely, the alleged resemblance had been an afterthought.

I sat for a while in the Internet café in Okhotny Ryad, read the news, answered long-overdue emails. Back in the street, the air seemed even cooler.

I reached Lubyanka with some twenty minutes to spare. At dawn, just before saying goodbye, Lena and I had agreed to meet outside Dyetsky Mir, the big toyshop on the north-western side of the square. To warm myself a little, I entered the shop. The spacious central atrium was deserted. I wandered among rows of plastic cars, skates, balls, dolls, stuffed animals. A couple of shop assistants hid behind the stands, avoiding eye contact with customers, as was the practice in Moscow. I passed through the bicycle section and, thinking that my legs could do with a rest, sat on a child-size stool near the entrance. Next to the stool, a low table was covered in piles of small plastic bricks, identical to those I'd played with in my childhood. I gathered a few colourful pieces and, without giving it much thought, began interlocking the bricks to form a wall. I then built four corners, joined them into a square which could serve as the base of a tower. I kept adding bricks, layer by layer, enjoying the simplicity of the task, trying not only to create a solid foundation for my tower, but also to match the colours in symmetrical patterns as the structure grew taller.

'Do you need more time to finish?'

I looked up. Lena was wearing a dark green anorak and tight jeans. Her blonde hair was airier than the night before.

I wasn't sure how much time I'd spent playing with the bricks. I stood up, awkward and embarrassed. 'I thought we were meeting outside,' I said. 'What's the time?'

Lena stared at me in silence, her blue gaze so intense that I had to look away, afraid she could read my thoughts.

'Come with me,' she said finally. 'I'm going to show you my favourite place in Moscow.'

She grabbed my arm and walked me out of the shop. As we crossed the street through the underground passage they called perekhod, I told her about my unusual Russian lesson in the morning, and how Nadezhda Nikolaevna and I had been kicked out of the café.

'Moscow is changing,' Lena said. 'In soviet times, communism gave us values to live by, a sense of community. People helped each other. That's gone now.'

She spoke deliberately, aware of my language limitations. I was glad to notice that, in broad daylight, without vodka, I still understood most of what she said.

'Russia is lost,' she continued. 'People here need guidance. First we had God. Then we had Lenin. Now we have nothing.'

We emerged on the other side of Lubyanka.

'See that?' Lena was now pointing at the square. The enormous roundabout was circled by dozens of vehicles that poured in from all over Moscow. Across the square, opposite the dreamy world of Dyetsky Mir, stood the infamous headquarters of the secret services, where, I had been told, thousands of people had been tortured and murdered.

'The Lubyanka building,' I said, nodding, frowning, trying to convey my understanding of the historical suffering associated with the building.

'Not that,' Lena said. 'I mean in the middle of the round-about. What do you see?'

All I saw among the fuming vehicles was an empty traffic island.

'Nothing,' I said.

'Exactly. There used to be a statue. Dzerzhinsky, founder of the soviet secret services.'

'I see.'

'The statue disappeared with the perestroika,' Lena said. 'It was never replaced. That's what I mean: after the fall of communism, Russia's soul is empty, like Lubyanka Square.'

We walked along Nikolskaya, then turned left into a narrow side street crammed with double-parked cars. I had visited these old streets of Kitay-gorod at night with the brothers, searching for clubs, but in daylight the entire neighbourhood felt like part of a different, sleepier city. Lena stopped in front of a residential building that had no signs.

'Here we are,' she said, indicating a brown metal door.

She rang a bell and the door was opened. Descending a flight of stairs, we entered a dimly lit underground room. A young bearded man with a ponytail sat behind a counter, reading in near darkness. He greeted Lena with a curt nod, seemingly annoyed by our interruption, and reluctantly placed his book on the counter next to a burning incense stick. The counter was covered with cheap booklets on Buddhism, Taoism, meditation, yoga. All the books bore handwritten price tags.

We removed our shoes and handed over our coats. Lena was wearing a white woollen jumper. At the sight of her curves, I had a sharp feeling of inadequacy – as if Lena were a real woman and I were just a boy pretending to be a man.

We were led into a larger underground room – the only light provided by candles flickering in the dark. The candles stood on eight or nine low tables, each of which was surrounded by piles of cushions. The floor was covered with rugs from wall to wall, giving the entire setting a gloomy oriental feel. All the tables were unoccupied, except one at the far end, where another couple cuddled and spoke in murmurs.

Lena placed our order with the bearded man. We sat among the cushions, our backs leaning on the wall. Gentle sitar music filled the air. The atmosphere was sepulchral, holy.

I put my arm around Lena. She leaned her head on my shoulder. Absorbing the sweetness of her perfume, my mind flashed back to Propaganda. An hour or so after we'd met by the bar, I had followed Lena outside the club, through a side alley, into an old building. After climbing a few flights of unlit stairs impregnated with the stench of cat piss, I had found myself perched on a rooftop – Lena was showing me the night-time view over Moscow. Look how beautiful and special this city is, she'd said. It was dark and cold, and I was wasted, but I understood what she meant.

A waitress in a kimono slid into the room carrying our tray and kneeled at our table. The tea ceremony Lena had ordered involved hot water being poured from a large jar into the teapot, from the teapot into thimble-sized cups, then all back to the jar. The circulation of steaming water had a hypnotic effect on me. At some point, tea leaves were ceremoniously added to the teapot and, after a minute or so, we were presented with two tiny cups of green tea. Lena grabbed her cup with two hands, bowing slightly, and expertly placed it under her nose. 'Beautiful,' she said.

I lifted my cup with the tips of my fingers. The tea had a damp-earth aroma and, once in my mouth, a faint taste of mud.

'I love this place,' Lena said after the kimono lady was gone. 'So quiet and peaceful, you wouldn't believe we are in the centre of Moscow.'

Lena spoke in whispers, which made the sound of her Russian serene, soothing.

'Moscow is full of surprises,' I said.

'Moscow is the best place in the world. The city has its own cosmic energy, you can feel it through your entire body.'

Lena took care of refilling our teacups. As I took a sip, I felt the strength draining away from my limbs. I placed my cup on the table and lay down among the oriental cushions, my head on Lena's thigh. Lena stroked my hair, her nails making sweet ripples through my skin. There was a reassuring tranquillity about Lena's presence, her mellow voice and graceful gestures. It was as if her body had a different density and she were forced to move in slow motion.

With my eyes closed, I drifted towards unconsciousness, floating in that graceful state before sleep. Images of colourful plastic bricks began to pop into my head in time with the notes of the sitar.

The spell of the moment was broken by a beep from my phone. Message from Colin. *Hey, lost you last night. banged the blonde dyev? Tonight: drinks at stepanov's at 9.*

I switched off the phone without answering.

When I returned from the toilets, I found Lena staring at the empty teacups, her face illuminated by the faint glow of the candles. The other couple had left — the dark cave was entirely ours. I sat between Lena and the wall, my legs around her waist, my arms beneath her breasts.

Lena didn't move when my hands found their way under her sweater, or when my fingers slipped under her bra. She sat in silence, her eyes on the candle.

I kissed her neck. My heart was beating fast now. 'It's getting late,' I said, 'why don't you show me where you live?'

For a long minute Lena kept gazing at the candle. 'I can't,' she said at last. 'Not today.'

We remained silent, listening to the sitar, my entire body focused and expectant.

All of a sudden, Lena turned round and grabbed my face with two hands. 'Promise me something,' she whispered, staring straight into my eyes. 'I want you to always remember this moment.'

Next thing I knew, she was unbuttoning my jeans.

6

TRUTH IS, IT WASN'T Pushkin who introduced me to Russia. It was Katya. She was not even Russian Russian. Katya was from Minsk. I'd met her at a university party in Amsterdam and within two weeks she'd moved into my apartment, an arrangement that was partly down to the city's housing scarcity. Though only two years older than me, Katya was, in my eyes, a real woman. She wore feminine, grown-up clothes and plenty of make-up. In the street, Katya didn't walk – she paraded, her long black hair falling in waves over her shoulders, and I took pride in the way other men turned their heads to look at her, my Slavic goddess.

We lived in the small flat I was renting in Fokke Simonsz-straat, a central Amsterdam street with no canal, on the third floor of an old house with narrow stairs that, like many buildings in the city, was tilted to one side. At home you could feel that the floor wasn't entirely level, that there was a slight slope from the couch to the TV, and this, I think, might have contributed to the sense of instability I suffered from at the time.

It was Katya who introduced me to Russian thought. Not to philosophers or great writers – although she'd read them all in school – but to the way Russians look at life. She also taught me my first Russian words. You are such a babnik, she'd say, every time she caught me looking at other women. A babnik, she explained to me, was a man who liked women and was liked by women. Katya had a scary sixth sense for these things and, whenever we both walked into a student party or a bar, she would immediately spot the girl I was going to feel attracted to, even before I'd seen her.

I also learned many practicalities from Katya. She patiently instructed me on the endless medicinal applications of vodka; headaches, indigestion, insomnia – there was nothing a bit of good old vodka could not cure. Katya also used the magic liquor as stain remover, shoe polish – anything, really. Katya rubbed vodka on her forehead and tummy for a couple of days each month – the most effective method, she maintained, to relieve her atrocious menstrual pains.

With her spectacular beauty and her unique way of seeing the world, Katya embodied the promise of a vast cultural universe to be discovered. It was only after she'd gone from my life and I'd started my research in Moscow that I realised Katya must have been my first maternal whore. The maternal whore is a concept I kind of came up with later in my research, a recurring female character in Russian literature:

a beautiful woman who uses her natural, God-given wisdom to nurture her man, to instruct him in the ways of life, without demanding a conventional commitment in return. Think of Raskolnikov's Sonya in *Crime and Punishment* — except, of course, Sonya was also an actual whore.

So it was Katya who showed me the light. She was the prophet of my new faith, the beacon of my new world. For that, I'm grateful. Without Katya, Russia would have remained nothing more than a frozen far-off land that belonged to Cold War films and dusty history books.

7

CHOOSE ANY STREET IN Moscow. Stand at the kerb. Raise your arm. In a few seconds you have two or three cars at the side of the road offering their services. Set the price. A hundred, a hundred and fifty rubles, depends on the distance to be covered, the time of day, how shitty the car is. A ten-minute drive and you are in, say, Kitaisky Lyotchik. The Chinese Pilot.

The Lyotchik is a popular bar, at least among students and the arty crowd. They often host performances and live music. Great place to start the night. But if for some reason it's not happening in the Lyotchik you all have a couple of drinks, maybe accompanied by a plate of chicken wings, take a piss, walk out and flag another car, perhaps a Volga this time, that will take you to Karma Bar.

You want to hit Karma just before midnight, when the

dyevs are drunk but not taken. If you are lucky, the Volga's radio is playing old soviet songs, Vysotsky or Okudzhava, but most often it will be blasting out trashy Russian pop, the kind of synthesiser sound abandoned by the West in the mid-1980s.

Colin is in the front seat talking to the driver.

Colin says, it's from taxi drivers you learn about the real Moscow. Drivers are typically well-educated men – engineers, doctors, professors – whose jobs have become superfluous in the new Russia, and who need the extra cash to make ends meet. Often, the driver will admire Colin's proficiency in Russian and his knowledge of local customs – surprised and pleased to hear he's American – and, if we've grabbed the car after a few drinks, Colin and the driver often end up singing Russian songs, reciting poetry or telling anekdots, which are the equivalent of Western jokes but without a funny punch line.

Stepanov, Diego and I sit in the back seat. The car drops us outside Karma and we add a fifty-ruble tip to the agreed price. The driver wishes us a good night and we walk into the club.

Two hours in Karma. That's four rounds of drinks. Colin doesn't like wasting time. With the first drink in his hand, and while the rest of us stand at the bar, he carries out a complete inspection of the premises, scanning, taking mental notes. Then he returns and says, 'Guys, let's move to the back of the dance floor, between the Buddha and the small bar. That's the spot tonight.'

We leave Karma and take another car, this one a zhiguli with a cracked windscreen and a chatty Georgian driver.

Now we have Oksana and Irina squeezed into the back seat. Colin's gone – it happens sometimes, a brother leaves the group, only to be met hours later for breakfast at Starlite Diner or the American Bar and Grill. Oksana is clearly Stepanov's, but, at this point of the night, Irina remains up for grabs.

Our nights begin at Stepanov's place, a high-ceilinged apartment on a side street off the Old Arbat, lavishly decorated in the late soviet style: piano in the living room, tapestries on the walls, a hand-coloured portrait of Brezhnev – chest covered in military medals. The tapestry above the couch depicts a popular Russian painting I've seen in one of my language books – three knights on horses, wearing pointy metal helmets. The knight in the middle, seemingly the leader, is riding a black horse, his hand shielding his eyes, gazing into the horizon.

Stepanov's flat is his grandfather's flat. Stepanov's grandfather had been important in the Communist party, a proud member of the nomenklatura, Stepanov tells us, but he passed away in the early 1990s, together with the Union of Soviet Socialist Republics. We often toast in his honour because, Stepanov says, his grandfather remains our host. At Stepanov's place we do vodka shots, play old vinyl records, decide which clubs to visit, talk shit.

To make sure we are not missing out on the best party, Colin makes us spend a great part of the night on the road, moving across the city, following rumours, searching for the finest crowd. It's an endless journey, from club to club to bar to café, back to a club, exploring the hundreds of establishments that stay open all night, buying drinks, talking to dyevs, collecting phone numbers.

Colin says, in Moscow you don't hunt, you gather.

The problem comes at the end of the night. Visitors are not allowed into the university residence, so, if it turns out to be a good night and a girl I've met in a club wants to come home for a cup of tea, I have to take her to Stepanov's place, where we'll spend the rest of the night on his couch, next to the grandfather's piano, under the strict vigilance of comrade Brezhnev.

Stepanov says, you're welcome to fuck anyone in my grandfather's flat.

But it's not ideal. Next morning I'll have to wake up early, walk the girl to the ring road, put her in a car before I take the long metro ride to Universitet for my three-hour language class.

Exhausting.

8

IT WAS KATYA WHO suggested that I should add Moscow to my application form. 'You'll increase your chances,' she said. 'Nobody wants to go to Russia. People are scared, with all these awful things they show on the news all the time. There'll be no competition.'

I didn't particularly care about academic life. But I was about to finish my degree in languages and literature and I didn't know what to do next. A friend told me that a PhD was nothing more than the usual academic assignment, just with a very long deadline. It sounded like something I could do.

Moscow. Why not. After all, I had taken an interest in Russian books. During my studies I'd read Dostoyevsky, Gogol and even a couple of chapters of *War and Peace*. Then, for my birthday, Katya had bought me an old English edition of selected short stories by Chekhov – the only book I later took to Moscow – and for a couple of weeks we had read the stories to each other in bed.

As Katya had predicted – and despite my mediocre grades – a few weeks after sending in my application I found myself facing a panel in the literature department of the University of Amsterdam. It was never really explained to me why I wasn't being considered for other universities which were top of my list – when they had asked me to submit a developed research proposal, I was told it was Russia or nothing.

At the interview I was invited to elucidate how my proposed research topic – the evolution of the female character in Russian literature – would contribute to the West's understanding of modern Russia. Following Katya's advice, I'd taken two shots of vodka before the interview – a trick Russians always use to speak in public, she'd told me. I felt confident and eloquent. I will certainly define the research topic further, sir, of course I think there is room for a fresh look at the subject, yes, a twenty-first-century view of Russian literature. I'm planning to expand my sources, indeed, will definitely take into account these latest gender-sensitive theories you mention, madam, I mean professor, I will use them all. Russian language? Da, da, I'm looking forward to learning Russian, certainly. I would be immensely grateful, I said at the end – trying to conclude my interview as solemnly as I could – if I were awarded this prestigious scholarship to study at MGU, the famous Moscow State University.

By the time I was offered the scholarship, another few

weeks after the interview, I had no reason to stay in Amsterdam. In fact, I was desperate to get out.

All friendly break-ups are alike; each painful break-up is
painful in its own way. Katya certainly made sure of that. At
first I was shocked, the entire thing had caught me off guard.
The days passed and I saw no improvement in my heart's
condition. I couldn't understand where the pain was coming
from. Had I really cared that much about her? Then, in the
middle of this unexplored emotional territory, confused and
disoriented as I was, I received The Letter. Dear applicant, we
have the pleasure of informing you that, and so on.

It was only later, when I read *Nest of the Gentry*, that I recognised the dramatic potential of my situation. In Turgenev's
book, Lavretsky, too, finds himself in similar circumstances
and ends up fleeing to Russia looking for solace. Of course,
now, when I look back, I wouldn't dare compare my Katya
to Varvara Pavlovna. Despite her glamour and beauty, Katya
lacked the old-school refinement of Turgenev's femme fatale.

So it was that, with a few warm clothes, a Russian–English
dictionary and my copy of Chekhov, I left Amsterdam for
good. Sitting on an Aeroflot plane bound for Sheremetyevo,
ready to start my post-Katya life, I found myself for the first
time totally surrounded by real Russians. They looked like
decent, honest people. I was glad to hear the unsmiling air
hostess addressing me in Russian, obviously mistaking me
for one of her own. Fish or meat? I'd been studying the language for a few weeks with a book Katya had bought me, but
the air hostess's question – which, granted, she'd posed while

holding two trays of warm aeroplane food in her hands — was my first successful encounter with the Russian language in a non-textbook context.

My confidence boosted, I began to look forward to my life in Moscow, my self-imposed exile, where I'd be enjoying, I thought, a rich academic and intellectual life. In the mental rendition of this new chapter, I saw myself sitting for hours in the library, meeting other students, reading profound books. If I managed to make the right acquaintances, perhaps I'd also be invited to a real dacha, where I'd drink endless cups of tea from an authentic samovar, and I'd discuss the meaning of life with bearded intellectuals who looked like Dostoyevsky or Tolstoy. A peaceful life of study and contemplation, I thought, as I glanced through the window and observed our plane gliding above the clouds towards a vast darkening horizon.

9

I WAS TOLD INTERNATIONAL students had been assigned language classes in the morning so that we could spend our afternoons researching in the library and meeting our supervisors. I wasn't quite keeping up with this arrangement.

Most days, after my language class with Nadezhda Nikolaevna, I would grab lunch at the main stolovaya with Diego, then walk back to my room in Sektor E to catch a couple of hours' sleep. In the afternoons I would typically take the metro to the centre, where I would have arranged to meet a dyev on the platform of some monumental metro station.

Walking around the streets of the centre, dyevs often insisted on holding hands and, as uncomfortable as this made me feel, I tried to oblige for as long as I could. They would take me to Red Square and the Old Arbat and other touristy places that I had, by now, visited several times. But I appreciated their efforts, and I would follow them obediently, showing interest, asking questions, saying how very interesno everything was. These walks were good for my Russian and, if the dyev I was meeting didn't live with her family, after two or three encounters she would invite me over to her place for a cup of tea.

By mid-December, three months into my stay, I started to worry about my academic research. I could sense that Lyudmila Aleksandrovna, who I was meeting once a week to discuss my project, was disappointed by my performance.

'Martin, you are a very slow reader,' she said once, while we were drinking tea and discussing Gogol in her office. She had a point, I thought, as I reclined cautiously on the wobbly chair, careful not to spill any tea. I had read some of the articles she'd recommended. Three, perhaps two, from a list of twelve. I told her it was hard for me to read faster, as most of the articles were in Russian. This was not entirely untrue.

On another occasion, Lyudmila Aleksandrovna mentioned how this other research student she was supervising, a Pole or a Czech, was making so much progress. 'He is so dedicated, such a hard worker,' she said.

It was true that, as things turned out, I was dedicating less time to my research than I'd initially intended. Not that I didn't appreciate the intellectual stimulation of academic life, or Lyudmila Aleksandrovna's mentorship. It was simply a question of scheduling. Free time was scarce in Moscow—my weeks came with a number of fixed appointments. Tuesday night was of course ladies' night at the Duck. Wednesday night we were expected to attend the Moscow-famous Countdown at the Boathouse, where, if you arrived early enough, you could get up to four drinks for the price of one. Thursday night was Propaganda night. Unmissable. And then, come the weekend, we had new clubs to explore, but also the old ones, which we still had to keep up with: McCoy, Karma, Dirty Dancing, Beefeater, Papa Johns.

One day Lyudmila Aleksandrovna handed me a reading list on Lermontov, which we were supposed to discuss at our next meeting. A week later I showed up in her office apologising for not having read the articles.

'But these articles were mostly in English,' she said, gazing at me from behind her thick glasses. 'You shouldn't have any problem reading them.'

'I know,' I replied. 'I just didn't have much time this week.'

'Don't worry, Martin, go back to the library right now and come back tomorrow.'

She was pissed off.

I decided not to go out that night and focus on Lermontov instead. After dinner, I sat in my room trying to read the articles, a selection of texts about the sociological and historical context of *A Hero of Our Time*. The articles were interesting but I found it hard to concentrate. As I lay on my bed, taking a break from the reading, trying to focus on Mikhail Yuryevich's life and times, my head kept flashing up images of Propaganda. The dance floor, the chilled vodka, the pretty dyevs. It was Thursday night and, by now, the brothers were probably getting into the club. I thought about the night I met

Lena, when we left Propaganda and she took me to the roof-top to show me the view. I recalled how, at some point, I put my arm around Lena, and, before we kissed for the first time, I had to listen to a long exposition on the importance of meditation and yoga in her life.

Back at my desk, I tried to channel my thoughts from Propaganda back to Lermontov and the articles I had spread in front of me. But my mind rebelled, fought back and drifted to Propaganda.

What was the point of coming all the way to Moscow if I was going to stay in my room reading articles?

I began to think about the ultimate purpose of my academic work. When I'd first discussed my research with Lyudmila Aleksandrovna, she'd suggested that I also use non-literary sources. 'If you are going to study the female characters in Russian literature,' she'd said in our second meeting, 'you could start by analysing the situation of women in Russia.' She then suggested that I read demographic studies, opinion polls, media analyses, and use all this scientific data to extract a clear picture of the role of women in Russian society. 'This could help you understand the real-life context in which literary heroines are born,' she'd said.

I could certainly check those sources, I now thought. In fact, if Lyudmila Aleksandrovna's point was that I form a clear picture of Russian women, I might as well adopt a more direct approach. I could add, for instance, a primary source of qualitative data. It then occurred to me that meeting dyevs could well be considered, to some extent, part of my academic research.

I stood up and began pacing around the small dusty room, contemplating the possibility of leaving Lermontov aside for the night and joining the brothers in Propaganda. From an academic point of view, I told myself, it would be interesting to discern to what extent Pushkin, Lermontov, Gogol, Turgenev, Tolstoy, Dostoyevsky, Chekhov – the whole bunch, really – were describing Russian women as they *were* in real life, and to what extent they were describing *their own ideas* about Russian women. The more dyevs I met, I told myself, the better I would understand the defining characteristics of real Russian women.

Thrilled with my breakthrough, I took a quick shower, put on a black shirt and a thick coat, and headed for the street. In the taxi I continued to think about my research. I was aware, of course, that my new methodology brought with it some technical difficulties. To begin with, I could anticipate a high degree of cross-contamination between the two populations of my study: heroines from Russian books and women from Moscow's nightlife. While it was surely real women who had inspired the heroines of the Russian literary canon, the opposite was also true: Tatyana Larina, Anna Karenina, Natalya Rostova, they had all influenced the way Russian women saw themselves.

I paid the taxi fare and strode towards the queue outside Propaganda. I needed to start meeting dyevs in a more structured way. I needed to learn about their lives, their ambitions, their fears. In a later stage of my research I could merge the qualitative data obtained from these encounters with the quantitative data I could gather from scientific sources, such as sociological studies. That would give me a complete picture of Russian women that I could compare with the behaviour of heroines in Russian literature.

Of course, at this stage, I didn't need to share these details of my research with Lyudmila Aleksandrovna, I told myself as I walked past the bouncer and entered Propaganda — it would be my own methodology, my unique approach, my very personal path into the core of the Mysterious Russian Soul.

10

AN INITIAL MISTAKE I made was not taking notes on my encounters. This caused me a great deal of confusion. Dyevs had diverse and interesting stories and I could at first identify some Tatyanas and Kareninas, but soon their backgrounds began to merge into one single narrative in my head and my many meetings turned into a continuous conversation with a changing interlocutor.

I often found myself in the awkward position of asking a dyev about a friend or a job she'd never had. When I noticed their confusion, I blamed my faux pas on my poor Russian. They seemed happy to correct me but, to avoid further embarrassment, I began to carry notebooks so that I could keep track of my meetings. Now, on long metro journeys, or sitting alone in cafés, I would take one of the red notebooks I'd purchased at the university, and I would scribble thoughts and bits from my conversations. With time, these notes – my field observations, so to speak – became particularly useful, as they allowed me not only to quickly recall the background of each girl I met, but also to identify common features of the Russian woman, the kind of information that could become handy at a later stage of my research.

I also wrote down the new words and phrases I encountered. Thanks to my regular meetings, my vocabulary was being expanded by intriguing concepts, such as sudba, a word that was used often, meaning fate or destiny, but in a distinctively Russian way. Events in life, I learned, were either ne sudba, when they didn't happen and therefore were not meant to be, or sudba, which implied a supernatural predestination against which simple human will was powerless. Once I understood the importance of this concept, I tried to use it as much as I could. And so I often found myself walking along the Old Arbat or sitting in a café, holding a girl's hand and telling her how I thought our meeting had been such a huge sudba. They liked that.

11

MIND THE CLOSING DOORS. Next stop: Chistye Prudy.

I was heading north on the red line, rocked from side to side, observing the other passengers, not thinking of anything in particular.

As the metro clanked through endless tunnels, I began to reflect upon the sheer size of the city, how nobody could tell me how many people lived in it. More than in Paris or London or New York, I was often told.

Every day, millions of unsmiling Muscovites navigated their way through the underground arteries of the city. Silent strangers in dark clothes, crammed into wagons yet trying to avoid human contact, staring at their newspapers, at their books, into the air. Not a smile. Every passenger in Moscow's metro seemed deeply unhappy.

Mind the closing doors. Next stop: Krasnye Vorota.

You could hop on any metro line and get off at a random station, and you would always resurface among wide streets and identical buildings. Each suburb had a different name, often related to communist lore, but they all looked pretty much the same. Stations had their own makeshift markets, which sold cheap clothes and newspapers and chocolates and flowers and gloves and hats and scarves and pirate CDs and, later on, mobile phones.

Mind the closing doors. Next stop: Komsomolskaya.

When we first met, some three weeks after my arrival, Ira was about to start working part-time as a secretary at an American firm. Wanting to improve her English but unable to afford language classes, she'd pinned a handwritten ad on the announcement board of my faculty. *You want to practise Russian?*

On Tuesdays we spoke in English and on Thursdays we spoke in Russian. That was our arrangement. We would meet in the first-floor cafeteria at MGU, where they only served a local variety of instant coffee and the price of a cup changed according to the amount of sugar you wanted in it.

Ira had a boyfriend, a piece of information she'd forced into the conversation while we were sipping our first cup of coffee, and this was good, I thought, as I could do with a real Russian friend. Besides, I wasn't attracted to her. Ira was plumpish, and her eyes, an undefined watery colour, were always framed by dark circles. Her hair was thin, short and messy. By Moscow standards, Ira was what Colin referred to as below average.

Mind the closing doors. Next stop: Krasnoselskaya.

So we became friends, Ira and I, and she introduced me to another side of Moscow – not the clubbing scene or expat hang-outs, which she didn't really know, but the cultural side of the city. She showed me the places where the young intelligentsia gathered, and she used those words, young intelligentsia, by which she meant, I realised, other cash-starved students. Ira introduced me to some of her girlfriends. They were very nice but, for some reason which defied the rules of probability, not one of them was above average.

Ira and her friends taught me modern slang and expressions I would not learn at language class with Nadezhda Nikolaevna, who was a hundred years old and probably didn't know them. From Ira I also learned Russian swearwords, which proved useful with time, when I began to take on rude waitresses and shop assistants.

It was Ira who first showed me Café OGI, the underground establishment, famous in Moscow, that later sprouted two separate cafés with similar looks and names – all selling cheap books, cheap food and cheap drinks. But Ira took me to the original one, on Chistye Prudy, and it was dark and smoky, out of a Dostoyevsky novel, and, as I sipped on a warm beer, I glanced around at the colourful clientele, trying to identify the philosophers, the schemers and the impoverished students with murderous intentions.

Mind the closing doors. Next stop: Sokolniki.

I jumped off the metro, took the escalator up to the street. It was a cold December day. I wandered in the snow for ten minutes, holding a hand-drawn map in my gloved hands, trying to recognise, among the indistinguishable blocks and entrances, which one corresponded to the one where Ira had drawn a cross. It was dark and by the time I found the podyezd, as they called the entranceway, it was quarter past eight. I tapped in the entry code, as written on Ira's instructions, and took the lift to the third floor.

'Happy birthday,' I said when Ira opened the door. 'This is for you.'

I handed her a bottle of expensive French wine I'd bought in Eliseevsky.

'What else?' Ira asked.

'Was I supposed to bring anything else?'

'Of course not,' she said, laughing. 'This is great. What I mean is, what else are you going to tell me? Or is happy birthday all you wish me?'

I took my shoes off, placed them at the end of a line of shoes ranged neatly along the wall. 'What's wrong with happy birthday?'

'Martin, in Russia you can't only wish someone happy birthday.'

I handed my coat to Ira. 'You can't?'

'Happy birthday is just a formula,' Ira said, hanging my coat on a rack bulging with winter clothes. 'You need to tell me what you wish for me in the next year, like happiness, love or success, you know.'

'Sorry, I didn't know. I do wish you all that as well.'

A pungent smell of cabbage wafted in from the kitchen.

'This is Sergey's mother,' Ira said, pointing at the older lady who had just appeared. 'Aleksandra Olegovna.'

Aleksandra Olegovna had clearly made an effort to look festive. Her hair was blown out, in the fashion of 1980s pop singers, and she was wearing a black dress and a thick necklace with pearly stones. She was in her late forties or fifties, I could never tell with older Russian women.

'Come in, come in,' Aleksandra Olegovna said. 'Apologies for the small apartment.'

It was customary among Muscovites to apologise for the size of their apartments. Colin said it was yet another manifestation of their inferiority complex vis-à-vis foreigners that, in the minds of untravelled Russians, all Westerners live in big houses. The thought made me laugh as, in Amsterdam, I'd been living in the smallest of flats, with a cupboard shower at the back of the kitchen and a sink I used both for shaving and piling up dirty dishes.

I was led into the kitchen, where I was introduced to about a dozen people. Ira's cousins, aunts, friends, a young couple I'd met before and Sergey. All Russians. All crammed around the table in silence, under a bright neon light. There was no music – you could hear the rattling of the old fridge. Realising that I was the last one to arrive, I wondered if the others had been asked to come earlier.

The table was covered with a flowery tablecloth and blanketed with food: mayonnaise-based salads, smoked salmon, beef-tongue jelly, pickled herring, salted cucumbers, mushrooms, boiled potatoes with butter and dill, smetana. Everything was untouched.

At the centre of the table stood three bottles of vodka.

Sergey's mother offered me a chair at the head of the

table, which, I guessed, she must have been using before my arrival. I refused, but she insisted and, to avoid further awkwardness, I accepted. She sat on a stool next to the fridge.

'Dear comrades,' Sergey said, 'let the party begin.'

For some reason everybody laughed.

Sergey stood up, opened a bottle of vodka, filled all of our glasses. 'I would like to dedicate this first toast to Ira,' he said, 'my beloved girlfriend, whose birthday we are celebrating today.'

He was talking in a rather formal tone – I wasn't sure if it was for real or meant to be a joke.

He looked at Ira. 'Irinochka, lyubimaya, I would like to wish you a long happy life full of love and friendship and success, professional, personal, spiritual. May all your wishes come true. To Ira!'

'To Ira!'

Sergey kissed Ira. We all drained our glasses of vodka and placed them back on the table.

Sergey did not correspond to the image of Sergey I had formed in my mind. Ira had told me how he'd quit university to become a professional photographer, and for no particular reason I'd imagined him tall, blond, Slavic-looking. But Sergey was short and dark-haired, with black eyes and thick eyebrows. His chin was black with stubble. I imagined he must have some Caucasian background, Georgian or Armenian perhaps, but I decided not to ask.

'Kushaite, kushaite,' Sergey's mum was telling me, 'you need to eat. Take some salatik.'

'Thank you, Aleksandra Olegovna,' I said. 'This looks very nice.'

'I feel so old,' Ira said. 'It was only yesterday that I finished school and here I am, almost done with university, with a new job. Life goes so quickly.'

Sergey was now refilling the glasses with more vodka.

'If you only knew,' Aleksandra Olegovna said. 'One day you wake up and realise your life is almost gone and what have you done with it? Nothing. Because there is nothing you can do. We just survive year after year as we get old—'

'Mama, don't start,' Sergey interrupted.

'I remember when I was your age as if it were yesterday,' Aleksandra Olegovna continued, looking at Ira. 'Of course things were different back then. I already had my little Seryozhka.' She placed her hand on Sergey's shoulder.

Sergey shook off his mother's hand and stood up. 'Dear friends,' he said, 'I would like to propose another toast. Let us drink now to peace and friendship among the peoples of the world.'

We raised our glasses and, as I was about to pour the vodka down my throat, I realised with panic that everybody was staring at me. It struck me that I was somehow considered by those around the table as a kind of international envoy to Ira's birthday. For a few seconds I wondered if I was expected to give an acceptance speech in return for the toast. My Russian wasn't up to the task, I decided, so I just raised my glass again, smiled and glanced around the table, indicating with my silent but sincere gesture that I was honoured to accept the toast on behalf of my fellow non-Russians of the world.

We drained our glasses and soon the conversation split into different groups.

A few minutes later Sergey opened the bottle of French wine I'd brought and poured it into the water glasses around the table.

'This is great,' he said. 'French wine. Where did you get it?'

'I bought it in Eliseevsky, they have a wide selection.'

'Oh, but it's so expensive in there,' Aleksandra Olegovna said.

'I hope you like Bordeaux,' I said.

I held the glass under my nose. The wine had a pleasant aroma, woody and sweet. I had indeed invested a significant amount of time and money in procuring the bottle. It wasn't the kind of wine you could find in metro shops selling cheap Moldovan and Georgian varieties.

'We love French wine,' Sergey said. 'The best. This toast,' he went on, raising his glass of wine, 'I would like to dedicate to Ira's parents, who can't be here today, and to all of our parents.'

'To our parents!'

They all raised their arms and, to my horror, drank the Bordeaux as if it were a shot of vodka, in two, three gulps.

'That was a great wine,' Sergey said, wiping his mouth with the back of his hand. Then he took a bite of black bread.

'This was an excellent wine,' Ira said. 'Thank you, Martin.'

'Much better than the Moldovan crap we normally get,' Ira's cousin said.

Aleksandra Olegovna was looking at my glass. 'Martin, why don't you drink your wine?'

With the aged Bordeaux in my hand, I hesitated for a

moment. Now everybody was staring at me in silence. I forced a smile, took a deep breath and drank the wine in one.

'So,' Sergey said, 'Ira tells us that you are doing some research on Russian literature?'

Ira placed her hand on my shoulder. 'Martin is trying to figure out why Anna Karenina throws herself under a train.' She laughed.

'It's about how Russian heroines behave,' I said, slightly annoyed that nobody seemed to take my research seriously. 'I'm first trying to identify some common characteristics between Russian heroines and real Russian women.'

'That sounds very interesting,' said Aleksandra Olegovna. 'How do you like our dear Pushkin?'

'Pushkin,' I said, 'of course.' I was thinking which of the stories proving my devotion to Pushkin I was going to tell, pondering if reciting a few verses would be appropriate at this point in the evening, when Ira's cousin stood up, clinking his glass with a fork.

'Let me propose another toast,' he said, in a sombre tone. 'All of us around the table are good people with big hearts.'

Ira looked at Sergey and rolled her eyes.

'Today,' Ira's cousin continued, 'we are celebrating Ira's birthday. It's thanks to Ira that we are here today, and if so many good people are around the same table because of Ira, well, that means that Ira herself is a great person.'

I wasn't sure I had understood everything right.

'Of course I *am* a great person,' Ira said.

We all laughed.

'To friendship!' Ira's cousin said, raising the vodka in his right hand, and hovering his left hand over the rest of us, as if to indicate that the effects of the toast were limited this time to friendship among those present in the kitchen.

'Thank you, thank you,' Ira said.

'That's beautiful,' Aleksandra Olegovna said with tears in her eyes.

We drank up.

Soon, the three bottles of vodka were empty and three more bottles appeared on the table.

Someone told an anekdot and, although I understood all the sentences, I couldn't figure out what was funny about it. But I nodded along to the story and, when everybody laughed, I joined in. Suddenly, the thought of being in Ira's kitchen laughing at a Russian joke I hadn't got seemed hilarious to me. To my surprise, my forced chuckle turned into real laughter, which in turn made everybody else laugh louder.

Sergey patted my back, seemingly in approval.

As we continued drinking, my understanding improved significantly. At some point I found myself totally immersed in the Russian conversation, almost unaware that I was speaking a foreign language. It was not that I knew more words, but I seemed more able to grasp the overall narrative – filling in the language gaps with my own drunken version of whatever was being said at the table.

Sergey put an arm around my shoulders and said, 'I really respect you.' He then thanked me for helping Ira with her English. 'You are such, such a nice guy. You could be Russian.' He stared at me in silence. His breath smelled of vodka and herring.

'Spasibo,' I said, smiling.

Sergey's gaze was somehow lost in a space behind my head, and for a second I was afraid he was about to hug me or kiss me, but at that moment Ira's uncle stood up on the other side of the table and proposed a new toast. This one to the women in the room, to their beauty and their pure hearts, and to something else which I didn't get but included, I thought, the Russian word for air or for breathing. We all drank up and had a bite of bread and salad.

'So,' I said, turning to Sergey, 'Ira told me you are now working on a project, black and white photos.'

'Not black and white – I'm using different tonalities of grey. With loads of shadows. It's a series I've called *Moscow's Soul*.'

'Interesno,' I said, digging my fork into my mushroom salad.

The salad tasted of damp earth and fresh dill, and, as I swallowed, I was overcome by a tide of positive feelings towards my physical surroundings. I glanced around the kitchen, my eyes unable to focus on any particular point, and I perceived everything in a warmer light – a blurry vodka gleam cast over the salad bowls, the flowery tablecloth, the rattling fridge, the flowers in the kitchen sink, the reddened faces of the other guests. It felt as if all the parts of the kitchen had become one single entity – coherent and meaningful. Then, peering through the window into the darkness, I discerned the crazy air-bound dance of fresh snowflakes.

'You know the statue of Peter the Great?' Sergey asked.

'You mean the big statue in the middle of the river?'

'Yes, Tsereteli's statue,' Sergey said, munching on a piece of cucumber. 'I'm trying to capture all of its ugliness in one single frame.'

He laughed.

I laughed too. 'I see.'

'The statue is very symbolic,' Ira said. 'It's representative of the new Moscow.'

'Why Peter's statue?' I asked.

Sergey moved closer to me, lowered his voice. 'Tsereteli's statue represents the banality of modern Moscow.'

'I find the statue hideous,' I said.

'Exactly,' Sergey said. 'Everybody in Moscow hates the statue. Only the mayor likes it. But the main thing is, the statue is not what it looks like. It's a fake.'

Ira placed a boiled potato on my plate and one on Sergey's plate. 'Seryozhka,' she said, 'eat more. You shouldn't have drunk before we started the party, now you are drunker than the rest of us.'

'A fake?' I asked. 'In what sense?'

In what sense, v kakom smysle, was a useful expression I'd learned to drop into a conversation every time I got lost. It was particularly handy in a situation where a question was addressed to me, an answer was clearly expected, but my comprehension skills had let me down. Instead of asking for the question to be repeated, which would have cast doubt on my credibility as an interlocutor, I would just ask, 'In what sense?' It was such a useful phrase that, with time, I also began to use it when I didn't know what to say and wanted more time to think. In what sense?

'The statue wasn't meant to be in Moscow,' Sergey said.

'It wasn't?'

'The statue was meant to be in the United States. It was commissioned as a present from the Russian people to the American people at the end of the Cold War. Americans didn't like it so they said no thank you.'

'Why would the Americans want a statue of Peter the Great?'

'That's the whole point,' Sergey said. There was a bit of sour cream stuck on his thick eyebrows. 'When the statue was made, it wasn't Peter the Great. Originally it was a statue of Christopher Columbus, and it was meant to symbolise the union between the two sides of the Atlantic, or some shit like that. When the Americans refused it, nobody knew what to do with a giant Columbus.'

'A waste of money, if you ask me,' Aleksandra Olegovna said.

'So,' Sergey continued, 'the mayor asked Tsereteli to turn Columbus's head into the head of Peter the Great. And he fucking did! But they couldn't find a place in Moscow to erect such a monster, you know, all the squares are occupied by Lenins and soviet stuff, so in the end they decided to plant the thing in the middle of the Moskva river.'

'Martin, try the herring and beetroot salad,' Sergey's mum said. 'It's a typical Russian dish.'

'Thank you, Aleksandra Olegovna, everything is delicious.'

Sergey began refilling the glasses with more vodka. 'Mama,' he said, 'let him eat whatever he wants.'

'So,' I asked, 'the statue in the Moskva river is not Peter the Great but Christopher Columbus?'

'Exactly,' Sergey said. He wiped his eyebrows, seemed puzzled to find sour cream on his fingers. 'If you look closely you'll see he is standing on an old vessel, from Columbus times, not from the times of Peter the Great.'

'It's a botch job,' Ira said.

Aleksandra Olegovna stood up, started to clear some plates. 'I can hardly recognise the city any more.'

'This is Moscow today,' Sergey said, putting a hand on my shoulder. 'We are losing our soul and nobody gives a shit.'

12

LENA LIVED IN AN old kommunalka not far from Chistye Prudy, sharing the communal bathroom with three families and her bedroom with a girl from Tula. They had some kind of arrangement, I imagined, as the Tula dyev was never around when I visited and Lena and I could always enjoy a couple of hours of privacy.

Lena's bedroom was a total bardak, a mess. The bedside tables, like every flat surface in the room, were completely covered in piles of books, old magazines, food leftovers, make-up paraphernalia, old cups of tea. The room always smelled of incense, which Lena kept burning in my presence – whether for some spiritual purpose or to mask other smells, I couldn't tell.

One cold evening in late December we were lying on Lena's bed, naked, listening to music from an Asian lounge compilation she liked to play when I was around. I had picked up a book from the pile on her bedside table, a cheap paperback on compassion, written, according to the back cover, by his holiness the Dalai Lama. I thumbed through the pages, many of which were dog-eared, reading the bits that Lena had underlined and trying to decipher the comments she had scribbled in the margins. It struck me that the Russian word for compassion, sostradaniye, derived from the word suffering, stradaniye, and literally meant co-suffering. A compassionate person was, in Russian, a co-sufferer. Considering this a valuable insight, I jumped out of bed and grabbed the red notebook I was carrying in my backpack.

I lay on the bed writing about the word compassion. Lena was staring at the ceiling in silence – her fingers fiddling with her golden chain, her perfect breasts swelling and ebbing with each breath, like waves in the ocean.

We hadn't had sex. At least not sex sex. We had never talked about this but, as far as I understood, Lena didn't enjoy the most primal aspects of human sexuality. For her, it wasn't about gathering momentum and losing control. Lena approached sexual intimacy as a flat sensory experience, as a slow succession of caresses and kisses, which often remained at the level of touching. It wasn't shyness or prudishness. Lena felt comfortable with her body. As soon as we were alone in her bedroom, she would often take her clothes off and go about her tasks in complete nakedness – making tea, lighting incense, moving piles of clothes from one bed to the other, fully aware of the powerful effect her naked body had on me. But once my own clothes came off, she would immediately apply herself to me, with precision, without pause, as if deactivating a ticking bomb. On the rare occasions when she had allowed me to get inside her, she had insisted on keeping the lights on and staying beneath me, her blue eyes fixed on my face. A few times, at the beginning, in the heat of the moment, I had tried to wrestle her on top of me, to give her more control, to fully appreciate the weight of her breasts, but she had always climbed off right away; and once, when I'd tried to stay beneath her body for a few seconds, she had abruptly jumped out of bed and run off to the bathroom — to return a few minutes later, her eyes red from crying. On that occasion I'd asked her what was wrong. Nothing, she'd said. But ever since that day, I always followed Lena's lead, her tempo, her moves, adapting my own expectations to whatever she was in the mood for — afraid to cross a line that, I suspected, originated in some obscure episode of her life.

I circled the word compassion in my notebook and dropped the pen. I turned to Lena, grabbed her golden cross. 'What's this?'

'From grandmother.'

'Beautiful.' I found Orthodox crosses aesthetically interesting, the slanted lower crossbeam breaking the symmetry of the design.

'Do you believe in God?' Lena asked, staring at the ceiling.

I was aware of Lena's spiritual side, but it had never occurred to me to raise the question myself.

'No, I don't,' I said. 'You?'

She thought about it for a few moments, as if she were

considering God's existence for the first time. Then she turned to me. 'I believe there is good and there is evil.'

'What about God?' I said. 'You know, the all-powerful creator.' I extended my arm and grabbed the New Testament from the pile of books on her bedside table. 'The God from your Bible.'

'There is no God,' Lena said. 'The Bible is a beautiful fairy tale – a skazka.'

'Why do you wear the cross then?'

'You don't need to believe in God to be a good Christian.'

I dropped the New Testament next to the pillow, leaned over Lena's body, kissed her stomach, then her breasts. 'A good Christian?' I said.

Lena burrowed her fingers in my hair. 'I believe in the values of Christianity as preserved by the Russian Orthodox Church. I believe in forgiveness, in compassion, in resurrection.'

My tongue was now toying with her nipples. 'If you ask me,' I said, looking up, 'I find resurrection the weakest part of the Gospels. You know, coming back from the dead. Bit of a stretch, don't you think?'

'You shouldn't mock this,' Lena said, now placing her hand over the New Testament. Like most of her books, the volume was encrusted with plenty of bookmarks. 'It gives my life a sense of direction. Trying to be good is a daily struggle.'

I kept playing with her breasts.

'Resurrection,' she continued, 'is of course a metaphor. Flesh is flesh, when it dies, it dies. But a dead soul can return to life. Bad deeds can be redeemed.'

My lips caressing her skin, I glanced up at her face. 'What about Yeshua?'

'Yeshua?' she said.

'Christ, you know, Jesus. Yeshua, like in *The Master and Margarita*.'

'I think the Gospels are beautiful.'

'But you can't believe they actually happened.'

'I don't. The New Testament was written by men. But I think Christ, the historical figure, must have been an incredible man who walked the Earth with a beautiful message. I believe in the message.'

Trying to keep her exact words in my head, I turned over and reached for my red notebook. These were the kind of thoughts I could find a use for in my research.

'Leave your notebook,' Lena said. 'Please.'

Lena didn't like my notebooks. When I began carrying them around, I'd tried to explain how it was important for me to understand her way of seeing the world so that I could compare her views with those of literary heroines. I'd thought she would feel proud to be useful, to take part in my research. But instead, she had developed an unexplained aversion towards my notebooks, and I could feel, every time I took one of them out of my backpack, that she didn't appreciate my taking notes.

'I just want to write something quickly,' I said, looking for a blank page.

With sudden violence, Lena ripped the notebook from my hands, and threw it into the air. The red notebook flew across the room, hit the wall, and landed on the other bed, next to a pile of dirty clothes.

I didn't know what to say.

'Martin, right now you are with me.'

It was often the case that I couldn't make much sense of Lena's actions. I decided to let it go and move on. I kissed her lips, caressed her hair, and tried to continue with our conversation.

'I don't think you need any bible to tell you what's good and what's bad,' I said. 'If you are a good person, you don't need religion.'

'And how do I know I'm a good person?'

'You are,' I smiled. 'Trust me.'

'I don't know if I'm a good person, really. That's why I need to search.'

'Search for what?'

She didn't answer.

I pushed my body against hers, kissed her neck, her ear. She didn't react. Her eyes were moist.

'For chrissake, Lena, why can't you just enjoy life as it is?'

'Because,' she said softly, 'without the search, life is a lonely and meaningless thing.'

Those were her exact words — a lonely and meaningless thing. I know because, later that night, I wrote them down in my mistreated notebook.

And now, so many years later, the smell of incense still brings me back to Lena's room in the kommunalka — the piles of clothes, the old bed, the worn books — and I feel an emptiness in my chest because life since hasn't been anything like so complete, so full of promise, so void of pain, and, even if I didn't know it, back then I could extend my arms, reach out, and almost touch happiness.

PART TWO

Irina's Dreams

13

In 1900, Anton Pavlovich Chekhov, by that time very sick and living in Yalta, wrote a play about three sisters who were stuck in a provincial shithole and spent their days dreaming about moving back to Moscow. *Three Sisters: A Drama in Four Acts* is not a story of sweeping mad love or tragedy. It's about boredom and dullness and the futility of pursuing happiness.

Olya, Masha and Irina live in a small town, absorbed in the insignificant tasks of daily life, watching time pass by, reminiscing about a happier past and dreaming about a brighter future. For the three sisters, who feel they don't belong in the provinces, there is only one way out of their dull existence: Moscow.

Moscow is the place where they could be happy again.

The three sisters, each in their twenties, had left Moscow

eleven years earlier, when their father — a general, now dead — had been awarded the command of a regiment in the provinces. They have a brother, Andrey Sergeyevich, who plans to return to Moscow to become a university professor, taking his sisters with him.

At the beginning of the play, Irina, the youngest, is radiant and hopeful. While her older sisters can't help being moody, Irina's dreams infuse her naive soul with endless optimism. It's in Moscow, she believes, that she will find true love and they will all be happy.

To the great disappointment of the three sisters, their Moscow plans never seem to take off. As the play advances and the sisters begin to understand that they might be stuck in the provinces, Moscow becomes less real, more ethereal. A spiritual aspiration.

Moscow represents where they want to be, both the past and the future. Moscow is everywhere, except here and now.

In *Three Sisters*, Anton Pavlovich exposes the very human weakness of believing that both the past and the future are better places to be. And holding on to the illusion that things will get better is our way of coping with life's dullness.

A series of visitors, mostly military officers from the battalion in town, come to see the three sisters. Among them is Vershinin, a colonel, who at the beginning of the play has just arrived from Moscow and impresses the sisters with his sophistication.

Masha, the second sister, married at eighteen, is now bored

of her husband. Whining about her life, she says that if only she lived in Moscow she would not even care about the weather. In response, Vershinin tells her the story of a French political prisoner who writes with passion about the birds he sees from the window of his cell, the same birds he never noticed when he was a free man. In the same way, Vershinin tells Masha, you will not notice Moscow once you live there again. We want happiness, he concludes, but we are not happy and we cannot be happy.

Masha, deeply impressed, starts an affair with Vershinin.

Irina talks about finding meaning in life through labour. But when she starts work at the local telegraph office she realises her life has no more meaning than before. Time goes by and Irina, too, loses her spark, drifting into ennui. As the dream of Moscow evaporates, she accepts her sudba and agrees to marry an officer she doesn't love.

At one point, Masha realises that she can hardly remember the face of her dead mother. Their own mother, who died young and is buried in Moscow, is being forgotten. And we will all be forgotten one day, Masha says. Yes, Vershinin replies, they will forget us. That's our destiny, our sudba: things that we believe serious, meaningful, very important, there will come a time when they will be forgotten or will seem unimportant.

At the end of the play the local battalion moves out of town and Vershinin has to leave with the other officers. Masha returns to her husband, who accepts her back despite his knowledge of the affair. This being Chekhov, there is no judgement, no punishment.

The sisters realise they will never go back to Moscow. They will grow old in the provinces. And they accept their destiny — settling for less than they had hoped for.

If life has meaning, it's not something within the grasp of Chekhov's characters. They are imperfectly human, short-sighted, and yet fully aware of their own insignificance. Life is a succession of dull moments, sometimes interrupted by short bursts of joy, always full of irrelevant thoughts that keep us distracted as we get older, dreaming of better lives but gradually accepting the unimportance of our own existence.

Then, one day, we die and everything is forgotten.

14

RUSSIA CHANGED FAST DURING the first months of my stay. On the last day of the year, as the world prepared hysterical celebrations for the arrival of a new millennium, Russia's president – widely regarded as an endearing old man with a drinking problem – went on national TV and, to everybody's surprise, announced he was resigning from office. As successor, he appointed the latest of his many prime ministers, a relatively unknown politician with an obscure background in the secret services.

At first, Muscovites didn't seem to give much significance to this. 'Nothing will change,' Nadezhda Nikolaevna had told me when we resumed our language classes after the holiday break. 'They are all thieves anyway.'

But things did change. In fact, it seemed to me that the country had entered a new era.

By early spring everyone had stopped talking about the economic crisis. TV news, which I watched often to exercise my comprehension skills, showed endless footage of the new president, looking young and sober. We could see him every night on the news, practising judo, riding a horse, reprimanding under-performing ministers or winning, pretty much single-handedly, a nasty war in the Caucasus. According to the national media, Russia was now doing great. Overnight, the country had become rich, confident and assertive.

These changes were quickly reflected in Moscow's clubbing scene. The city entered the elitni era. A new club opened every weekend, each more select than the last. Nightlife was no longer the exclusive realm of dyevs and expats. Russian oligarchs began to show up at the doors of the latest elitni clubs, first in limousines with tinted windows, then in black humvees, always accompanied by an entourage of drivers, okhrannikis and whores.

The nightlife crowd became known as the tusovka, each of us a tusovschik. For some reason that was never explained to me, it was around this time that cafés and clubs began to serve sushi or, rather, a local version of the Japanese delicacy, which in Moscow included plenty of cream cheese, smetana and dill. To keep up with the trend, the tusovka had to learn to use chopsticks.

Elitni clubs came with their own elitni sections, cordoned-off VIP areas, which were only accessible if you spent a few hundred dollars on champagne. It soon became hard for us, humble expats, to get into these clubs. We would be turned away at the door by bouncers who spoke no English and didn't care that we did.

But we didn't give up. We, determined Westerners, who had won the Cold War by standing for decades against Russian bullying, were not about to accept defeat without putting up a fight. So now, when out with the brothers, we would always try to make it into the latest of elitni clubs, many of which were no longer called clubs but 'projects'. Sure, we had to adapt to our new status, make a few concessions, adopt a less prominent profile. We would now ask our taxi driver to drop us round the corner, as the sight of a crumbling zhiguli would instantly kill our chances of passing face control. We would approach the front door of the club in small groups, walking purposefully, radiating self-confidence, barely acknowledging the bouncer, looking as wealthy and as Russian as we could.

Sometimes it worked. And nothing compared to the feeling of gliding through face control, those first seconds after the bouncer has casually beckoned you in, and you step firmly onto the carpet, and you enter a pafosni universe prohibited to mere mortals, chosen because you are handsome, special, and you walk towards the boom-boom beats with your heart full of anticipation and excitement — feeling that you belong in Moscow and Moscow is the centre of the world.

When we were turned away, which was increasingly often, we would hail another car and move to one of the clubs whose prime had passed and which had been forced to adopt a more lenient door policy.

Colin said, you find the best dyevs in these clubs, hot enough to make it through a second-rate face control but not as demanding as in trendier places. But some nights, for reasons we never understood, even these démodé establishments would not let us in, so we would end up in safe old Real McCoy, or Karma Bar, which for years maintained an all-expats-welcome policy and were always packed with young students.

These nights didn't come cheap. I had to buy rounds of drinks for the brothers when it was my turn, but also for pretty dyevs and their entourage of not-so-pretty friends. I also bought new clothes at the shopping mall in Okhotny Ryad, black shirts and shiny shoes, to fit in among the increasingly exclusive and well-uniformed tusovka.

I was blowing my stipend money fast, and it was meant to last the entire academic year, so, when Stepanov offered me a part-time job, I accepted it at once.

'It'll only take you a few hours a week,' Stepanov said. Then, with a smirk, he added, 'I'm sure it won't distract you from your research.'

That was how I started working for Stepanov.

My job description: show up at business meetings wearing a suit, mutter a few words in English, hand out business cards with a smile and a strong handshake. Nothing else, really. Director of Marketing, Insight Investments International, my business card said, good old Latin letters on one side, flashy Cyrillic on the other.

Other than Stepanov and me, Insight Investments International had two staff members, Pavel and Vova, Stepanov's schoolmates. I was the third 'I' of the firm, the International, a Western face investors could trust. But Stepanov was always the one to talk the talk.

I never fully grasped the intricacies of the business but, as far as I gathered from the meetings I was asked to attend, Insight Investments International sold Russian companies, or parts of them, to foreign investors.

In business mode, Stepanov would try to hide his boyish face behind three-day stubble and sunglasses. He always wore a dark suit and a black shirt, a popular look among Russian men at the time, inspired by TV series and movies where the protagonists were always Russian criminals.

'I think the sunglasses might put some investors off,' I told him once. We had just met a group of French business-men who wanted to buy a dairy factory and produce brie and camembert for the Russian market. The conversation had somehow drifted – the French businessmen seemed more interested in nightclubs than in Stepanov's exposé of Russian cheeses.

'Bullshit,' Stepanov said. 'They love the sunglasses. That's how they know that I'm well connected, that I really under-stand business in Russia.'

Every time a deal went through, Stepanov handed me an envelope stuffed with dollars. I was never told how my salary was calculated but, with time, Stepanov's envelopes got thicker, and I ended up with plenty of cash to spend.

15

'HERE'S A QUESTION,' COLIN SAYS. 'If you had to choose only one club to go to for the rest of your time in Moscow, the one place you're allowed to visit, which one would you choose?'

'Only one?' I ask.

'Only one. You could not get into any other club. The only place for you to get drunk and meet dyevs.'

'Propaganda.'

Colin takes a long sip and finishes his Long Island iced tea. His eyes are shiny, his half-smile wider than usual. 'Come on, you must be kidding.'

'I'm not,' I say. 'You know I like Propaganda.'

It's Friday night and the Real McCoy is packed. The air is hot, shirts are sweaty. The windows by the entrance are coated in a layer of condensation. We are on our third Long Island iced tea, in good spirits.

'Sure,' Colin says, 'we all like Propaganda, but, come on, before McCoy? Be serious, man. We've met so many nice dyevs in here.'

'Don't get me wrong,' I say. 'I really like the McCoy. What the fuck, I *love* the McCoy. Moscow wouldn't be the same without it. But the McCoy would probably be my second choice. Or my third, after Karma. If you ask for one single club, for me it's Propaganda.'

Colin points up at two dyevs dancing on top of the bar, their high heels pounding away next to my drink. 'You don't get this atmosphere in Propaganda, the McCoy is always a feast. This is the real Moscow, man. Wild and fucking honest!'

At that moment, as if to prove Colin's point, the two dyevs, who are wearing short skirts and leather boots, start kissing each other. People around us raise their arms and cheer.

'There're plenty of hot dyevs in Propaganda,' Colin says, 'I give you that. The difference is, dyevs go to Propaganda to be seen, the Real McCoy they come to to get laid.'

'For an easy score,' I say, 'the Real McCoy is unbeatable. It totally deserves its three fuckies. But think of all the great nights we had in Propaganda. Propaganda's a Moscow legend.'

Colin is now ogling the dyevs dancing on the bar. 'We *had* great nights in Propaganda,' he says. 'Not any more. Now it's going all pafosni and exclusivni like the rest of the city. These days you walk in and you could be in any club in the world. It's been sanitised, Westernised. If that's the type of club you enjoy, you may as well go back home. Propaganda has lost the wildness of the real Moscow. If you think about it, how many Prop dyevs have you fucked lately?'

'I met Lena in Propaganda.'

'Yeah, all right, but how many *new* dyevs? You met Lena in Propaganda ages ago, soon after you arrived. She doesn't count. There is nothing like McCoy, man.'

Colin leaves the glass on the bar and – grabbing the leather boot of one of the dyevs – points at it so that she is careful not to kick it. The dyev looks down at us and smiles.

The music is now deafening.

'Remember that dyev I met last week in Zeppelin?' Colin asks. He's sweating, rolling up the sleeves of his silky blue shirt.

'The one with the big nose?'

'But great legs, right?'

'If you say so.'

I wave at the waiter and point at our empty glasses. He looks up and acknowledges my order.

'So I met her on Tuesday. What a bitch!'

'She did look bitchy,' I say.

'We'd agreed to meet in Teatralnaya, outside the Bolshoi. I came straight from the gym, so I was carrying my sports bag, and guess what the first thing this bitch said when she saw me was, before hello or anything? "You are not bringing that ugly bag with us, are you?"'

'Your sports bag?'

'Yeah, my fucking sports bag.'

'Why would she give a shit?'

'Fuck knows,' Colin says.

The waiter places two new glasses between the leather boots of the dancing dyevs, fills them with crushed ice and various shots. He then tops up the glasses with coke from a hose and a splash of lime juice. I pay for the round, clink my glass with Colin's and take a sip. The air feels balmier now, lacking oxygen. I welcome the freshness of the drink.

'These drinks are loaded,' I say.

'Try getting a Long Island like this in Propaganda. These are the best drinks in town, I tell you. Anyway, so the dyev told me something about how carrying a sports bag around is so working class, not kulturno in Moscow.'

'What the fuck.'

'I know,' Colin says. 'I told her I'd just been to the gym and I had nowhere to leave the bag. So we walked up Petrovka and I took her to this new café on the corner with Stoleshnikov, you know, the new place with white tables and white chandeliers and the hot waitresses dressed in black. All pafosni and nice, right?'

'Sure,' I say. 'I like it.'

'This bitch didn't. She asked me why I'm taking her to a café and not to a restaurant when I had promised to take her to a restaurant.'

'What's the difference?'

'Fuck knows. I told her, "Listen, there's nice food in here and a good atmosphere," but she was all whiny because of my working-class bag and because I wasn't taking her to a real restaurant. Then we get the menu and the bitch starts complaining about the food. She orders a glass of French champagne, which was of course the most expensive item she could find on the menu.'

'Classic,' I say. 'What did you do?'

'Wait.' Colin drinks from his Long Island. 'I told her I'd go home quickly to drop my bag and get changed, and be back in fifteen minutes to take her to a proper restaurant. She seemed happy with that. So I go outside, take a taxi and, when I'm on my way home, I write her a text telling her to go fuck herself because I'm not coming back and I don't want to see her ever again.'

'Well done, man, that's great.' I slap Colin's back. 'You made her pay for her own champagne.'

'Not really,' Colin says, shaking his head. 'I did pay the bill on the way out. She was probably not carrying any cash. Anyway, you should write about this in your PhD, or if you ever write your book about Moscow. I think it's very representative of the new Russia.'

A popular Russian song from the 1980s comes on. Everyone in the club is now singing along and dancing. People gather, forming a circle, arms around each other, revolving around the dance floor.

'The city is changing fast,' Colin shouts in my ear. 'Not what it used to be. Remember when you could take a dyev to McDonald's and expect to get laid in return?'

'Come on, it was never like that.'

'It was, maybe before you arrived. Things are no longer the same, the good times will soon be over. One day we'll look back on this time and realise that we got to live in this special historical moment. We're witnessing the disintegration of an entire society. We're in the midst of a social and sexual revolution. Moscow is a jungle, man. People just care about getting rich and getting laid. Money and sex. It's all new to them.'

I take a sip of my drink. 'Money, perhaps. But they must have fucked during soviet times.'

The ring of bouncing people, reaching critical mass, surges towards the bar, a human tornado razing everything in its path. To avoid a collision, Colin and I have to step back. A drunk girl is now on the floor, her skirt halfway up her waist, a long rip in her tights. Colin helps her to her feet. She laughs, says spasibo and, singing along, rejoins the crowd.

Colin is holding his glass up in the air, so as not to spill it over his silky shirt. 'In soviet times they only fucked for reproduction purposes,' he says. 'Free sex is one of those things brought by the perestroika. That's why Russians embraced the uncertainty of political change, because at least they were getting some. Hence the Duck.'

'What has the Duck got to do with this?'

'The Hungry Duck symbolised the social and political changes. Dyevs in the Duck were crazy sluts because sexuality was oppressed for seventy years by the old regime. Their sluttiness was a form of unconscious protest against oppression.'

'That's crap,' I say. 'Look at Chekhov's plays, everybody fools around.'

'That's in books,' Colin says. 'Free sex in real life is something new.'

At the end of the song, as the music quietens down, a table

is knocked over at the back, glasses shattering on the floor. The crowd is silent for two seconds. Then someone screams vsyo khorosho, everything's good, and there is laughter and the dancing goes on.

'Some things never change,' I say. 'One day, we'll be gone from Moscow, but other guys will come to this very bar to pick up dyevs, and new dyevs will come to get drunk and have fun. It's the circle of life.'

'No way,' Colin says, undoing a button on his shiny blue shirt. 'Come here in ten years and see. There might be a Real McCoy, but it won't be like this. Look what happened to the Duck.'

'That's different,' I say. 'The Duck was too wild. It couldn't last.'

'Nothing good lasts, man. Life's a short bitch and we have to enjoy every fucking bit of it.'

I nod, taking a long sip of my drink.

'This Moscow,' Colin says, his arm hovering over the McCoy crowd, '*our* Moscow, will also disappear.'

16

WITH THE WARM WEATHER, the trees around the university campus, which had been bare all winter, turned lush and green. The city was flooded with a bizarre soft light that revealed a mesmerising range of faded colours, and you could now see pale pinks and greens and blues on the façades of old buildings. They were all turning into white, these colours, sun-bleached, and Moscow at this time of the year felt polaroid-faded, dreamlike. Walking the older streets of the centre I was often under the impression that my surroundings belonged to a discoloured guidebook.

You could find plenty of dyevs strolling around Okhotny Ryad and Aleksandrovsky Sad, or manoeuvring their high heels across the cobblestones of Red Square. They wore impossibly short skirts and no bras, ate ice cream, and stared straight into your eyes for as long as you could hold their gaze.

To combat the heat, terraces and kiosks across the city sold bottles of beer which men carried proudly in their hands as they strolled along the boulevards or sat on park benches. If you ventured under the archways of old buildings and into their courtyards, you would sometimes discover hidden cafés, temporary wooden structures that sold grilled shashliks and dried fish.

In the months I had spent in Moscow, new coffee shops had sprouted around Tverskaya, Bolshaya Dmitrovka and Bolshaya Nikitskaya, and in the smaller streets around Kuznetsky Most and Kitay-gorod. They sold expensive cakes – eclairs, Napoleons, carrot cakes, brownies – and, for the first time in Russia, freshly brewed coffee. Dyevs sat in these trendy cafés for hours, stuffing themselves with sugar and caffeine, reading women's magazines and Akunin books, redoing their make-up every twenty minutes with the help of pocket mirrors. But they were never fully focused on their reading, I realised. Even if seemingly absorbed in a book, dyevs were always attentive to their surroundings, ready to look up at any minor disturbance, like gazelles on the savannah who don't let their guard down while drinking from a pond.

On Saturdays I played football. Our team played in blue shirts and was called the Blues Brothers, which was why – I seem to recall – we had started referring to ourselves as the brothers. I'd met them through Colin at the beginning of my stay. We played an expat league but the rules allowed two Russian players per team. Stepanov was a solid midfielder. Colin played up front with me and Diego spent most of his time on the bench, happy to come out for ten minutes and then enjoy the drinks.

We had played all winter on a covered pitch in Dinamo but now that it was warm and dry we played in Kazakova, a small park east of the ring road. The grass pitch was surrounded by woodland and the ruins of a pre-revolutionary palace. A green oasis — it didn't feel like Moscow.

It was the Dutch expats who managed the football league. They'd arrived in the mid-1990s, recruited by Russian oligarchs who didn't trust local employees to run Moscow's casinos. They were all a bit older than the rest of us and most had Russian wives and kids. The Dutch booked the pitch, paid the referees and brought local casino employees every Saturday to serve shashliks and salads and cold beers after our matches. So Saturdays were lovely, especially when it was sunny, and the players brought their wives, girlfriends and mistresses to watch our games.

I would bring Lena and no one else. She would stand on the side of the pitch in her skimpy summer dress, her short blonde hair gleaming under the sun. She would pace on the grass, along the sideline, following the game with attention, but I never heard her shout or cheer, not even on the rare occasions when I scored a goal. After the match, I would grab a bottle of beer from the ice bucket, and lie on the grass to watch the next game with my head on Lena's lap, feeling the sun warm my cheeks while she stroked my sweaty hair.

By mid-June, the nights were so short that the sky was bright until midnight, when we entered the clubs, and bright again when we came out onto the street a few hours later.

Clubs opened their own gardens and terraces, and it was around this time that the party boat started to run on Friday nights.

The boat was an elitni affair, and the point and time of its departure one of Moscow's best-kept secrets. It was Stepanov who would find out on Friday which embankment the party boat would depart from that night. After a few warm-up drinks in Stepanov's place, we would get on board and, because we were in the know, we were always allowed in. There would be plenty of New Russians on the boat, models and actresses and TV people, some of whom even I recognised, and the boat would drift all night up and down the Moskva river, stopping every now and then to load and unload beautiful people.

On board, we felt part of Moscow's tusovka, the chosen ones, gathering to spend the nights in communion with the city. We drank, talked to dyevs, made best friends, and I would often meet the dawn dancing on the top deck, as the boat glided gently over the dark waters, blasting its mellow techno music under the enormous statue of Peter the Great or Christopher Columbus, and the chocolate factory, and the House on the Embankment, with its giant Mercedes-Benz star, and my heart would beat faster as the boat passed under the Bolshoy Kamenny Bridge – where we would all duck for no reason – and emerge by the earthy walls and golden domes of the Kremlin as the city was brought to life by a warm orange sun rising over the east.

Oh Bozhe, how I loved Moscow!

17

AT THE BEGINNING OF July, about ten months into my stay, I rented a studio on Tverskaya, on the top floor of an old soviet building. The landlady requested that I pay in cash, which suited me fine as all I had was the stack of dollars I was getting from Stepanov. Rents in the centre, which would skyrocket later, were quite reasonable at the time.

My flat had no bedroom, just a living room, half of which was occupied by an enormous corner sofa that unfolded into a bed. Once I'd got the landlady to change the carpet, the place looked pretty decent. Above the couch, I hung an Indian tapestry that Lena had bought me for my birthday and had previously adorned my university room. The tapestry showed Lord Ganesh, in browns and yellows, surrounded by white dots. Handing me the present, Lena had told me the story of how the Hindu god had had his head chopped off and replaced by that of an elephant. She assured me that Lord Ganesh brought good luck, that he used the little broom in his hand to remove obstacles from the path of life.

The kitchen, a separate room with wood-clad walls and a small dining table, was functional, warm and cosy. On top of the table, next to the wall, I placed an old electric samovar. Lena insisted that the samovar – a silvery soviet model I'd bought at Izmailovsky – made better tea than any modern kettle. I liked its polished look, which made me think of a well-deserved trophy, and the way the lid rattled furiously when the water reached boiling point.

Both balconies, the kitchen one and the living-room one, faced not Tverskaya but the courtyard, which in warmer weather was half occupied by the tables and chairs of the summer terrace at Scandinavia. Because the other constructions around the courtyard were only two or three floors tall, the view from my sixth-floor balconies spanned all the way from Barrikadnaya to the buildings of the New Arbat, which may or may not have represented open books, but were, for some reason, loved by Muscovites and Christmas-lit all year round. If I stood on either of my balconies, I could gaze at a vast urban scape, an endless extension of rooftops, twisted antennae, old pipes and tangled cables and – if the day was clear – I could follow the sun setting on the horizon, behind the redbrick chimneys of the old soviet factories. Breathtaking.

I was now living in the heart of Moscow. Everything I needed was here: shops, restaurants, cafés, cinemas. Most places stayed open all night and it felt great to know that I could walk down to the street at midnight to buy milk or books or blinis. There were always plenty of people on the street, day and night. So much life that you never felt alone.

My building stood just a few steps away from Pushkin-skaya. This was convenient because, as I had discovered during my first months in Moscow, Pushkin's bronze monument at the centre of the square – the very statue Dostoyevsky had unveiled in 1880 – was Moscow's favour-ite meeting point for couples, being both centrally located and, in a Russian way, romantichno. On warm days I would often wait for a dyev beneath the petrified but somehow dis-approving regard of Aleksandr Sergeyevich. I would be the only man in the square not holding a bouquet of flowers, stingy foreigner, and I would be scanning the faces of arriv-ing dyevs, trying to recognise the one I had met a few nights earlier, with whom I had probably exchanged a couple of kisses on the dance floor of a nightclub and a few messages in the days that followed.

If I didn't remember what she looked like, which was often the case, I would wait patiently beneath Pushkin's statue, looking distracted, leaving her the task of recognising me. Then, once we saw each other, we would say privet privet and I would take her across the square to Café Pyramida, which had an actual glass pyramid for a roof and lounge music and sushi and cocktails, and dyevs liked it, and we would chat for a while. If after an hour or so things were not happening, I would walk the dyev back to the metro, say poka poka, and that would be, most likely, the last time we saw each other. But if the dyev was friendly, and she didn't

105

order the most expensive thing on the menu, I would invite her for a cup of tea in my apartment, conveniently located across the street, with that enormous couch that I usually left open as a bed, and the spectacular views of the west of the city.

18

As hard as I tried to understand her, I could never predict Lena's outbursts. Nor could I grasp the reasons behind her frequent mood swings. One moment she was sweet and calm – the next she was hurt or hostile.

One hot summer evening we were in my apartment getting ready to go out for dinner. I had just showered and slipped into my jeans, and Lena was waiting for me by the door. I rushed around the flat, shirtless, looking for my mobile phone. I turned over the cushions and pillows on the couch, looked in the kitchen, checked the pockets of the trousers piled on the old leather armchair. The phone was nowhere to be found. The air in the apartment was warm and I was losing patience. 'What the fuck,' I said, in English.

'What are you looking for?' Lena asked.

'My phone. Have you seen it?'

'Did you check your pockets?'

'Of course.'

'Let me call you.' Lena extracted her phone from her handbag and rang me. In a few seconds a faint ringtone emerged from a pair of jeans that lay draped over the wooden stool by the front door. Lena took my phone from the pocket and handed it to me.

Twenty minutes later we were sitting on cushiony white sofas on a new summer terrace on the Boulevard, waiting for our salads. I was having a beer, enjoying the warm evening. The sky was bright, pinkish, almost purple behind the buildings. But Lena was not in the mood. She was sipping her glass of chilled white wine, hardly speaking.

I knew she wanted me to ask what was wrong with her. But I didn't want to ask. I didn't want to reward her childish attitude. If she had a problem with something I'd done or said, let her bring it up. So I kept talking, pretending not to notice the way she was avoiding conversation.

I was saying something about how nice it was to live in the centre, how glad I was that I'd moved out of the university. Then I told her about my idea of writing a book about Moscow, a fictionalised account of my life in the city. She was looking down at her glass of wine, her blonde fringe, which she'd let grow a little, falling over her eyelashes and covering her eyes.

When I took a long sip from my beer, she finally jumped in.

'Martin, tell me, why does it say Lena Propaganda in your phone?'

So this was it. The cause of her misery.

'What do you mean?' I said.

'When I called you before, in your place. On the screen of your phone, it said Lena Propaganda.'

'That's where we met,' I said. 'Propaganda. Remember?'

'You could just write Lena.'

I smiled. 'It's not such an original name in Moscow, you know.'

Her eyes remained fixed on her glass of white wine. I grabbed her hand across the table. 'I just want to be sure it's you I call.'

She removed her hand and stared at me – her big blue eyes now moist.

'Who are the other Lenas?'

'I don't know. Old friends. I'm no longer in contact with them.'

'Why do you keep their numbers then?'

'Does it bother you?'

'I don't want to be Lena Propaganda.'

'If it makes you happy, I can change it. Would you like me to add your surname? Or perhaps your patronymic?' I took the phone out of my pocket, placed it on the table, between my beer and her wine. 'What is it? Sergeyevna? Borisovna? What's your father's name?'

'I don't want you to write anything but my name.'

'Is it my fault that so many girls in Moscow share the same few names? It's all Katyas, Mashas, Lenas, Tanyas, Olyas, Natashas.'

She looked at me, now on the verge of tears. Then, in a shaky, soft voice she said, 'I just want to be Lena.'

'In my heart,' I said, 'you're just Lena. Besides, it could be worse. You could be Lena Beefeater, or Lena Hungry Duck. Propaganda is classy, elegant, refined.'

'It's not funny, Martin. I know I'm not that important to you, but at least I would like to think that I'm more than just someone on a list.'

'But, Lenushka, you *are* important to me. Otherwise we wouldn't be here, right now. Listen, if I ever write my book about Moscow, you'll be the only Lena in it. I promise.'

'You have no heart,' she said, a tear rolling down her cheek. 'And my mistake is that I let you have me too easily.'

'What do you mean?'

'You never had to fight for me.' She took a sip of wine, then placed the glass in front of her. 'You never bought me flowers.'

'When the hell was I supposed to buy you flowers?'

She didn't answer. She lifted her glass, swirled it, drank all the wine at once. 'Now it's too late,' she said, eyes down, shaking her head. 'For you, I will always be Lena Propaganda.'

In a way, Lena, you were right. Now I know. Had we met anywhere else but Moscow — had there been no other Lenas in my mobile phone — things would have turned out differently. Truth is, Moscow brought us together, but Moscow kept us apart. What can I say now? Sorry, Lena, I wish I'd bought you flowers.

19

THREE WEEKS AFTER MOVING into my new flat, I decided to drop my language lessons. The daily commute to the university took up too much of my time – I had to free my agenda from unnecessary distractions.

I knew I would miss Nadezhda Nikolaevna. I would miss the hours in which we inhabited the structured world of language textbooks. I would miss her enthusiasm and dedication – which kept me awake, most of the time, despite my hangovers and chronic lack of sleep – and I would also miss the little sweets she brought me once a week, usually on Fridays – blinis, syrnikis, home-made preserves. She, too, must have felt sad about finishing our classes because she wept a little when we hugged goodbye after our last lesson.

Without language classes to attend, I only had to visit the university to see Lyudmila Aleksandrovna and discuss my research. Following my suggestion, and despite her initial resistance, we had now agreed to meet less often – once a month. She had taken some convincing though, as I hadn't really told her about my plans to use the Russian women I met as a primary source for my research, an original approach I suspected she would disapprove of.

My discussions with Lyudmila Aleksandrovna, which covered the more orthodox aspects of my investigation, helped me understand the different interpretations that scholars had given to crucial events in Russian novels. Reading the articles she recommended, I understood that every Russian literature scholar had to develop an original opinion about the key moments of seminal novels.

Why, ultimately, had Anna Karenina thrown herself under a train?

This question was discussed at length in several papers, with so much fervour that I often wondered if the fact that Anna Karenina was a fictional character was lost on the authors. But talking to Lyudmila Aleksandrovna I realised it was expected of me, as a prospective expert on Russian literature, to come up with my own unique interpretation of these fictional events.

With my mornings free, I would now sit in central cafés to read Russian books with the help of a dictionary, taking notes in my little red notebooks. I tried to understand why Russian authors made their heroines behave the way they did and, ultimately, how these heroines tried to make sense of the world they lived in. In the long term, I thought, all I needed to do was to compare these notes with my observations on

Russian women, which were conveniently written in the same red notebooks.

I gave a lot of thought, for instance, to Tatyana's actions at the end of *Evgeny Onegin*. Her decision to reject Onegin, which seemed so true and inevitable in the context of the story, had originated, after all, in Aleksandr Sergeyevich's mind — a mind moulded by his particular life experience.

Something worried me. When talking about Tatyana in the Pushkin Speech, Dostoyevsky had endowed her with the capacity to choose, the possibility to decide her own destiny. This didn't feel totally credible. Not just because Tatyana is a literary character at the mercy of her creator — in itself a major obstacle to choosing your own path — but because, unlike in books, real life doesn't always involve such clear choices.

And yet, any other ending to *Evgeny Onegin* — one in which Tatyana had not been presented with clear alternatives — would have lacked the literary quality that gave Pushkin's work part of its greatness.

Tatyana's story, her lesson to the world, only made sense as long as she had a choice.

20

WHEN I FIRST SAW YULYA Karma she was over by the fat Buddha statue, taking a break from dancing, leaning against the wall. Roundish Slavic face, enormous eyes. Even in the darkness of Karma's underground dance floor, Yulya's bright eyes, framed by thick eyeliner, resembled pure crystal. A glance at her eyes and I could feel a revolution raging in my chest, a horde of tiny Bolsheviks taking over my entire body, making Yulya the one concern of my night. I approached her and we chatted, and she seemed naive and shy, probably because her friends were around, I thought, and at some point she told me she was nineteen. When her friends were distracted at the bar, Yulya gave me her phone number, which she asked me to memorise without writing it down, so that nobody noticed. At the end of the night, just before heading out of the club, I found her again and, when nobody was looking, I stole a kiss. Her lips were full and soft and in the days that followed I couldn't stop thinking about her.

We arranged to meet a couple of days later, at Pushkin's statue. She was as beautiful as I remembered, even if, in plain daylight, her round figure was edging on plumpness. I took her to Pyramida. We had a drink and she told me about the elitni economics institute she attended, the best in Moscow, she said. She was interested in politics, and in what I, as a foreigner, thought about Russia's shaky transition to democracy. She told me she read international newspapers online, to practise her English and to keep up with global affairs. I found her smart and witty but, the more she talked, the more I felt she was uncomfortable, as if something were nagging at the back of her mind. When we finished our drinks and our shared tray of sushi, I suggested we go to my place for a cup of tea.

'Sure,' she said, 'but I have to tell you something.'

Then, as we walked through the perekhod, Yulya Karma informed me that first, she had a boyfriend, for two years now, and second, she didn't intend to leave him. She did say first and second, and I imagined this formal way of convey-ing what she considered essential information was the result of her privileged schooling.

'Right,' I said, not knowing how to react.

'And another thing,' she added, as we came out on the other side of Tverskaya and walked towards my building. 'Today I have my period.'

'Your period?'

'Yes,' she said. 'We won't be able to have sex.'

I was taken aback.

Yulya clutched my arm.

'It doesn't mean that I can't see you again another day,' she said, smiling.

Up in my flat, I poured fresh water into the samovar and plugged it into the wall socket. While the samovar was heating up, I joined Yulya in the living room. She asked about the Indian tapestry on the wall. I told her the story of Lord Ganesh, how he got his elephant head, and how he used the small brush in his hand to remove obstacles from the path of life. I didn't mention that the tapestry was a birthday present from Lena.

'Interesno,' Yulya said. 'So you hung an elephant above your couch to make your life easier?'

'It's not an elephant. It's a Hindu god. He brushes all my problems away.'

'What a boring life you must have,' she said, laughing.

The samovar rattled. Back in the kitchen, I carefully opened its tiny tap and poured boiling water into two mugs. I returned with the steaming mugs to the living room. While the tea was brewing, we stepped onto the balcony. Yulya was impressed by the view from my flat.

'You can even see the New Arbat from here,' she said, pointing at the cluster of buildings to the south.

'I love how the buildings in the New Arbat look like open books,' I said, as I stepped behind Yulya and put my hands around her waist.

She pushed my hands away, turned, and kissed me. We kissed for a couple of minutes on the balcony, then moved inside to the couch. I took her shirt off. But when I tried to unfasten her bra, she stood up and said, 'Ne nado.'

Ne nado. It meant no need or don't bother, except Muscovites used the expression all the time, in awkward and quite diverse situations. Ne nado, I don't need the change back. Ne nado, I can walk myself back to the metro. Ne nado, I'm not giving you my phone number. Ne nado, you are not getting laid today.

'I told you,' she said, 'I have my period. Wait for next time.'

I was sweaty.

'Davay pit' chai,' she said, sitting forward on the couch. Let's drink tea.

I took the tea bags out of the mugs and placed them on a napkin. She took a sip of tea, then placed her mug back on the coffee table. She grabbed my hand and smiled.

'How often would you like to see me?' she asked.

'In what sense?' My heart was still pumping fast.

'If we become lovers,' she said, 'how many times a week would you like to see me?'

I wasn't sure I understood. 'I don't know,' I said.

'One, two, three times a week?'

'Twice a week,' I said, without giving it much thought.

'Good,' she said. 'I'll tell my boyfriend that I'm taking English lessons. Then I can come to see you on two different days for a couple of hours.'

And so Yulya Karma started to visit me on Mondays and Wednesdays from five till seven. The second time she came, after tea, we went down to the Moskva Bookshop in Tver-skaya and I bought her two English language books, one with grammar lessons and one with exercises, and also a small Oxford dictionary. From then on, when she came to my place, she always carried her English books. And a few times she did bring some essays she'd written in English for her studies, things on international trade or finances, and we would go through the text lying on my couch and later, when she was getting dressed, she would say, 'Very nice class, professor.'

One day Yulya Karma broke our schedule. She sent me a text on a Thursday around midnight saying *I miss you* and asking if she could come over. She showed up at my place an hour later, wasted, barely able to stay on her feet. She'd been drinking cocktails with some girlfriends, she said. For the first time, she spent the night in my flat.

Next morning, as she was getting ready to leave, she asked if I had a spare toothbrush. I looked around but couldn't find one.

'You are not ready for all your lovers,' she said, which struck me as odd because we had never talked about other people.

The next time she came to my place – Monday at five, as per the schedule – she brought me a present. 'Open it,' she said, excited. It was a box containing a set of colourful toothbrushes. In fact, after a closer look, I realised the box contained only one toothbrush handle but five different heads, identical in shape but different in colour.

'This is for you and all your lovers,' Yulya said, laughing. 'You can change the heads. Each of us can have a different colour.'

'Spasibo,' I said. 'Very thoughtful.'

'I pick red,' she said and at the end of the two hours, as if to mark her territory, she fitted the red head to the handle and brushed her teeth before leaving.

For weeks I left the multiheaded toothbrush next to my sink, and offered it to anyone who came home. When dyevs asked which colour they could use, I would say that any colour was fine, they were all new. This was, I thought, the right thing to say. They didn't seem to notice that one of the brushes had been used and, for some reason I never understood, they all picked red and ended up brushing their teeth with the same head.

I enjoyed the regularity and predictability of Yulya's visits. It was easy to arrange my days around our encounters and I appreciated not having to deal with the logistics of bringing a new dyev home, sending text messages back and forth, the initial exchange in Pyramida and all that work.

Besides, the clandestine nature of her visits — the fact that she came to my flat to cheat on her boyfriend — made me think of *The Master and Margarita*. I saw myself as the master and this notion gave our entire arrangement a certain literary quality, as if Bulgakov himself were giving us his blessing.

I found Yulya Karma attractive but, despite my efforts, rather unresponsive in bed. She would lie on my couch, naked, relaxed, smiling, but hardly moving or moaning, waiting patiently for me to finish. At first I tried to be creative but after a few attempts I gave up.

Yulya's breasts were large and heavy but, once she was fully undressed, so were her thighs and her buttocks. I never mentioned this to her – I really didn't care – but she would bring it up herself often.

'I was so much thinner before,' she said one of the first times we met.

'You are thin.'

We were lying naked on my couch, which I had recently covered with blue washable fabric. Through the balcony, the summer breeze carried the sounds and smells of traffic into my flat.

'I could eat whatever I wanted,' she said. 'Really, I never used to put any weight on. I was so thin, you should have seen me. Now, even if I starve myself for a week, I can't get rid of the extra kilos. I hope it's just a phase.'

'Perhaps you could join a gym,' I said, staring up at the wall, my eyes fixed on Ganesh.

'You think I'm fat?'

'Not at all, I like your figure. You are very sexy.'

'Thanks. I don't have time to go to a gym.'

One day, at the end of our two hours, Yulya was slipping into her jeans when she told me she had started to visit a masseur twice a week. The masseur, she said, massaged her thighs for an hour to release the excess fat and redistribute it within her body. I told her that this method of losing weight was unknown in the West and that, to me, it didn't sound very scientific. She insisted that these massages were the latest fashion in Moscow, but I found myself wondering if this was true or if the masseur was perhaps just another guy she was also fucking on a fixed schedule.

21

ON WARM EVENINGS THE air inside my flat became stuffy and I'd have to open the balcony doors. If there was a breeze, the air from the street was fresh, but, when the evening was still, the smoke from the grill at Scandinavia reached my sixth-floor balconies and the entire flat smelled of burnt animal fat.

The summer terrace at Scandinavia, I'd learned, opened every year as soon as the last snow of the season had melted. At first, when the evenings remained chilly, they provided blankets and mushroom gas-heaters but, as the days got warmer, the blankets disappeared and the clientele, mostly expats, flocked to the terrace, attracted by cold beer on tap and hamburgers that were grilled until midnight.

The Exile said Scandinavia made the best burgers in town.

Sometimes, when I walked into my building, I would see guys I knew from football chilling out on the terrace. I'd have to stop to greet them and, if I wasn't alone, they would ogle my companion, usually nodding in approval – an approval I had not sought, and which annoyed me, really. Later, at night, from my living room, with the balconies open, I could hear their voices which by then would be drunk and loud.

I enjoyed it when Lena spent the night. She brought me old soviet films that she'd seen a hundred times, comedies usually, the jokes mostly lost on me, and when she saw that I didn't laugh she would pause the film and try to fill in the cultural and linguistic nuances she thought I was missing. I found her explanations interesting because they revealed, if not Russian thinking per se, at least a great deal about soviet aesthetics. But, despite Lena's efforts, I rarely got what was comical about the scenes, which to me seemed clown-like and childish, and at a certain point I had to pretend that I, too, found them funny so that we could move on and watch the rest of the film.

At night, before falling asleep, we would lie reading on the couch. She was always nose-deep in some spiritual book or self-help manual, Lena, about the power of meditation or compassion or friendship, and every time she encountered a new concept – an insight she found revealing – she would read it aloud to me, hoping that I'd embrace it at once as she had, and she would get pissed off when I teased her and didn't take her books seriously. It seemed to me that most of Lena's books talked about the same crap – about refusing temptation and attachment and material pleasure, about how we all needed to focus instead on the spiritual world around us.

We also listened to music.

One afternoon, in early August, Lena and I were lying naked on my couch, listening to an album I had recently bought at the Gorbushka pirate CD market. The sun was setting over Moscow. Orange sunlight poured into my living room, over the coffee table, the couch, the wall tapestry. Bathed in the evening sun, Lord Ganesh almost came alive. It felt good to be there with Lena, calm and quiet.

The balcony doors were open. In between songs, I could hear the permanent roar of the city, mixed with the chattering of people and the clinking of glasses that came from the Scandinavia terrace, but also, at some point, the distant sound of sirens.

I was enjoying the album, a pirate compilation from an indie rock band I'd recently discovered. I couldn't keep my eyes off Ganesh, his elephant head and twisted arms looking mystical under the warm sun-rays. It was in these moments of serene nudity that all my senses were at their most receptive.

'I love this album,' I said.

'Very nice songs.' Lena had her head on my chest and one leg between my legs.

'You know what,' I said, 'I'm going to give you this CD. You can have it.'

'Why?'

'A present.'

'What for?'

'You just said you like it.'

'I do. But it's your CD.'

'This is a pirate copy,' I said. 'I bought it in Gorbushka. But I really like it so I'll buy the licensed CD in the official shop.'

'Why would you buy a licensed copy of a CD you already have?' she said. 'Licensed CDs are very expensive.'

'I know, but it feels different. When I really like an album, I prefer to have the original thing.'

For a few seconds we remained silent, listening to the music. Abruptly, Lena untangled herself from my body and rolled away from me, facing now the back of the couch. Her blonde hair, cut short at her neck, shone brighter in the sun.

I could hear more sirens howling in the street, louder now, closer – an unsettling sound, but, back then, a sound unrelated to my own pain.

'Strange about those sirens,' I said.

Lena didn't answer. She was covering her eyes with an arm.

Lena was crying.

'What's wrong?' I asked.

'Nothing.'

'What have I done?'

'Nothing. It's OK.'

'It's not OK, you're crying.'

'It's nothing.'

'Is it something I said?'

Lena got up, stomped to the other side of the room. She took a tissue from her handbag, blew her nose, came back and sat on the other side of the couch, staring at the sunset. She was still naked, but now out of my reach; biting the golden cross on her chain.

'Maybe something bad happened in the street,' she said. 'An accident.'

'Lenushka, tell me, what's wrong?'

'I don't know,' she said. 'I guess I'm just stupid.'

'Is it about the CD?'

Silence.

'What is it?' I said.

'Yes, Martin, it's about the CD.'

For a few seconds I tried to understand the situation. Then I moved along the couch and held Lena's hand.

'Lenushka,' I said, 'I don't know what I was thinking. I'm not going to give you a pirate copy. I'll buy two copies of the original CD, one for me and one for you.'

Gazing out through the balcony, Lena shook her head slowly, in silence. Then she turned to me.

'Martin, I don't want your fucking compact disc.'

'Lenushka, what's wrong?'

'Why the hell would I need a CD that you have?'

She stood up. The rays of setting sun illuminated her beautiful breasts and sparkled on the golden cross that hung above them.

'Has it crossed your mind,' she said, failing to hold back her tears, 'that maybe one day we could move in together, you and me, as a real couple, and then we would not need two copies of the same album?'

The next day I learned about the sirens. A bomb had gone off at the perekhod in Pushkinskaya, about two hundred metres away from my building, killing thirteen people and injuring more than a hundred. The news on TV showed images of broken glass, people screaming, a pool of blood. It seemed the blast, which I hadn't heard, had occurred at the southern entry of the perekhod. The police said it was the work of Chechen terrorists.

It felt unreal to see the mayhem on TV when all the action had been taking place only a minute away from my building. The bomb had exploded in the very heart of Moscow, a few steps from Pushkin's statue, on the route I took almost daily, the route Lena had probably followed, before the explosion, to get to my place. I wondered if, at the time of the bombing, people on the Scandinavia terrace had noticed what was going on on the other side of the building, while they were drinking beer and gorging on the best burgers in town.

For a few days I avoided the underpasses at Pushkinskaya. I would cross at street level, using the zebra crossing on the Boulevard. The first time I went back to walking through the perekhod, I saw a plaque on the wall commemorating the victims and, from that day on – and for the rest of my stay in Moscow – every time I passed by there would be flowers and candles on the ground under the plaque, and I would be forced to remember the day I failed to hear the deadly explosion from my flat – the day thirteen people were killed in Pushkinskaya and Lena thought we didn't need two copies of the same CD because maybe we could move in together.

And yet, other than the plaque and the flowers and candles, everything in Pushkinskaya looked exactly as it had before the explosion. Muscovites rushed in and out of the metro, stopping at the kiosks to buy knock-off watches, sunglasses and chocolates. Up at ground level, young couples met beneath Pushkin's statue, exchanging flowers and kisses, as they had done before the explosion, and as they would keep doing, I imagined, for many years to come.

22

ON 12 AUGUST, LESS than a week after the bomb in Pushkinskaya, a Russian nuclear submarine sank in the North Sea
with its entire crew on board.

I only learned about this the day after, while I was watching the news on TV. It was early in the morning and, despite
the bright light coming in from the balcony, I was yet to
reach a state of complete wakefulness. I lay stretched on
the couch, in my underpants, drinking coffee. As far as I
understood from the news, the submarine was now lying at
the bottom of the sea, the survivors trapped inside the hull.
The Russian president, who had decided not to interrupt
his holidays by the Black Sea, had ordered the deployment
of a rescue team.

I finished my coffee, turned off the TV. After a cold shower,
I put on a pair of jeans and a white T-shirt and took the stairs

down to the street. I had agreed to meet Stepanov for breakfast at the Starlite.

It was a lovely summer morning. The sky was clear, the air fresh. As I walked towards Mayakovskaya, I found myself thinking about the Russian sailors who, at that very moment, were trapped underwater, with little oxygen, probably in darkness. When I reached the Akvarium Garden I found it prettier than ever. It was all green and full of life – a smattering of red tulip-like flowers had sprouted around the Apollo fountain at the back of the park.

A waitress I knew by sight was setting up the terrace of the Starlite, opening the sun umbrellas and placing ketchup bottles and napkins on the tables. As I passed, she greeted me with a smile. 'Your friend is inside,' she said.

'Thanks.' I stepped into the diner and found Stepanov slouched at a corner booth, wearing a pair of gold-rimmed sunglasses I'd never seen before, sliding eggs and bacon around a greasy plate.

'Sorry, brother, I couldn't wait,' he said. 'I needed something solid in my stomach.'

We shook hands and I sat opposite him. 'You look like shit,' I said.

'Yeah, fucking great night.'

Because we'd met through the brothers, Stepanov and I always spoke in English. I found this slightly disconcerting, as if, by using a foreign language instead of his native Russian, Stepanov was trying to be something he was not. It was an unfair thought, I knew, because to Russian native speakers, my simplified version of their language would also sound artificial.

A waitress approached our booth. I ordered a salmon and cheese omelette and a cup of coffee.

'Straight from the club?' I asked.

Nodding, Stepanov forked a piece of egg into his mouth. 'You should have come. We ended up in this new place, next to the river, on the south bank. They've installed a huge tent. It was real elitni, full of celebrities.'

'Sounds good.' I had decided to take a night off and stay at home. Now I wondered whether I should have gone out instead.

'Plenty of models and actresses, all very exclusivni. Pasha Face Control on the door.' Stepanov swallowed his last piece of egg and dumped his toast on the plate to soak up the grease.

'If you want the best crowd,' I said, 'it's gotta be Pasha on the door.'

'He was on top form. He turned a minister away.'

'Good for Pasha. A government kind of minister?'

'The fucking minister of housing or social issues or something like that.' Stepanov took a bite of bread and, still chewing, a sip of coffee. 'He showed up with this great-looking baba, surely a prostitute. Pasha didn't let him through, so the minister started to make a scene, shouting that he was going to call the president at the Kremlin, shut the club down.'

'Pasha held his ground, I hope.'

'Of course,' Stepanov said, 'but the minister kept on screaming that he knew everybody personally, the chief of police and all that. Pasha remained calm and said something like, "Sorry, your Excellency, but this is a private party."'

'"Sorry, your Excellency"?'

'Yes.' Stepanov laughed. 'Can you imagine? So the minister got furious and took his phone and started to make calls. He shouted for a while, saying someone needs to cut the legs off this fucking kid, looking at Pasha, you know.'

'Sure.'

'But no one ever arrived. In the meantime, Pasha was letting other people into the club. We hardly had to wait.'

The waitress brought me a steaming mug of coffee.

'Before I forget,' Stepanov said, 'this is for you.' He placed a brown sealed envelope on the table.

I took the envelope and tucked it into the back of my jeans.

'The deal with the Americans went through,' he said.

'Congratulations. Breakfast's on me.'

Insight Investments International was a firm with no office – all business meetings took place in bars and restaurants. The Starlite was kind of our corporate headquarters. Stepanov was of the opinion that, being an American diner, the Starlite put Western investors at ease.

'That last meeting went very well,' Stepanov said. 'You did a good job.'

'Those guys seemed pretty interested.'

'They *were* interested. It's always so much easier to do business with Americans. Americans know how to make money. They trust people. Trusting mode is their default position. Unlike fucking Europeans. Europeans are always suspicious, thinking all Russians are crooks. They don't get that foreign investors need our help to understand the local business environment.'

The waitress topped up my mug of coffee, which was almost full, and smiled at me.

I smiled back. 'Spasibo.'

'It's normal that foreign investors are cautious,' I said. 'They better be careful doing business in this country. Russia is a lawless jungle.'

'That's bullshit,' Stepanov said. 'Russia might be a jungle, but even jungles have their own laws. There are many rules here. It just happens that they are different rules from yours, and most of them are not written. In the end our system is no worse or better than the West's. Just different.'

I could see Stepanov was still drunk. 'Maybe you're right,' I said.

'Anyway, foreigners are getting more reluctant to invest in Russia. The sweet chaos of the 1990s is over. They're afraid of the new political climate, intimidated by all this posturing and nationalist shit from our politicians. It scares them off. So I want to start tapping into the local market.'

'What do you mean?'

'Oligarchs.' Stepanov was pointing his fork at me. 'They've got the real money these days. And they don't know how to spend it. I've been looking into car dealerships. With the cash from Insight Investments we could set up an operation to import luxury vehicles from Europe.'

'Not easy, I presume.'

'There are ways. I found out I can avoid customs duties if the firm I set up is legally owned by a handicapped person. Some bizarre old rule. I just need to find a cripple to own the firm on paper. Of course I can let you into the business if you are interested. Oligarchs love to mingle with foreigners.'

'Always happy to help.'

The waitress came with my omelette and a side bowl of chips I hadn't ordered. 'On the house,' she said, in English, pointing at the chips with a smile.

'Have you heard the news about the sunken submarine?' I asked. 'Poor bastards.'

'They're all dead by now.'

'But they said there might be some survivors.'

'I bet you, no survivors,' Stepanov said. 'No one gives a shit about those poor fuckers. Most sailors are peasants, poor people who join the navy because they can't afford to live normal lives. Nobody gives a fuck about them.'

'But they sent a rescue team,' I protested. 'I saw it on TV.'

'I doubt it. That's what the government says to keep the mums and babushkas happy. They probably don't even know where the fucking submarine is. This country is a joke. In soviet times we had the best navy in the world. We were feared and respected. And look, now, outside Moscow, the country is in ruins. We can't even keep our ships afloat.'

In the afternoon, after a short nap, I watched the news. They were now saying that the rescue team had reached the sunken submarine and had heard noises and tapping from inside the hull. According to the news, government experts were considering different options to get the sailors out alive.

But now I wondered if the government was making all this stuff up – if, as Stepanov had told me, it was all a media montage to keep families happy and to pretend they cared. They interviewed a handful of experts, who said that the survivors had just a few more hours of air left. I turned off the TV.

I texted Lena and asked her to come over for dinner. I hadn't seen her since the day of the bomb in Pushkinskaya. She came over and was in good spirits. I was glad she didn't mention the CD incident. After tea on the couch, we moved to the kitchen to prepare dinner. My fridge was almost empty so we boiled some frozen pelmenis and served them with smetana. I opened a bottle of wine.

While we were eating at the kitchen table, I mentioned the submarine.

'All the sailors will die,' she said.

'Why?' I asked, irritated by so much Russian negativity.

Lena looked confused by my question. She placed her fork on the plate and took a sip of wine. 'Because we are in Russia,' she said. Then she went back to eating her pelmenis.

Catching sight of my own reflection in the silvery surface of the samovar, it dawned on me that Russians regarded tragedies, deaths, not as extraordinary and avoidable events, but rather as an integral part of normal existence. The expected.

As if listening to my thoughts, Lena grabbed my hand and, with a sad smile, added, 'That's how things always end up here.'

*

After dinner, we moved back to the couch to watch a film. It was an old soviet film I had read about and insisted on watching. It turned out to be in black and white — long, slow, arty. Lena fell asleep before the end. Through the open balcony door I could hear the murmur of expats having drinks at Scandinavia.

Lena had a soothing effect on me. When I was concerned about something in particular, or when my thoughts were drifting towards a darker place, it was enough for me to check that Lena was there, next to me. For some reason, the physical proximity of her body gave me a reassuring sense of calm.

In fact, I often found myself wishing that Lena were at home with me. With another girl I would chat for a while, have tea, and that would be nice but, at some point during the evening, I would be struck by an irrepressible urge to be alone. Sometimes, if the dyev was perceptive, she would sense my mood darkening and would leave the flat on her own initiative. But often the dyev would insist on staying around. In those cases, I would grow irritable, my Russian would become sloppy and, as the evening advanced, communication between the two of us would deteriorate. The dyev would then try to bridge the emotional gap, now evident to both of us, with physical contact, but, at this point, physical contact would no longer work for me.

Lena, on the other hand, knew when I needed space. Maybe it was something she'd picked up from her readings on compassion and all that spiritual stuff. She never forced herself upon me.

With Lena, I talked about films and books and food and current news, about everything, really, aside from other girls. Not being able to discuss girls with Lena was a nuisance, since it ruled out the most important part of my research and a large proportion of the time I wasn't spending in her company. In a way, I wished I could talk to Lena about other girls because for me they were not that relevant, and they certainly did not affect the way I felt about her. But she never asked, at least not in a direct way, and I assumed we had somehow agreed to avoid the issue.

Over the next couple of days I followed the news about the submarine, wishing for a happy ending for the sailors, until, finally, it became clear that they were all dead.

A few days later I learned that Britain and Norway had offered technical assistance and modern equipment to rescue the Russian sailors. From his retreat in Sochi, the Russian president, reluctant to allow foreigners inside the secret nuclear submarine, had respectfully declined the offer.

23

ONE DAY LENA TOLD me she wanted to show me the beautiful side of Russia. She used those words, beautiful side of Russia, as if all I had seen up to that point were the ugliest bits of the country.

'Let's get out of Moscow for a weekend,' she said. This came as a surprise, as we had never spent more than a few hours together, a night at most, and it was always my idea to meet. But I was intrigued, so we made plans to spend a couple of nights in Suzdal, a small city on the Golden Ring I absolutely had to see, unreachable by train but only four hours away by bus, a place untouched by the buzz of Moscow.

So, on a Friday morning in mid-September, we got on an old bus at Shchyolkovskaya, at the end of the dark blue metro line. After leaving the station, the bus passed through endless rows of identical buildings with grey façades and I tried to imagine the lives of their inhabitants, so far away from central Moscow. Who were they? How did they spend their days? After a while, the road turned greener, and there were dachas and warehouses. Then the forest.

We were sitting near the back of the bus, Lena and I, a row behind two old men who seemed to be sleeping. The bus stopped for a toilet break and, once we were back on, one of the old men, white beard and deep wrinkles, turned round and, pointing at me, asked Lena, 'Does he drink?', as if asking permission to feed a dog.

'You can ask him,' Lena said, and, before I had time to prepare a clever excuse in Russian, I was pulled out of my seat, finding myself in the very back row, which had been previously unoccupied, sitting with the two men and a bottle of vodka.

When you are the victim of a vodka ambush there is no polite way to get out of it, even if you're on a bus and it's only ten in the morning. I had no choice but to join them.

The younger of my two sobutilnikis, my drinking buddies, took a pocketknife out of his bag and began to slice bread and kolbasa. He prepared little buterbrods, which I was instructed to bite after every shot of vodka. He was sickly thin, with pockmarked cheekbones, missing most of his front teeth. We drank out of plastic glasses, toasting first our vstrechu, then friendship, the usual stuff.

They wanted to know if I liked Russia, if I liked vodka, if I liked Russian women. The first bottle was finished and another bottle made an appearance and at some point I realised I must have drunk more than I'd thought because we were singing Russian songs that I was learning as we went.

We arrived at Suzdal around lunchtime and, standing outside the bus, I said do svidaniya, first shaking hands but then with a hug that, to my surprise, became quite emotional, as if instead of strangers on a four-hour journey we were old comrades returning from war. I was given a phone number so that we could call and visit them in Suzdal before we went back to Moscow. I said we would and, before parting, the older man with the white beard told Lena that I was such a khoroshi paren, that he respected me, that I could be Russian.

Suzdal was gorgeous. It was sunny but not too warm and the centre of the town was crammed with beautifully coloured onion-shaped churches, blue and gold and yellow, and at first I thought it could have been the setting for one of Chekhov's short stories, perhaps an unnamed provincial town, a town called simply S., where life passed without much drama. But as Lena and I walked around the centre, it occurred to me that Suzdal was more spiritual, more mysterious, more Dostoyevskian, and it wouldn't have surprised me to see one of the Karamazov brothers, Alyosha maybe, turning a corner and walking towards me.

We checked into our hotel, which happened to be a monastery that rented out some izbas to visitors. The izbas, tiny cottages, were located at the back of the monastery, within the walled compound behind the central chapel. Inside, the izba was very clean, with an old wooden bedstead. We left our bags and went for a walk.

Being wasted is a great way to visit a place for the first time, I realised — everything is illuminated in a special light and the impressions are much stronger. Outside the monastery we bought cabbage pirogis and salted cucumbers from a babushka who kept them in a bucket under a piece of cloth. The pirogi was oily but warm and it felt great when I bit into it. We walked into a church, which was dark and moist and smelled of burnt wax and incense. Lena covered her hair with a scarf. She lit tall, thin candles, crossed herself, kissed the icons. Despite her unusual approach to religion, I hadn't expected Lena to follow these rituals. As she went around the church performing her Christian duties, I stayed behind, admiring the tranquillity of the place, listening to the faint crackling of the candles, breathing the holy air of the temple. I was feeling a growing tickle in my heart, a hint perhaps of my own spiritual awakening, and somehow I ended up wondering what it would be like to start a new life as a monk, spending hours in meditation or prayer, believing in something good, big and supernatural.

After visiting two more churches, we were out in the air again and walking among rows of small wooden houses, which were like the dachas I'd seen outside Moscow, but better kept. The windows had ornate wooden frames. Now I thought about what it would be like to live in these places, comparing the two experiences, living as a monk or living as a Russian peasant, and I couldn't decide which of the two was more idyllic. In a dacha I could live with Lena, who would cook while I repaired the roof and cut wood for winter, and, walking along the unpaved streets of outer Suzdal, I fully appreciated the beauty of that simple existence, even though I'd never cut wood or fixed a roof in my life. Yet in a monastery, I thought, I could receive spiritual stimulation, and I imagined having someone like Zosima, an elder, a saint, a spiritual leader and mentor to guide me through life, and then I realised I was too drunk to make any sense of my thoughts.

We passed the last row of dachas and then we were in a small park that ended in a forest. Among the trees, I took a few pictures of Lena, who was looking gorgeous, and I asked her to take her shirt off, then her bra. She glanced around to check, then did as I'd asked. She posed for me, topless, her jeans on, her arms extended above her head, pulling her breasts upwards, and I'll always remember Lena like this – leaning on a tree, her breasts like perfect forest fruits – because, so many years after that day in Suzdal, I still keep those photos, and I look at them often, and Lena looks younger than I felt she was when the pictures were taken.

In the late afternoon, as the effects of the vodka dissipated, I was hit by a wave of exhaustion. I suggested we go back to our monastery and have an early night.

Back in the izba I kissed Lena. We lay on the bed but, when I was about to unzip her jeans, she said, 'Sorry, not today.' I was disappointed because it was our weekend away and I was having such a great time – I was feeling spiritual, high, and I thought it could be a special occasion. Now I knew the weekend would not be perfect. Then Lena said, don't worry, I'll do my best, and she – who had spent the entire afternoon praying, lighting candles and kissing icons – crawled down the bed, dragging the golden cross of her necklace over my shirtless body, pulling my jeans off, together with my underwear.

24

AT THE END OF summer the days remained mostly sunny but you could feel a chill in the air, especially late in the afternoon, and you knew that winter was forming somewhere deep in Siberia, gathering strength, preparing to descend on Moscow. Local girls, though, defied the change of seasons and continued to wear miniskirts as they paraded up and down Tverskaya.

I'd been living in Pushkinskaya for a couple of months now, closely observing life in the square, which I saw as a window onto the entire country.

Sometimes there were demonstrations, with a dozen, twenty protesters at most, who stood stoically across from McDonald's, next to the Kroshka Kartoshka kiosk, unperturbed by the smell of baked potatoes, holding banners against the war in Chechnya and exhibiting black and white photographs of what I assumed were victims of the conflict. Often, though, the protesters were older and held pictures of Lenin and Stalin and red Communist banners or, occasionally, Orthodox crosses and religious icons with what looked like biblical quotes painted on them.

Sometimes I would see a bunch of demonstrators and, despite my best efforts to understand their cause, I could not figure out what they were protesting against, and nobody stopped to talk to them anyway, at least not the normal people, who just walked by and looked at them as if they were mental patients who had escaped from a madhouse.

I started to go for long morning walks. I tried new routes every day, venturing further away from the centre, discovering parts of the city previously unknown to me. Sometimes I would find myself walking in some remote neighbourhood, along wide avenues, past endless rows of concrete buildings, lost in a soviet landscape that was both shabby and monumental. When I lost my bearings, I would have to ask for directions to the nearest metro station to return to the centre.

Later, overwhelmed by the dimensions of the city, I began to take my walks closer to home, reducing my Moscow to manageable proportions — Pushkinskaya becoming the centre of an imaginary circle whose limits I no longer crossed. Mayakovskaya in the north, Tretyakovskaya in the south, Smolenskaya in the west, Chistye Prudy in the east. I would only venture out of these invisible urban borders, by taxi or metro, to attend university or to find new clubs with the brothers.

At some point I noticed that I'd settled into a fixed routine, turning always at the same corners, down the same alleyways, somehow finding comfort in the familiar details I encountered every day as I moved through the heart of the city.

After breakfast each morning, I would typically walk along the Boulevard, under the trees, then turn left at Bolshaya Nikitskaya, keeping to the left pavement, passing the old houses and the small church on the corner, until I reached the Tchaikovsky conservatory. At this point, I would often cross the street and sit on the terrace of Coffee Mania, where I would spend one or two hours drinking coffee and reading books in Russian with the help of a dictionary, writing down words and thoughts in my red notebooks.

I was now reading Chekhov in Russian. I had bought the collected works of Anton Pavlovich, a soviet edition from 1970, eight volumes in blue hardcover. The books, which I had acquired for a decent price in the basement section of the Moskva Bookshop, were lovely and smelled of ancient paper. A colour picture of a pensive Anton Pavlovich adorned the first page. I always carried one of the volumes in my backpack, usually the one with the dramaticheskie proizvedenya, all the plays, or the one entitled *Rasskazy i Povesti 1895–1903*, which included Chekhov's best-known stories. I liked reading the plays because they were subtle, understated, particularly the big four, and I admired the way Anton Pavlovich didn't seem so much interested in telling a story as in conveying a nastroeniye – a mood or atmosphere.

Anton Pavlovich is the master of nastroeniye, Lyudmila Aleksandrovna had told me, and he certainly was, capturing in his writing the essence of late nineteenth-century Russia.

Sitting on the terrace of Coffee Mania, scribbling random thoughts in my notebook, I often found myself wondering what Chekhov would write, how would he manage to capture the nastroeniye, if he were to write scenes not about nineteenth-century provincial life but about the life of expats and dyevs in today's Moscow.

25

'IT's BEEN RAINING FOR two weeks,' I say, looking through the window. It's dark and the rain is falling with violence. 'Everything is so dirty out there, I can't wait for winter to arrive.'

Stepanov stands by the turntable, flipping through his records. He's been playing Russian bands all night. 'Winter should come soon,' he says. 'Last year by this time we had plenty of snow.'

I return to the sofa, slump down next to Colin. 'How young do you think is too young?' I ask.

Colin holds his empty glass up to the light, peers through it from different angles, as if judging the quality of its craftsmanship. 'What do you mean?'

'For a dyev.' I notice comrade Brezhnev staring at me from across the room. Serious eyes. Bushy eyebrows.

Colin places the glass on the table and leans forward, half smiling. 'To fuck her?'

'No,' I say. 'To *be* with her. When do you think a dyev is too young for that?'

Diego is sitting on a chair, wearing his furry shapka, his large paw-like hands typing on his mobile phone. Black shirt unbuttoned, you can see his chest and facial hair meeting at an arbitrarily shaved line halfway up his neck. 'How old is she?' he asks.

'Young,' I say.

Stepanov flips the record on the turntable. Then he crouches and lowers the needle with precision onto the edge of the vinyl. 'How young?'

I regret bringing up the subject. 'Is this KINO?' I ask, when I hear the first beats of the song.

'Fuck yes!' Stepanov mimics guitar playing, then drops onto his leather armchair. 'The *Black Album*.'

'Sounds good,' I say. 'Is this before or after *Gruppa Krovi*?'

'Their last album,' Stepanov says. 'Released after Victor Tsoy died. That's why it's called the *Black Album*, the rest of the group decided not to name it. You know, some people think Tsoy was killed, that his car crash was no accident, because he was against the system and all that.'

'So Martin's banging a little girl,' Colin says. 'What's the legal age in Russia anyway?'

'I don't really know her age,' I say. 'She's not *that* young.'

Stepanov takes the bottle of vodka and fills our four glasses. 'I don't think we have age limits in Russia.'

147

'Where did you find her?' Diego asks, not bothering to look up from his mobile phone.

'At the Moskva Bookshop,' I say. 'A couple of weeks ago. She was standing by the foreign language books.'

'The foreign language shelves are a great spot to pick up dyevs,' Colin says. 'In Dom Knigi there are always hot dyevs around the foreign books. It's like just by being there they are giving you a green light.'

Diego looks up. 'Why's that? I don't think *you* need much encouragement to hit on a girl.'

'You know,' Colin says, 'if they are trying to learn English, they are more willing and interested in meeting expats.'

'So you took her home right away?' Diego asks, now looking at me.

'I took her for a cup of coffee,' I say. 'She's a lovely girl, but a bit shy. Next day we went to the new sushi bar that just opened in Bolshaya Dmitrovka.'

'Haven't tried that one yet,' Colin says.

'Don't.' I stand up and walk towards the large piano in the middle of the room. 'The sushi's crap. But it was Polina's first time, so she didn't notice.'

'I had a Polina two or three months ago,' Colin says. 'From Irkutsk. Or was it Tomsk?'

'So Polina tried to eat with chopsticks,' I say, 'but she kept dropping the sushi. At some point the sushi fell onto the soy plate and the splash stained her shirt. Instead of running off to wash the shirt she just blushed and apologised.'

'That's cute,' Colin says.

'I told her she could use her fingers. She seemed relieved.'

'I can't understand the whole sushi revolution,' Diego says. 'What did they eat before in Moscow?'

'So from the sushi place you took her home?' Colin asks.

'Not really,' I say. 'Next day I took her to the cinema in Pushkinskaya. Then I asked her to come up to my apartment.'

Colin smiles. 'Man, your apartment has the best location in town.'

'Guess what she tells me when she's undressed?'

'I need to move to the centre,' Colin says. 'Get a flat around Tverskaya.'

'Martin,' Stepanov says, 'don't tell us she was a virgin.'

I nod. 'I didn't know, of course. So she's lying naked on my couch and I can see from her face that she's kind of panicking. So I asked her, "Are you OK with this?"'

'Man,' Colin says, 'you should never ask.'

Diego looks up from his mobile phone. 'If she's a virgin you are supposed to ask.'

'Good fucking etiquette,' Stepanov says, laughing.

'Seriously,' Diego says, 'you want to be sure she's really up for it. Wouldn't you?'

'Anyway,' I say, 'she just told me to be careful because she'd never been with a man before.'

'Who gives a fuck about age anyway,' Stepanov says, standing up and raising his glass of vodka. 'If she's into you, why not.'

I raise my glass. 'That's right.'

'Let's drink to our friend,' Stepanov says, pointing his glass at me, 'Humbert Humbert.'

Diego and Colin laugh.

'Fuck you,' I say.

We all drink up. Stepanov starts to sing along to the next song. Colin joins in for the chorus.

When the song is finished, Colin turns to me. 'Remember Marusia, from the Real McCoy?'

'Of course,' I say. 'The TV presenter.'

Colin shakes his head. 'She's driving me crazy, man.'

'Haven't banged her yet?'

'She's just playing with me. I took her for dinner twice, to expensive places. But she's so used to this kind of treatment, must have plenty of guys after her. She would not put out, the bitch.'

Stepanov is pouring vodka into our glasses. He realises he's miscalculated the amount of liquor left in the bottle and there's not enough to fill the last glass. He takes his own glass and pours half of his vodka into Diego's.

Diego lifts his glass, now full to the brim, takes a small sip. 'Is that one of the famous half-German sisters?'

'Yeah,' Colin says. 'That was a great night, when we met them.'

'You've told us the story a hundred times,' Diego says.

'If only you had slept with her that first night,' I say, pointing at Colin, 'you wouldn't give a shit about her right now.'

'If only,' Colin says. 'But shit, we were so wasted, remember? And now I can't get her out of my mind. If I could fuck her just once I would be able to move on. Maybe we could double-date them again?'

'I'm done with the sister,' I say. 'She's so messed up. Anyway, they are too high maintenance, the kind of dyevs who end up with oligarchs.'

'Listen to this song,' Stepanov says. 'The best on this album.'

'If only I could fuck her once,' Colin says, to himself, gazing despondently into his glass.

Stepanov stands up and raises his glass. 'To tonight.'

We drain our glasses.

Diego has now pocketed his mobile phone. Then he asks about the bomb in Pushkinskaya. 'So close to your place,' he says, looking at me. 'Did you hear anything?'

'Only the sirens. It all happened underground, the earth must have muffled the blast.'

'Poor people,' Diego says. 'I don't understand why Chechens do this.'

'I doubt it was the Chechens,' Stepanov says.

Diego shrugs. 'That's what I heard on the news.'

'You guys shouldn't bother watching TV news,' Stepanov says. 'It's all propaganda. TV in Russia is where the government says whatever they want the people to believe.'

'That's true,' Colin says. 'Fucking weird, if you take Russians individually, one by one, they are the most honest people on Earth. They are so direct, so straightforward, they just can't lie. Not in their genes. Russians can't do hypocrisy, not like Westerners. That's why they come across as rude. It's not rudeness. It's fucking honesty. But, shit, when it comes to the public sphere, that's another story. Everything in this country is a big fucking lie.'

Stepanov lowers his voice. 'True. The bomb in Pushkin-skaya was most probably planted by our guys. Nashi.'

'What do you mean your guys?' I ask.

'You know, the FSB, the secret services. It's like the building they blew up last year in Pechatniki. They killed dozens of people, just to make a point.'

'What point?'

Colin turns to me. 'To show the common people that Russia has enemies.'

'Precisely,' Stepanov says. 'You need to understand that for Russians to feel united we need an enemy, someone who wants to destroy us, an external threat that helps us come together. Mongols, Poles, French, Germans, Americans, anyone will do. It's a tradition, it has always been like this.'

'I see,' I say. 'Like *War and Peace*.'

'I guess,' Stepanov says. 'Haven't read it.'

'You never read *War and Peace*?'

Stepanov shakes his head, looking down at the coffee table. 'I started it a couple of times. Too fucking long.'

'Russians can't live without existential fear,' Colin says. 'They are a screwed-up nation.'

'I wouldn't put it exactly like that,' Stepanov says.

'They have an enormous inferiority complex,' Colin continues, now pointing at Stepanov. 'With all their shit about being a special nation and all that, if you scratch under the surface, all Russians are jealous of the West. Of America in particular.'

'Have *you* read *War and Peace*?' I ask Colin.

'I saw the movie,' he says. 'What I mean is, making enemies

is how Russia tries to overcome its inferiority complex. The hostile attitude, the political whining, it's just a façade, it makes Russians feel more valued, or, at least, less ignored. That's why they came up with the whole communist fiasco and put up with it for so long. They knew it didn't work, but they liked the feeling of being feared.'

'I thought communism was about giving life some meaning,' I say. 'Through sacrifice and suffering.'

'Bullshit,' Colin says. 'It was about prestige. Like the unpopular kid in school that turns into a bully. He's never going to be one of the popular guys, so he'd rather be a bully than a nerd. That's Russia.'

'Communism was awesome,' Diego says. 'It would have been great to live here twenty years ago, when people believed in those things. Social justice, ideals. The fall of the Soviet Union was a historical tragedy for the entire world. No wonder Russia is such a mess now. And the people are so confused.'

'That's what makes Moscow so fucking interesting,' Colin says. 'The confusion, the chaos. We're just lucky to be here at this moment in history. In a few years it'll all be sanitised and clean like the West. I would die of boredom now if I had to live in the States.'

Stepanov stands up, walks towards the turntable. 'Russia will never be like the West.'

'Let's hope not,' Colin says.

Stepanov takes the KINO record from the turntable and slides it into its black sleeve. 'We see the world in a different way.'

'Vodka's finished,' I say. 'Should we start moving?'

'How are we getting there?' Diego says. 'We don't even know the address. I don't want to walk around in this rain.'

'It's somewhere behind Lubyanka,' Stepanov says. 'We'll ask the taxi to drive around until we find it. It's opening night, there'll be people outside.'

We stand up. Diego helps Stepanov take the empty bottles and glasses to the kitchen. We start putting our shoes on.

Diego readjusts his shapka in front of a wall mirror. 'I'm looking forward to seeing this place,' he says.

'It's gonna be awesome,' Colin says.

Stepanov takes his sunglasses from the coffee table, switches the lights off. We leave the apartment and head down to the street.

26

IN THE EVENINGS THE rain fell frozen, heavy, and for two weeks all the streets around Pushkinskaya were covered in mud and slush. The floors of perekhods and metro platforms were smeared in black sludge, wet and slippery – the underground air swamped by the smell of damp earth. Then, one day in late November, temperatures dropped below freezing, the wind and the rain stopped, and dry snow started to fall over Moscow.

The snow began around noon and went on until late in the evening – falling in silence and piling on the stack of plastic chairs on Scandinavia's terrace, on parked cars, on the bare trees of the Boulevard, on Pushkin's bronze shoulders.

Lena stood by the balcony door, staring at the snowfall.

'I love Moscow in winter,' I said. From the couch I could not see her face but I knew she was crying.

'The snow will cover all the shit until spring,' she replied.

She was in her underwear, red lace knickers and matching bra, holding a cup of tea that had long gone cold.

'Come here, Lenushka.'

'I'm going home.'

'Stay, please.'

She turned to me. 'What for?'

'It's late. And cold outside. Come back to the couch. We can talk about everything tomorrow.'

The flat was dark, but for a solitary candle flickering on the coffee table, next to an empty wine bottle.

'Martin, you said you might write a book about your life in Moscow.'

'Maybe after my PhD, something more personal.'

'If you write about me,' Lena said, 'please make it a sad story.'

'All Russian stories are sad.'

'True.' Lena took a sip of cold tea and continued crying in silence. I knew she would not let it go. Once Lena had found a reason to cry she did not stop.

'I don't think I want to see you tomorrow,' she said. 'I don't think I want to see you again.'

I sat up on the couch, draped a blanket over my shoulders. 'What's wrong?'

'You really don't care about me, about how I feel inside. You have no capacity for compassion.'

Compassion. Sostradaniye. Co-suffering. Lena didn't like it that I wasn't able to suffer with her.

She placed the cup of tea on the table, picked her crumpled jeans up from the carpet, shook out the legs.

'Lenushka, please.'

'Can I ask you something?'

'Please.'

She was holding the little cross of her necklace. 'Do you love me?'

I grabbed my glass of wine from the table, had a sip. 'In what sense?'

'Why is it so hard for you to say I love you?'

'Everybody says I love you. It means nothing.'

'Maybe it means nothing where you come from. Here it means a lot. I love you, Martin. I'm not afraid of saying it. I'm connected to my emotions. I say what I feel. But you never said you loved me. Not even once.'

'What's your point?'

'I want to know that you have feelings for me,' Lena said, 'that I'm important to you. Not just someone you sleep with.'

I didn't know what to say. I tried to come up with some smart words, something revealing the depth and complexity of my feelings for Lena without falling into the tackiness of a forced love confession. Something witty, honest, simple – worthy of a Chekhov character. But the words didn't quite form in my mouth.

Lena slipped into her jeans, wiped her tears with the tips of her fingers.

I stood up, grasped her hand.

'Lena, I really like spending time with you. You know that. I love it when we are together. Let's go to sleep, please.'

I tried to kiss her but she turned her face away. I wrapped my arms around her waist and pulled her gently towards me – her breasts now pressed against my body.

We embraced and on my cheeks I felt the damp warmth of her tears. I kissed her neck. Lena didn't budge. We stood skin to skin, in the darkness. Not knowing what to do, I retreated to the bathroom for a quick shower.

When I came out, Lena was standing by the double front door, zipping up her high-heeled boots. She was wearing a white woollen hat and a matching scarf. In high heels Lena was a bit taller than me.

'The metro must already be closed,' I said. 'Do you need money for a taxi?'

'Martin, I'm not a whore.'

Lena stood motionless, waiting for me to open the doors. Tears had smudged her mascara – she had black smeared all over her face. I tried to wipe her cheeks but she pushed my hand away. I unlocked the doors and she walked out.

Lena didn't take the lift. Instead, she stomped down the stairs, her boots tapping loudly all six floors down to the street. I closed the doors, wrapped myself in the blanket again and stepped onto the balcony. The air outside was icy and crisp – Moscow was covered in fresh snow. I saw Lena coming out of the entrance below, looking small and remote. She opened the metal courtyard gate, turned left, and disappeared under the archway beneath my building.

I stood on the balcony, my nose going numb with the cold. The snowstorm had paused for a moment but tiny snowflakes kept on swirling in the darkness, sparkling around the street lamps.

Winter had arrived.

27

LENA, HERE'S MY BOOK about Moscow. I imagine these days you don't have much time to read books. But if destiny puts these pages in your hands – the way it brought us together so many years ago – I can tell you now what I was thinking back then, on my balcony, when the first snow of the season fell over Moscow and you left my flat in the middle of the night. Fuck you. Fuck you and your sad stories and your endless search for pain. And fuck that troubled soul of yours that I was never Russian enough to understand.

PART THREE

Anna's Punishment

28

UNLIKE PUSHKIN'S TATYANA, WHO stays with her husband despite having a thing for Onegin, Anna Karenina decides to dump both husband and son so that she can pursue her affair with Vronsky.

These two stories, arguably the best-known love stories in Russia, have rather different endings. Two married women love another man. Married woman number one, Pushkin's Tatyana, decides to stick with her husband. Married woman number two, Tolstoy's Karenina, ditches her husband and elopes with her lover. Married woman number one lives virtuously — if not happily — ever after. Married woman number two falls into disgrace and ends up throwing herself under a train.

Thing is, we know Anna Karenina could've got away with her affair, if only she hadn't been such a drama queen.

Tolstoy makes sure we understand as much, by showing us that other women in Anna's milieu were having affairs — discreetly, without major repercussions. But Karenina makes a big fuss about her story with Vronsky and ends up messing everything up.

As a result of her public infidelity, Karenina gets a bad reputation, and all of a sudden it's uncool among the elitni tusovka to be seen near her. She loses her friends. All she has now is Vronsky. Vronsky likes Karenina, but she becomes so clingy and dependent that, at some point, he feels suffocated. Who could blame him.

So Vronsky does what anyone in his position would do: he tries to cool things off. He lets Anna know that he would like her to go and get a life of her own, but of course now she can't because she has become a social outcast. Vronsky still has his friends, because he is a man, and in nineteenth-century Russia — as in twenty-first-century Russia — men can fuck around and remain respectable members of society.

Anna is now jealous and kind of paranoid and she whines all day. She becomes a bore. So Vronsky tells her, what the fuck, Anna, just chill out. But Anna Karenina, who's a sufferer, makes a scene about Vronsky's every move. Is Karenina proving the extent of her love through her suffering? Vronsky won't have any of it, and she becomes more desperate — unbearable. She has nowhere to go. In the end, she can't stand it any longer and, in what's probably the most famous scene in Russian literature, she goes and throws herself under a train.

Tolstoy shows us a parallel storyline, that of Levin and

Kitty, who enjoy a stable if somewhat dull marriage that is based not on carnal love, but on mutual respect and sacrifice. Is Tolstoy against the idea of romantic passion?

Kind of. Levin, Tolstoy's alter ego in the novel, is motivated not by his passion for Kitty, but by the intellectual notion of domestic life, the concept of creating a family.

Anna Karenina is punished by Tolstoy, who writes the story from an omniscient God-like point of view. In a way, Anna's punishment is to be expected – Lev Nikolaevich had forewarned readers by giving his book an epigraph of a scary Bible quote: 'Vengeance is mine, and I will repay.'

So Anna Karenina pays, first with her social status, then with her sanity, finally with her life. All because she made the wrong choices. But what are those wrong choices? What is, in the end, the fateful decision Anna has to pay for?

She doesn't pay for having an extramarital affair. Nor does she pay for abandoning her child, something Tolstoy would not have considered particularly wrong. Karenina is punished for betraying her own nature, her Russianness. Trying to feed her romantic and sexual desires, Anna Karenina forgot Tatyana's lesson: that life is not about happiness – it's about meaning. For that, she deserves to be crushed by a train.

29

THE MORNING AFTER THE first snowfall I awoke to the sound of metal shovels scraping the asphalt in the street. I made coffee and toast and sat by the balcony. Down in the courtyard, street sweepers in orange uniforms were gathering piles of snow, then loading the snow onto their trucks. The sky was cloudless, cosmos blue. The roofs of the city were covered in white.

I checked my phone and saw that Lena had not replied to my text message. I showered, put on winter clothes, went down to the street. In the metro, I prepared mentally for my monthly meeting with Lyudmila Aleksandrovna. Typically, after talking about the weather, I would tell her what I was reading, which, to her disappointment, was rarely academic books or articles but mostly novels, the classics, which she thought I should have known by now. She would then give

166

me some pointers for my research, recommend further reading and, when we ran out of things to say, we would discuss politics, history or whatever was in the news.

I had to admit that I wasn't dedicating much time to my research, at least not to the more conventional part – reading scholarly papers, meeting professors, visiting the library. Come to think of it, I hadn't been to the library in weeks. Not that I wasn't working, but getting to know Russian women was taking up most of my time. Why should I bother with dusty old literary theories – I thought, as the metro sped through the tunnels – when I can spend my time reading Chekhov and meeting real women?

I arrived at the university before eleven, just in time for our meeting. When I entered her office, Lyudmila Aleksandrovna was reading at her desk, hidden behind stacks of books and papers.

'Please sit down,' she said. 'Let me boil some water.'

She approached a side table under the bookshelves, switched the rusty kettle on. The water must have been hot because it boiled in a few seconds.

'Finally, the snow,' she said, sitting at her desk with two steaming cups of tea before her. 'So late in the season. If the weather keeps changing year after year, soon we'll have no winter at all. You know, in soviet times winters were cold and dry. They always came at the same time of year.'

'Everything was better organised in the Soviet Union,' I said.

'Exactly,' she said, missing the irony of my remark. 'Every thing worked back then. Not like now. Don't believe what

167

they tell you in the West, Martin, life was much better then. Life was dignified.'

I sat across from her at her desk, keeping steady, afraid to lean back in case my wobbly chair fell apart. 'It must have been an interesting time.'

'Good times indeed,' she said softly, speaking not to me but to the tea bag she was taking out of her cup. 'You know, back in the 1970s, I used to travel a lot. I had to attend academic congresses and literary seminars all across the Soviet Union. It was wonderful. We even had seminars in Sochi, Martin, can you imagine?'

'Yes, Sochi.'

The fabled seminars in Sochi must have been important for Lyudmila Aleksandrovna, because she mentioned them almost every time we met.

'We stayed in a beautiful dom otdykha by the sea,' she went on, 'very quiet and peaceful, and we had academic discussions until late in the night. And everything was paid for by the trade union! Everything, Martin, can you imagine?'

'Everything.'

She took a sip of tea, placed the cup back on the table. She looked at me, her thick glasses steamed up. Her golden tooth was framed by a dead smile, her thoughts surely lost in the 1970s. Lyudmila Aleksandrovna belonged to the generation of Muscovites who were too old and too soviet to embrace the changes that the perestroika had brought to the country.

'Believe me,' she said. 'Train, accommodation, meals, everything was covered. And look at things now, with our pitiful

university salaries, we can hardly afford to buy bread and kolbasa. And the streets of Moscow are full of brainless oligarchs
driving expensive German cars. Russia is a bardak.'

'Some things seem to be better now,' I said, trying to
cheer her up a little. 'You know, with the new president.
The economy is doing great.'

'Nothing's changed. Don't be fooled because you live in
the centre of Moscow, Martin. Most people in this country
don't have enough to eat.'

I unwrapped a block of chocolate I had bought in the
metro, broke it into pieces and placed it on the desk, among
the stacks of books. Lyudmila Aleksandrovna took the biggest piece and bit it with gusto.

'Martin, you are going to have to work a bit harder, you
know. I haven't seen any real work from you in the last two
or three months.'

She took a sip of tea.

'I've been doing some interesting reading lately,' I said.
'I've gone through a lot of Chekhov, as you recommended.'

'It's good that you read the works of Anton Pavlovich,'
she said, 'but, as I told you before, proper research is not
only about reading the books. You need to read academic
papers, talk to experts, compare views. You need to check
those sociological studies of women that we talked about. I
suppose that's not what you do when you go out at night.
After all, Martin, you are in Moscow to write your thesis,
not to go to discoteks. This is MGU, the Moscow State
University. Students all over would kill for the chance you
have to work in this faculty.'

169

I straightened my back and gripped my cup of tea. 'You are absolutely right, Lyudmila Aleksandrovna. I do need to focus a bit more. But, you know, at this stage of my research I'm trying to learn more about real people.'

'In what sense?'

'Before writing about literary characters, I feel I need to learn about the real Russian mentality. You know, about the intricacies of the Mysterious Russian Soul.'

I'd learned by now that Russians loved to hear the expression *Mysterious Russian Soul*. It made them feel special, unique. The Russians I met often referred to the Mysterious Russian Soul to describe deep feelings that, I was told, a foreigner like me would never be able to comprehend.

'Martin, you have been in Moscow for more than a year. The Russian soul has no more mysteries for you. It's about time you started to put what you've learned down on paper. You need to write your thesis. Otherwise you might end up losing your scholarship.'

There was no point arguing with Lyudmila Aleksandrovna. In her long academic life, she'd surely seen too many students trying to bullshit their way out of work. I was not going to win her over with my revolutionary methodology of using dyevs as primary sources.

Then, out of nowhere, Lyudmila Aleksandrovna launched into a lecture about the lishniy chelovek, the superfluous man, a type of male character common in nineteenth-century Russian literature. 'Superfluous men,' Lyudmila Aleksandrovna was saying, 'are typically born into wealth and privilege. They are sensitive men, like you, Martin. They

are also very cynical. You know, they disregard social values.'
She took her glasses off and wiped them.

'Why superfluous?' I asked.

'They don't contribute anything positive to society. They suffer existential boredom. Often, they end up challenging other men to useless duels.'

'Existential boredom,' I said.

She put her glasses back on, now smiling. 'Of course the father of all superfluous men, the model to follow, is Evgeny Onegin himself.'

I glanced around the cramped office, at the piles of books on the floor, at the book-lined walls, at the small window, partly obscured by books. I remembered how puzzled I was when, during one of our first meetings, I'd spotted the brown adhesive tape around the window frame. By now, at the start of my second winter in Moscow, I'd learned that the tape was a necessity in old buildings, to avoid a freezing draught seeping in during the cold months.

Looking back at Lyudmila Aleksandrovna's smile, I couldn't tell if she was mocking me, or truly accusing me of being superfluous.

'There are other examples,' she said, 'of course. I presume you've read Turgenev's *Diary of a Superfluous Man*.'

'Not yet.'

'You could also say that our dear Pechorin in *A Hero of Our Time* is one of them. And, of course, our good old friend Oblomov.'

'*Oblomov*,' I said. 'I've read that.' Goncharov's *Oblomov* was the story of this guy who's so bored and uninterested in the world that he spends a large part of the book trying to get out of bed.

Lyudmila Aleksandrovna was now pointing her finger at me. 'Martin, tell me, are you a superfluous man?'

'I'm not into duels, if that's what you mean.'

'I'm serious,' she said.

'I don't know, Lyudmila Aleksandrovna. I admit that my contribution to society is rather limited. But existential boredom, I don't know.'

'Think about it,' she said.

In the end, I agreed to bring an entire outline of thesis chapters to our next meeting. We then talked about the impossible traffic in Moscow and she gave me a speech – a version of which I'd heard often from other Muscovites – about the city having the most efficient and beautiful metro system in the world.

Before leaving her office, I placed two theatre tickets on her desk – Chekhov's *Three Sisters* at Taganskaya.

'This is for you,' I said. I'd been told that MGU professors expected little presents every now and then from their students. She stood up and thanked me for the tickets, said she would take her daughter to the theatre with her.

As I left Lyudmila Aleksandrovna's office I was wondering who, among men, is not superfluous.

30

I HAD SOME SPARE TIME after seeing Lyudmila Aleksandrovna, so I decided to visit the university's second-hand bookshops. Browsing through the Russian literature section I found an edition of *War and Peace* in two volumes, printed in 1944, with cardboard covers and a beautiful old-paper smell. I bought the two volumes for a hundred and forty rubles, about the price of a vodka shot in Propaganda.

I had arranged to meet Ira for lunch at the main stolovaya. I found her standing outside the entrance, reading a book in English. We said hello and I showed her my purchase. She seemed unimpressed.

'Sergey's mum has so many of these old books,' she said. 'We store them at the dacha.' She dropped her book into a plastic bag. 'Let's eat. I'm starving.'

We stood at the end of the food queue. Ira looked thinner,

her watery eyes brighter. When we reached the front, a sour-faced babushka with a paper kitchen hat loaded our trays with borsch, chicken, buckwheat. To drink we each took a glass of syrupy kompot. At the cashier's desk I pointed at both our trays, but Ira insisted on paying for her own food.

'It's nice to be back at the university,' I said, as we sat at one of the big tables by the window. I could see the court-yard covered in fresh snow. 'I hardly come down these days.'

'How's the research going?'

'I'm reading stuff,' I said. 'Thinking, meeting people. Just not writing that much. What about you, how are things?'

'Not that good.'

I had learned by now that, whenever confronted by a 'how are you' or 'how are things', Russians rarely answered with a simple 'fine, thanks'. They saw the question not as a polite greeting formula, but as a welcome chance to enumerate the many problems life had recently dumped on them.

'What's wrong?' I was dissecting the chicken with my knife and fork, trying to extract some meat from the skinny thigh.

'Sergey.' Ira slurped a spoonful of soup. 'He does nothing all day, just drinks beer, watches TV.'

'What about the photography?'

'Not even that any more. Not inspired, he says.'

'What can you do,' I said, smiling. 'Sergey's an artist.'

'He's my boyfriend,' Ira said, gesturing at me with a piece of black bread, 'and I love him with all my heart, but I'm tired of his laziness.'

'Give him a break. He's probably just going through a difficult phase.'

174

She held up the piece of black bread, which seemed to stand for Sergey in our conversation. 'I don't care if he wants to do photography or painting or whatever he wants, but he could have finished his degree and got a real job as well. In the end all he does is talk and talk and no action. I don't know, sometimes I question the whole thing between us.'

I realised what looked different about Ira. She was wearing make-up. Eyeliner, shadow, powder – you could hardly see the dark circles around her eyes.

'All talk and no action,' I said. 'Sergey's a dreamer, a classic Russian idealist.'

Ira bit into her black bread. 'A what?'

'A Russian idealist. You know, a typical character in Chekhov's works. Nabokov writes about this in his *Lectures on Russian Literature*.' I took my red notebook out of my backpack and started to flip through the pages.

'You and your Chekhov. The world is not a book, Martin. There is literature and there is reality.'

'Here it is,' I said, pointing at my own handwriting. 'The Russian idealist, Nabokov says, is an intellectual who combines lofty dreams and human decency with an inability to put his ideals into action. Just like Sergey.'

I smiled.

Ira didn't. She stared down at my notebook, lost in thought. 'Sergey's a drunk,' she said. 'He has no lofty dreams, he just wants to drink all day and maybe, one day, if he feels like it, take his stupid black and white photographs that nobody needs.'

A group of young students sat on the other side of our table. 'Lucky you can support him.'

'I don't earn that much,' she said, lowering her voice. 'They exploit the Russian staff in our firm. American colleagues doing the same job as me get three or four times my salary. It's so unfair. In the end, after sending money to my family and paying the bills, I can't really save much. And, you know, I would like to rent my own apartment one day. Sergey's mother is very nice, but the place is too small for the three of us.'

'This chicken is all bone,' I said. 'There's no flesh.'

'Welcome to Russia,' Ira said, in English.

Through the large window, I saw five or six students having a snowball fight. They seemed to be having fun, running after each other. I thought it would be nice to join them. There was something about fresh snow, a promise of renewal and peace.

'By the way,' I said, 'Lena left me.'

'Again?'

I nodded. 'Yesterday. I think this time it's for real.'

'What did you do?'

'Nothing.'

'You must have done something.'

'I didn't *do* anything. She found a hair in my bed.'

'Another girl's hair?' Ira asked.

'I guess. Long and black.'

'You're such an asshole.'

'I told Lena it was probably an old hair caught in the blanket, but she didn't want to listen. She just started to cry.'

'And she left? Just like that?'

'First she asked me if I loved her,' I said.

'What did you say?'

'What was I supposed to say? Anyway, she was all emotional, not listening.'

'Western men, you're all pussies.'

'Then it occurred to me that the hair could be from my cleaning lady.'

'Is that possible?' Ira asked.

'Maybe, who knows.'

'You don't know what your cleaning lady looks like?'

'Perhaps it was her hair. Anyway, I told Lena I thought the hair belonged to the cleaning lady, but it was too late. She was too pissed off.'

'Of course,' Ira said, 'she didn't believe your bullshit.'

'It's not that she *didn't* believe me. She *chose* not to believe me.'

Ira put her empty soup plate aside. 'What do you mean?'

'I mean, she preferred the drama of finding another lover's hair over the triviality of finding a hair from my cleaning lady.'

'I see.' Ira shook her head. 'And, I presume, that's because she's a woman?'

'Not at all,' I said. 'That's because she's Russian.'

31

WHEN THE INTERCOM RANG I was lying on the couch, reading a book. I glanced at my watch – almost midnight. I placed the book on the coffee table, face down so as not to lose the page, walked over to the entrance, picked up the receiver.

'Martin, it's Sergey. Are you alone?'

'Sergey? Come up.'

I pulled a pair of jeans on over my underpants and opened the two front doors of my flat.

A minute later Sergey knocked at the open door.

'Come in, come in,' I said.

'Sorry to show up this late.' Sergey made sure he was fully inside the apartment before shaking my hand – some odd superstition about not greeting under a threshold. Since I last saw him, Sergey's thick stubble had grown to almost a full beard. His eyes were bloodshot. He smelled of vodka.

'Everything OK?'

'It's so hot in here,' he said.

'The heating is on high these days. I have to open the windows so as not to boil to death. It cools off later at night.'

'You're lucky to live in the centre,' he said, taking his shoes off. 'We don't get that much heating in the northern suburbs.'

I hung his coat behind the door and directed him into the kitchen. 'You all right?'

'It's good for your health to get some cold air into the apartment,' he said. 'Even now, in the heart of winter. My mum opens the windows every morning, it helps clean the air and get the infections out of the house.'

'It would be easier if I could regulate the temperature myself.'

Sergey glanced around the kitchen, as if searching for something. 'Do you have a beer?'

'Sure.' I opened the fridge, took out two bottles of Baltika and a plastic box of salt cucumbers. I sliced a cucumber and arranged the slices on a small plate. Sitting at the table, I moved a pile of books to one side and opened the two bottles.

Sergey stared at his bottle, saying nothing.

'Do you want a glass?' I asked.

'No, thanks. It's all right.'

'Davay,' I said. We clinked our beers.

'You know,' he said, 'in Georgia people never toast with beer.'

I took a sip. 'Why's that?'

'I don't know,' Sergey said. 'Bad omen, I suppose. Did you know my father was Georgian?'

'I didn't know.'

'From Gori, like Stalin. Came to Moscow in the late 1960s, to study at MGU. Of course back then it was all the same country so things were easier. Besides, half of Moscow's intelligentsia were Georgians. Artists, poets, singers. Many came to Moscow.'

'But your mum is Russian.'

'Half Ukrainian, half Russian. That makes me a perfect soviet specimen. Except of course there is no Soviet Union any more.' He glanced down at his Baltika and shook his head.

'You know,' he said, 'I was born in Moscow. I've lived all my life in this city, and yet I don't always feel I belong here. I get stopped in the street all the time by policemen hoping that I'm an illegal immigrant and they can squeeze some rubles out of me.' He took a sip of beer. 'They're kids, these policemen, illiterate drunks who think they're important just because they wear uniforms.'

I took a piece of cucumber. I could see Sergey's eyes were watery, tears waiting to be released.

'It's about Ira,' he said, head down, now brushing his thick eyebrows with his thumbs.

'Is she OK?'

Sergey lifted the beer bottle, drank a few gulps, placed it back on the table. He started to peel the label. 'She's fucking another guy.'

'In what sense?'

'An American asshole,' Sergey said. 'From work. She told me. Well, it's more that I caught her. My mobile phone ran out of credit so I used her phone to text a friend. When I went to check that my text had been sent, I saw a sent message in English. You know my English is not very good, but I knew what it meant.'

'Your English is good.'

'The message said *I miss you*. It was sent to this guy Robert S, her boss at the firm. So I asked Ira about the message and she started shouting at me, saying that I was breaching her privacy because I had looked at her mobile phone. As if *that* was the important thing.'

'I see.'

Sergey was staring at the bottle of beer, tearing strips from the label, placing them next to each other on the table. 'She told me they had just been flirting and nothing else but, when I insisted, she admitted that they have been sleeping together. For a few weeks.'

Sergey held the bottle to his lips and, as he began drinking, let out a sob. He choked and spat some beer on the table.

'I'm sorry,' he said, now openly crying.

'Don't worry.' I took a roll of paper towel and handed it to him. He made a ball of paper, wiped the table. Then he tore another piece of paper towel off the roll and blew his nose.

'I'm so fucking stupid,' he said.

'Calm down, man.'

'I'm wasting my life. I'm not doing anything meaningful. I left university so that I could work and take photos and now I'm not even doing that. Ira is the only thing I have.'

He covered his eyes with one hand and cried.

I searched for something appropriate to say but nothing came to mind.

'And now she's gone,' he said. 'She just packed a few things and said she'd go to a friend's place.'

Sergey finished the rest of his beer.

'Want another one?' I asked.

'Please.'

I got another Baltika from the fridge and opened it for him.

Sergey was silent for a while, staring at the samovar on the table.

'I'm sure the American guy makes tons of money,' he finally said, shaking his head.

'I don't think Ira is the type of woman who cares about that.'

'Of course she does. They all do. Women don't give a shit about a smart guy or an interesting partner. All they want is someone who earns enough to buy them stuff. That's why Russian babas run after foreigners.'

'But Ira has a good job. She can buy her own stuff.'

Sergey blew his nose again, took a slice of cucumber.

'Can you talk to her?' he said. 'Please.'

'I don't think that's going to change much.'

'You're her friend, she'll listen to you. I want to know why she did it, if she wants to come back to me.'

'I don't think my getting involved is going to help you in any way. Maybe it's better that *you* speak to her.'

'Please, talk to her. Please.'

Sergey's mobile rang. He glanced at it and silenced it without taking the call.

'It's my mum,' he said. 'She's been calling the whole day. She's worried I'm going to kill myself or something.'

'Maybe you should give her a ring.'

'Later,' he said. He looked around the kitchen, as if inspecting the walls. 'Expats have a great life. With all the money and the good flats, partying all day and meeting Russian girls.'

'Most of us work as well,' I said. 'It's not all a big party. My research takes up quite a lot of my time.'

From the books on the table Sergey grabbed my Penguin Classics edition of Chekhov's plays, translated by Elisaveta Fen.

'I thought you read these things in Russian,' he said.

'I like to read them in English as well, just to make sure I'm not missing anything.'

'Even Chekhov?' he asked. 'Don't you know these plays by heart?'

'There's always something new every time you read them. And it's interesting to see how translators go about concepts that don't really translate. For example, there is this quote in *Three Sisters*.' I took the book from Sergey's hands and opened it at one of the marked pages. 'Look here,' I said, pointing at an underlined paragraph halfway down the page. 'At the beginning of the first act, Irina says, "If only we could go back to Moscow." But if you read the Russian original, as Chekhov wrote it, what Irina really says—'

'I can't read fiction any more,' Sergey said abruptly,

looking not at my book, but at his beer. 'Such a waste of time. I haven't read a novel in years. There are so many interesting things to read about real life in newspapers and magazines or history books. Why bother reading something that someone made up?'

'I used to think like that,' I said, disappointed by Sergey's lack of interest. 'But in the end, if you think about it, fiction is not that different from non-fiction. Non-fiction offers a very partial view of reality. When authors choose what to say and what to leave out, they are already distorting facts. Because the biggest chunk of any story, real or fictional, always remains untold.'

'The book you plan to write about Moscow,' he said, 'will it be a memoir or fiction?'

'What's the difference?'

'Things either happen or don't happen.'

'Not that simple,' I said. 'Memory is very selective, it changes the past. In the end, all memoirs are fiction.'

Sergey closed his eyes for a couple of seconds.

'I guess,' I said, 'that if I ever write my book about Moscow, I'll just bury my own experiences within a fictional story.'

Sergey stood up, anchoring his hand on the wall to keep his balance. 'Need to go to the toilet,' he said, tumbling out of the kitchen.

When he came back a couple of minutes later he didn't sit down. He took the beer and finished it in three or four long gulps.

'I don't want to keep you up,' he said. 'It's very late, sorry to drop in on you like that. I'm heading home.'

He walked out of the kitchen, sat on the stool by the entrance and started to put his shoes on.

'Would you talk to her?' he said.

'I'm not sure it's going to help.'

'Please.'

'I'll see what I can do.'

Sergey put his coat on and we hugged goodbye. He kept hugging me for a few seconds, his beard scratching my neck. I patted his back, which was, I imagined, the manly and appropriate thing to do. When he had left the flat I cleared the beers from the kitchen, wiped the table and put the salt cucumbers back in the fridge.

32

LENA WAS NOT REPLYING to my messages or phone calls. As the days got colder and darker, I started to accept that she was no longer there, at the other end of the phone, waiting for my call.

Something strange happened to me. Now, when I was alone at home trying to watch a film, I would picture Lena lying at my side. Often, I would find myself staring at the Indian tapestry she'd given me, or at the empty couch, exchanging words with an imaginary Lena – comments about whatever I was watching: this is funny, ridiculous, I don't get it – then trying to imagine what Lena would have said in return.

Perhaps these divagations of my mind were due to the fact that, precisely at that time, I'd started to sleep badly. Regardless of when I went to sleep, even after a long vodka night, I would wake up early in the morning. As soon as I regained the smallest spark of consciousness — an awareness of who I was and where I was — my brain would be bombarded with dozens of fresh thoughts that grew out of control and then I couldn't get back to sleep. Lying on the couch, my eyes open, I often ended up thinking about Lena.

I also thought about Lena after a bad night out, when I hadn't met any promising girls and it was time to go home. As the music in the last club of the night stopped and the lights went on, and people gathered on the street, and new couples kissed, and phone numbers were exchanged, and taxis were shared — as the night was ending and a new Moscow day was about to begin — I would stand alone in the street and think about Lena. But I would not think about the drama or the tears. I would think about her body and I would visualise the exact moment when she unfastened her bra for the first time and offered her perfect breasts to me. This vivid image would produce a sharp pain in my chest. The night gone, I would take a taxi home, crash on my couch and wank myself to sleep.

33

It was dark outside, freezing, close to minus twenty. I walked down Tverskaya, wearing my heavy coat, scarf, hat and thermal gloves. I turned left at Kamergersky – the cold seeping up through the soles of my winter shoes, reaching my feet. By the time I arrived at Pirogi, my nose was frozen numb.

Inside it was warm and lively – all the tables were occupied by young people drinking beer, eating, talking loudly. I walked towards the back room, where the books were sold, but couldn't see Ira.

The day after Sergey's unannounced visit, I'd called Ira to see how she was doing. She'd suggested meeting on Thursday for dinner.

I walked down the stairs into the basement rooms and found her sitting at a small table at the back. In spite of her make-up, she looked tired, the bags under her greyish eyes darker than usual. We kissed hello. After taking my winter gear off, I sat at the table.

'Have you ordered yet?' I asked.

'Only tea. I was waiting for you. We should order right away, it usually takes ages in here.'

She beckoned the waitress. We both ordered mushroom soup, which Ira said was very good, then kotlety, salad and a bowl of pelmeni.

'So,' I said with a smile, 'what have you done to poor Seriozha?'

'What did he tell you exactly?'

'That you are sleeping with an American guy from work.'

'It's more complicated than that.'

'He was pretty drunk when we met. He didn't look great.'

'I'm sorry that he came to your place like that,' she said.

'It's OK, I just felt sorry for him.'

One of the other tables in the room was occupied by two girls in almost identical woolly brown sweaters. I noticed one of them staring in our direction, with a red lipstick smile. For a moment I wished I was with Colin, instead of Ira, so that we could chat the two girls up.

'This isn't any easier for me,' Ira was saying.

'So, what happened?'

'Not much,' Ira said. 'There's this guy at work. We became friends and he made it clear that he was interested in me. Then we went out a couple of times. And we started to have a thing. Nothing serious.'

'Who is he?'

'His name is Rob. One of the consultants.' Ira unbuttoned her cardigan, revealing a tight black top with unusually deep cleavage.

'Were you seeing him the last time we met?' I asked. 'You know, when we had lunch at MGU.'

'Yes.'

'Why didn't you tell me?'

'I don't know,' she said. 'I think I tried to tell you, but you didn't seem interested.'

The waitress brought two bowls. The cold from the street remained in my bones. I took my spoon and went straight for the soup.

'That was quick service,' Ira said.

'Moscow *is* changing after all. You cheat on Sergey. Quick service at Pirogi. What's going on?'

'Not funny.'

'This is delicious,' I said.

'I told you.'

'Creamy and tasty.'

'They make it with white mushrooms.'

We savoured the mushroom soup in silence. The dyev with the red lipstick kept staring at me. So did her friend now. They giggled and I wondered if they thought Ira and I were a couple. I hoped they realised she was just a friend.

'So,' I said. 'Who's this Rob? Married with kids?'

'Nope. Young, single. A babnik, like you.' Ira ate some soup. 'You might have met him in your nightclubs, he goes out with other expats.'

'I don't really hang out with Americans. Except Colin, of course, but he's been Europeanised.'

'Rob's fresh from New York. His first time abroad. He's been in Moscow for four months.'

'These things happen,' I said, hoping these words would close the subject. 'I just thought you were happy with Sergey.'

'This has nothing to do with Sergey.' Ira pulled her black top down, readjusting her cleavage.

'Whatever,' I said. 'It's fine. These things happen.'

I had promised Sergey I would talk to Ira. Done. Now we could move on.

'Really, it's not about Sergey,' Ira insisted.

I looked at the other table. The dyevs were emptying a jug of beer and seemed to be having a good time. If only Colin were here. Even Diego would do.

Ira was looking at me with an angry expression, as if reading my thoughts.

'But it *does* have to do with Sergey,' I said, trying to pick up the conversation where she'd left off. 'He was your boyfriend and you started to fuck someone else.'

'I can't believe my ears, Martin. Are you giving me lessons on fidelity?'

'I just mean . . . I don't know.'

'Sorry,' she said. 'I know you're trying to help.'

She placed her spoon on the empty plate. 'You know, Martin, I think sometimes you forget I'm a woman. I'm not only your friend but also a woman, even if, for whatever reason, that's not how you see me. I need attention and courtship. Someone to give me compliments. Rob likes me, he makes me feel appreciated, *as a woman.*'

As a woman. Kak zhenschina.

'So it's a serious thing, the American guy and you?'

'Of course not,' Ira said. 'He's an expat, he just wants to have fun, like all of you. He probably has other women on the side. But that's not the point. I know he's not crazy about me, but at least he cares enough to make an effort. Women need that. We need to feel that men try hard to get us.'

'And buy flowers.'

'It has nothing to do with flowers,' Ira said. 'It's about feeling wanted.'

'But Sergey worships you. He's mad about you. And you understand each other so well. Ira, you don't need other people to know how much you are worth.'

'But I do,' she said. 'I do need other people to tell me. I know I'm good enough to be Sergey's girlfriend or to be your "just friend". But maybe that's not enough for me.'

I finished my soup, pushed my plate aside. I took a sip of beer, trying not to look at the girls on the other table. 'What I'm saying is that sometimes it's better to be with someone who really appreciates you for who you are than with someone who just wants to sleep with you and have a good time.'

'Sergey is a great guy,' she said, 'but I don't want someone I need to take care of. I want someone who takes care of *me*. Sergey spends all his time complaining about his problems but doing nothing about them. Getting drunk is all he does. In the end, no woman wants that kind of man, Martin. At least before he was more fun to be around, but now he's so gloomy.'

'He has his moods. That's true.'

'I would like to have children one day. And I want a man who brings money home, a man who's hard-working and resourceful.'

'Sergey is going through a rough patch,' I said, 'but he'll find a job. It's not all about money.'

'Of course it's not all about money.' Ira buttoned her cardigan all the way up. 'The problem is not that Sergey doesn't bring in money. The problem is that he doesn't care about it. He's happy living at his mother's old flat, off my salary. He says we don't need anything more. He has no ambition. I love Sergey very much but I can't stand this situation any longer. I have to think about my own life.'

'And where does the American guy fit in all this?'

'Rob makes me feel good about myself.'

The girl with the red lipstick stood up, smiled at me again, and walked towards the toilet.

'Excuse me,' I said, getting to my feet, 'I'm going to wash my hands.'

Ira glanced behind her, at the table where now there was only one girl. She looked back at me, shaking her head.

'Martin, I really like you. But you are such an asshole.'

34

POLINA LIVED WITH HER parents in the south of Moscow, half an hour away from the last metro stop on the red line. When she came to my place, she would tell her mother she was staying with a girlfriend of hers. In the morning she would leave early to go to school.

She didn't talk much, Polina, but she seemed to enjoy the time we spent together. She smiled a lot, which was unusual in Moscow, and listened carefully to everything I said, always in awe, as if I were a professor giving a lecture. Unlike Lena, Polina never corrected my Russian, and even looked embarrassed when I asked her for a clarification or to repeat something she'd said – as if it were unforgivable for her to have used a word or expression that I didn't know. I attributed this to our difference in age.

One day when I had nothing to do, I asked her to come over.

Klassno, she texted back. *I've missed you. Will be there in two hours.*

I hadn't seen her for a week or so. I had spent the morning in Coffee Beans and, on the way back home, I had bought a pirate DVD at the perekhod, an American romantic comedy, the kind of film Polina liked.

I took a shower, changed the bedsheets on the couch and started to prepare a salad for dinner. I was chopping vegetables when I heard my phone beep. Surely Polina, I thought, perhaps she was running late. Picking up the phone, I was shocked to see Lena's name on the screen. It was the first time I'd heard from Lena since she'd left my flat on the first night of snow.

Privet, can I come to your place tonight?

My first thought was that it was an old message that, for some technical reason, got stuck somewhere. But I couldn't help feeling anxious about the possibility of seeing Lena again. The image of Lena's sensual body – so different from Polina's – flashed into my head. My heart was beating fast.

I replied: *Sure, come over.*

Less than a minute later I received a text back. *I'll be at your place around eight.*

I immediately called Polina to cancel our date. But now Polina's phone was out of reach, she was probably on the metro. Anxious, I kept calling every few minutes, hoping to catch her before she got to the centre. Her phone seemed to be switched off.

At seven thirty, Polina showed up at my flat, with the pink backpack she always carried full of schoolbooks and clothes for the next day. In one hand she held a bottle of wine.

She kissed me, smiled. 'I'm so happy to see you. I bought Georgian wine at the corner shop. I'm starving, what are we having for dinner?'

I didn't know how to tell Polina that I needed her to go back home, that she couldn't stay at my place.

I decided to be honest. She deserved that.

'Polina, a friend is coming to see me tonight,' I said, regretting, not for the first time, the gender specificity that the Russian language required. Podruga meant female friend.

Polina stared at me in silence.

'I'm so sorry,' I went on, 'but I shouldn't have asked you to come tonight.'

'What do you mean?'

'I've been trying to reach you. Your phone wasn't working.'

Polina looked confused, her smile was gone. She didn't seem to understand what I was saying.

'This friend,' she finally said, 'is she like a girlfriend?'

'No,' I said. 'Well, an old girlfriend. I haven't seen her in a long time.'

Polina's lips started to tremble.

'Polina, I'm really sorry.'

I grabbed her little shoulders. Her cheeks were red. She stepped away from me, picked up her pink bag from the chair.

'I really like you,' I said, 'but, you know, I have a thing for this other girl.'

Polina was now covering her face and sobbing, like a child.

'The thing is,' I said, 'I met her before I met you.' I thought this would somehow make things more understandable for Polina. 'It's mostly sexual attraction. Nothing serious, really. I like you, Polina.'

Polina went to the entrance of the apartment and tried to open the first door, but her hands were shaking – she could not turn the key.

'Why don't we meet tomorrow?' I said. 'We can go to TGI Fridays, and then to the cinema.'

Polina finally managed to open the door. She turned round.

'You are cruel,' she said.

Then she left.

Lena arrived an hour later. We hardly talked. After removing her hat, scarf, shoes and coat, Lena continued with the rest of her clothes, sweater, shirt, bra, jeans. She stood in the corridor, silent – wearing nothing but her necklace, her blonde hair uncombed, her breasts whiter than I remembered. Then she kissed me.

Thirty minutes later we were lying on the couch in silence. I was staring at the tapestry on the wall – at Ganesh's elephant head and his useless little brush. I didn't know what to say. Somehow, despite all the anticipation and all the longing that had built up over the weeks, being with Lena didn't feel as good as the thought of being with Lena. I could not understand why, but her body could not fill the emptiness inside me.

Then Lena dressed, kissed me goodbye, left.

I closed the doors and stepped into the kitchen. At the

sight of Polina's bottle of wine, a black void grew in my chest and sucked the air out of my lungs. I let myself fall onto a chair and covered my face, surprised to find a tear rolling down my cheek.

35

IN WINTER I WOULD OFTEN walk along Bolshaya Bronnaya, turning right into Malaya Bronnaya, keeping to the edge of the pavement where the snow was fresh and crunched under my feet. It was a beautiful walk along the quieter streets of the centre and I would focus my mind on the frozen air flooding my lungs, then steaming out my mouth in small white clouds. After fifteen minutes I would reach Patriarschiye Prudy.

I would stroll around the frozen pond, where children played with sleds or hockey sticks. Then I would walk back through Mayakovskaya into Tverskaya, descending towards Pushkinskaya and, often, when the cold had seeped through my many layers of clothing and had reached my bones, I would enter the Revolution Museum, which was always empty but warm. I would leave my coat, scarf, gloves and hat in the cloakroom, get a hand-cut ticket from a babushka at the entrance and wander into the exhibition galleries.

I passed through the initial halls, which contained old soviet flags, newspaper clippings and photos of Lenin, and walked straight into the rooms with soviet propaganda posters from the 1950s and 1960s, the wooden floors creaking under my feet. The museum had long lost its purpose, but there was a church-like tranquillity about it. I was usually the only visitor among the cleaning ladies and unsmiling dezhurnayas.

One morning, a couple of days after Polina's departure, I found myself standing in front of a poster depicting a blonde soviet woman. One hand shielding her impossibly bright blue eyes, the woman was gazing into the distance, perhaps, I thought, at the prospect of a socialist paradise. For some reason, the image reminded me of the painting of the three knights in Stepanov's place, who also gazed into the horizon, except that the knights were carrying swords and lances, while the beautiful soviet woman carried a basket of vegetables and potatoes.

'Comrades,' the poster said, 'come to the kolkhoz. Let's produce more potatoes and vegetables. Let's build our nation.'

I loved the naive and hopeful tone of the soviet posters — the way they portrayed a world based on work and sacrifice. I found it therapeutic to look at these images, at their beautifully faded colours, to see all those soviet men and women working together for a common goal. Women looked stunning in these posters, but not in a delicate dyevushka way – they were strong and maternal: you could not picture these women putting on make-up or complaining about the food in a café. These women were resilient, self-sufficient, forward-looking.

Where are they now? I asked myself.

I had read my share of Solzhenitsyn, and a couple of books on Russian history, and was aware of the darkest side of the soviet period. But, looking at these posters, I couldn't help but feel both sadness and nostalgia. I felt sad and nostalgic for a past I'd never lived, a past that, as far as I knew, had never really existed, at least not as portrayed in these posters. But looking at these images full of symbolism infused me with a sense of hope.

My first contact with soviet imagery had come through Khavronina's *Russian As We Speak It*, a language book Katya had given me as a present back in Amsterdam, a few weeks before we split up. It was a second-hand book with a faded blue cover that she had asked a friend to bring from Minsk.

'I've been told,' Katya said with the book in her hand, 'this is the best manual for beginners.' It was early in the morning and I was still in bed. Katya had already put on make-up and done her hair. I wasn't sure if I wanted to learn Russian, not knowing whether I would get a scholarship, but I loved the drawings in the book, depicting the simple, happy, soviet lives of Pavel and Marina.

Pavel was a chemist who worked in a factory outside Moscow and Marina a doctor who worked in a children's hospital. In lesson three, they talked about their apartment, which was plain but cosy. In lesson nine, they went to a restaurant, ordered chicken Kiev and spring salad, drank borzhomi water and then went dancing. In other lessons they went to the post office, to the countryside, to the supermarket, to the theatre. On Sundays, Pavel and Marina went to the park, where, the book said, the sun shone and birds sang.

Standing in the empty hall of the Revolution Museum, I now wondered if that was the Russia I craved – the simple and beautiful world of Pavel and Marina, and not the complicated Russia I had been thrown into.

But, as I had discovered early on in my stay, the Russia of my language book was fictional. There were no singing birds in Moscow. The birds I saw were crows or ravens – vorony, they called them – perched on the electric cables of Pushkin-skaya, screeching loudly, scavenging the rubbish bins in the square, going through the leftovers outside McDonald's.

Where had all the hope of the soviet years gone? Russians had been cheated, and, in a way, they had earned their right to be cynical. Poor old babushkas at the Revolution Museum, I thought, themselves a tragic part of the exhibits, working for a few rubles a month and then commuting to the outskirts of Moscow where they lived on a diet of beetroot, potato and mayonnaise. Poor cleaning ladies sweeping the metro, old Nadezhdas and Revmiras, whose hopes and ideals had been flushed away with the perestroika. Poor Sergey, a soviet man with no country. Poor Nadezhda Nikolaevna, scolded by a young waiter for not knowing the rules of the New Russia. Poor Lyudmila Aleksandrovna, who lived trapped in the 1970s, in her Sochi seminars, because she could not understand that, despite her admirable and firm denial, Russia was for ever changed.

The woman in the poster looked ahead with her confident regard, carrying the promise of a brighter future. In that moment, I felt a strong urge to join her and her struggle. Come with me, she seemed to be saying, stop wasting your life. I wanted to answer her call, cross the line that divides reality from historical fiction and meet her at the kolkhoz, where I would kiss her, marry her, co-suffer with her, and I would pick potatoes and vegetables all day long until my hands bled. I would do it for her, for her cause. For something to believe in.

PART FOUR

Olga's Soul

36

IN *DUSHECHKA, THE DARLING*, Chekhov tells the story of Olga Semyonovna, a loving and gentle soul, a person who – Anton Pavlovich tells us – lives to love. The short story is set in a provincial city, and begins with Olga Semyonovna – known as Dushechka, darling, or little soul – listening attentively to the angry ramblings of Kukin, a local businessman who manages an attraction park and theatre. Kukin is whining about how the public's bad taste and the bad weather are ruining his business. Dushechka, deeply touched by Kukin's despair, falls for him. Soon after, they get married.

Dushechka starts helping her husband at the theatre. Now, at every social occasion, she talks at length about the theatre business, shamelessly adopting her husband's opinions as her own. Soon, her life becomes one with that of her husband

207

and, in her role as devoted wife, Dushechka finds purpose, perhaps even happiness.

One night, while Kukin is in Moscow on a business trip, someone knocks at the gates of Dushechka's house. A telegram. With trembling hands, Dushechka opens the telegram and reads with astonishment that her husband has died. She is shocked but also confused, because, in a very Chekhovian detail, the telegram contains bizarre spelling mistakes. Dushechka is in pain.

Not for long though. Just three months later, while returning from church, Dushechka bumps into Pustovalov, a wood merchant, who offers her some words of consolation, death being the will of God and all that. We can see Pustovalov is hitting on the widow. Now Dushechka, always the sensitive soul, can't stop thinking about Pustovalov. She can no longer sleep. She is in love. So they go and get married.

Dushechka is happy again, able to devote her life to her new husband. She now talks endlessly about types of wood, the price of logs and all things related to her husband's business. Unlike her first husband Kukin, Pustovalov is a homely guy who doesn't really like going out. When some friends suggest they go out to the theatre, Dushechka — who, as Kukin's wife, had been the most ardent theatre devotee — now says, 'What's good about theatre anyway? We never go to the theatre, we are working people.'

Dushechka is a new woman because she is with a new man.

She lives happily for six years until one day in winter, after drinking hot tea, Pustovalov goes out without a hat, catches a nasty cold and, after four months of illness, dies.

Poor Dushechka. She retreats into isolation, with only the company of her cat. There is also the local veterinarian, who's separating from his wife and comes to visit Dushechka often. Although Chekhov doesn't really go into the details, he seems to hint that Dushechka and the vet are more than friends. We know this partly because Dushechka now bores people talking about animal diseases.

One day, to her despair, the veterinarian is posted far away and once more she is left on her own. With nobody to love, Dushechka falls into a depression. She grows old and grumpy. She no longer has any opinions. She doesn't know what to talk about or what to think. Her heart, Chekhov tells us, is 'as empty as her courtyard'.

The years go by and Dushechka's house grows shabby. She is now an old woman, who spends her summers sitting on the porch and her winters looking through the window at the snow.

Then, one day, the vet, now an older man, shows up in town with his wife, with whom he had reconciled. Dushechka lets them stay at her place, and somehow ends up taking care of their nine-year-old boy. In the child, Dushechka finds someone to love, a new purpose in life. Now she cares about the school curriculum and other child-related issues. With something to whine about and occupy her days, Dushechka is happy again.

As interesting as Chekhov's story is Tolstoy's interpretation, which gives us an original take on the mystery of Olga's soul. In a review of *Dushechka*, Lev Nikolaevich says that Chekhov, intending to mock the unsophisticated woman, had accidentally created an endearing character. Tolstoy goes on to accuse Chekhov of being harsh on Dushechka, by judging her intellect and not her soul. Olga's soul, according to Tolstoy, embodies the capacity of Russian women to love unconditionally, a virtue unknown to men. It is through this unconditional love, he suggests, that women achieve happiness.

37

YEARS LATER, I CAN SEE that the moment at the Revolution Museum, as I stood absorbed by the silent call of a woman in a poster, had the makings of a spiritual awakening – like the instant Raskolnikov finally realises he needs to confess his crime and move on with his life and his punishment.

If my life in Moscow had been a Dostoyevsky novel, Polina's tears at my apartment would have carried the seeds of my epiphany, and the dark feeling that accompanied me during the days that followed would have – perhaps at that very moment in the Revolution Museum – emerged at the surface of my conscience as clear regret.

But back then I didn't know. I couldn't know, really, distracted as I was by the city. Despite the odd doubt about the purpose of my life – despite the fatigue, the sleepless hours in bed, the morning headaches – come the weekend, I would put on a well-ironed shirt, drink shots of vodka and go out with the brothers to nightclubs. And in this way we spent our weeks, our months, and never did I stop to think that all of this could, one day, come to an end.

By late spring, Yulya Karma had stopped visiting me on a regular basis. We still saw each other for tea, but only every two or three weeks. It was nicer this way, because our bodies had time to get unaccustomed to each other, and we clashed with more zeal. One day, Yulya Karma told me she had decided to leave her boyfriend and proposed, in the same businesslike manner as when she'd first offered to be my lover, that she be my girlfriend. 'I think we are very compatible,' she said, 'we would be very good together, as a real couple.' I told her it wouldn't really work because, even though I was quite fond of her, I would never be able to fully trust her. I think she understood. And it was a pity, I thought, because I liked her and she had a touch of pragmatism that made her different from the other girls; so practical and focused, Yulya Karma, and she could have made a good girlfriend, were it not for her natural talent for deceit.

Colin said, in the end, we were all searching for the perfect girl, the Export Quality Dyev, as he put it — the perfect woman to take home with us the day we had to leave Moscow.

Maybe he was right. Perhaps all the going out was, after all, just a protracted search for someone we could keep. A futile search, I now understand, because, ever since Katya had left me in Amsterdam, I couldn't bring myself to define what I was looking for and, had I encountered it, I would not have known. What I craved was a particular thrill, a wave of euphoria, a resonance in my soul, which was becoming harder to feel with each new girl I met.

I lost contact with Ira. A couple of times we'd agreed to meet for coffee at the university but, for different reasons, I'd had to cancel at the last minute. We'd talked on the phone, and she told me she was considering leaving her American lover and getting back with Sergey. We agreed to go out for dinner to catch up, but I kept postponing, never finding the right time, until the plan faded away. It wasn't that I didn't want to see Ira, and at times I missed her company, but I found it hard to fit her into my life. We were out of sync, Ira and I. She lived at a slower pace, with her modest salary, going to Project OGI with her old friends, torn between Sergey and her one lover.

Stepanov's car dealership, which he had set up in just a couple of months, was booming. He imported luxury vehicles from Finland, where he bought them for almost half their Moscow market price. He managed to avoid customs duties by profiting from a mix of bizarre legislative loopholes and good old Russian bribery. The cars were exhibited in a spacious salon in Prospekt Mira, which Stepanov had named Miller & Stevenson Luxury Vehicles, suggesting foreign ownership. To emphasise the non-Russian nature of the business — which, according to Stepanov, allowed for the cars to be marked up at least ten per cent above their price in Russian-owned dealerships — I was asked to show up often, particularly when serious buyers were expected. Oligarchs,

213

flooded with enormous amounts of cash at the time, couldn't get enough of the cars, and, by June, Stepanov was selling about a dozen luxury vehicles a month.

He kept a black BMW for himself — a bumer, he called it — which gave him much to talk about but rarely left its parking place in Stepanov's courtyard. To the chagrin of those Muscovites who could now afford decent cars, it remained much easier to navigate the city by public transport or the large and very efficient fleet of unofficial taxis permanently cruising the streets.

We had a great summer that year. Truth be told, I don't remember much of the legendary nights of the summer of 2001. It's not that I forgot them — it's more that they never registered in my vodka-soaked mind. I only know what happened because I recall Colin, Diego, Stepanov telling and retelling our stories in Starlite, or at Stepanov's place, and the stories that weren't told back then were for ever lost, and, in the end, my memories of those great nights are not my own memories, but those I borrowed from the brothers.

38

IN SEPTEMBER RUSSIA changed again.

A week after the attacks in New York and Washington, in the midst of worldwide soul-searching and hysteria – as the Western media talked about the war against civilisation, or 'the day that changed the world' – *The Exile* came out with an article that caused a stir among expats. Under the heading 'Be Cool, America', the article said, more or less, that America had it coming.

Russians also seemed to have mixed feelings about these historical events, brought up as they were to hate their Cold War foe. Russian leaders, including the president, rushed to publicly offer condolences and assistance but, if you looked carefully at the TV while they spoke, you could detect a trace of a smirk on their faces.

These are the kind of people we have to deal with in

today's world, Russian politicians said, referring in the same breath to the war in Chechnya. But Russia went ahead and allowed America to use its air space to attack terrorist bases in Central Asia. Russia also shared intelligence from the soviet experience in Afghanistan. All of this was unprecedented, historical in fact, and, in the few weeks after 9/11, Moscow expats had the feeling that Russia was warming to the West. Russian leaders sounded more obliging, helpful and understanding than ever before, perhaps thinking that, if the world was to be split along a new Iron Curtain, they wished to be, this time, on the right side of history.

This geopolitical rapprochement cascaded down to our everyday Moscow lives, where we all perceived a small post 9/11 shift. Expats were in vogue again, and for a few weeks, we — the ambassadors of Western civilisation — were the recipients of kind words of support.

It didn't last long though. By the end of the year, as the images of the planes crashing into the towers lost part of their power to shock, things went back to normal. Russia redirected its course away from the West, disappointed perhaps that its friendly gestures had not been taken seriously. And, in Moscow, expats no longer deserved any particular sympathy.

Stepanov said the Americans had done this to themselves; not by provoking others, as *The Exile* had suggested, but by actually planning and carrying out the attack on their own soil. He maintained it was all a CIA conspiracy. This theory was widely held in Moscow at that time. It was a bizarre hypothesis which I couldn't understand until, at some point, after long drunken discussions on the topic, it dawned on me why Russians didn't know how to deal with 9/11. Russians were envious of Americans and regretted that 9/11 hadn't happened to them instead. They couldn't bear the fact that an event so full of suffering and historical meaning, an event that was to mark the fate of the new century, had happened to undeserving Americans instead of Russians – hungry and ready as they were for national tragedies.

39

READING *WAR AND PEACE* IN Russian was an ambitious project I had tackled several times but never managed to carry through. I knew I was no real expert in Russian literature – and, clearly, I lacked the intellectual focus to become one. But if I could at least claim to have read *War and Peace* in its original language, word by word as Lev Nikolaevich had written it, I thought I would somehow feel less of a fraud.

For the last few days, I had been going every morning to Coffee Beans. I would sit by the large front window and carefully arrange the two volumes of my 1944 edition on the table, next to a dictionary and one of my notebooks. I would ritually spend a few minutes holding my hot mug of coffee, observing how Muscovites fought winter in the street. For some reason, I took pleasure in the contrast between the two sides of the glass wall – the world of high ceilings, gilded mirrors and fresh coffee, and the world of crawling traffic, red noses, teary eyes and thick scarves. From the warm interior of Coffee Beans, listening to cool jazz, people in the street appeared to me as fictional characters.

I would take my time with every page, sipping coffee, flipping through the dictionary, struggling with bizarre Russian words I had never encountered before and, I suspected, I would never encounter again. I would take notes, my work occasionally slowed by my having to exchange looks with a dyev at a nearby table.

Every now and then, the thick double doors of Coffee Beans would open to let a new customer in, coat peppered with snowflakes, shoes caked with ice and mud. The floor of the café was constantly being mopped by diligent waitresses in a Sisyphean effort to keep winter outside, so, after passing through the door, newcomers would hesitate for a few seconds before defiling the shiny floors. To me it felt as if each newcomer were an intruder who had, for some reason, less right to be in the café than me.

A few days into my latest *War and Peace* attempt I realised that I wasn't making significant progress, that at this pace it would take me months, if not years, to finish Lev Nikolaevich's book. I decided to recalibrate my objectives. After all, I told myself, it's not that I had to read the *entire* book in Russian. A taste of the original language was all I needed, as long as I knew the story well enough to form some original opinions of my own. So, one morning, before entering Coffee Beans, I walked into the Moskva Bookshop and, overcoming a vague sense of guilt, I bought an English translation.

Now I would flip through the pages of the cheap Penguin Classics translation – which I kept half-hidden under the table – identifying interesting passages that I could later read in Russian in my beautiful soviet edition. I couldn't be bothered with the war bits. Lyudmila Aleksandrovna had told me that Tolstoy's battle scenes were masterpieces in their own right, the best depictions of violence in world literature, she said, so realistic and vivid. But when I tried to read them I would soon lose interest. I always ended up skipping those sections and looking for the passages about the lives of the characters in times of peace, analysing Lev Nikolaevich's take on his female characters.

One morning I sat by the window of Coffee Beans observing how snowflakes floated among the cables and banners of Tverskaya. They didn't seem to reach the ground, the snowflakes – they glided peacefully towards the street's surface, then hovered above it for a moment, weightless, as if having second thoughts, and were briskly swept away by the breeze, sideways and upwards, back into the sky. Of course the snowflakes had to reach the ground at some point, I thought – Tverskaya was covered in white.

I was reading the scenes in which Natalya Rostova made an appearance. At the beginning of the book Natalya is only twelve, but she already shows the features of a full dyevushka in the making. She's lovely, Natalya, and gracious – the pure embodiment of youth. I had read somewhere that Tolstoy had fallen in love with Natalya's character and I could see where that theory came from. Although she was not described as being particularly attractive, she was depicted in a special light. Was she Tolstoy's ideal woman? Unlike Pushkin's Tatyana, who was too good to be true, Tolstoy's Natalya felt real, alive. Natalya Rostova was capricious, coquettish and, in her own early nineteenth-century way, a bit of a tease. She would certainly fit in modern-day Moscow.

I was absorbed by these thoughts, taking some notes, when Colin walked in, holding a copy of *The Exile* that he had picked up at the entrance. He shook the snow off his coat.

'Beautiful morning,' he said as he placed the newspaper on my table and his coat on the nearby rack. He was wearing a black turtleneck sweater. 'Saw you through the window. Another cup of coffee?'

'Sure.'

When he came back with two mugs of fresh coffee, I shared my thoughts about Natalya Rostova.

Colin listened attentively, stirred his coffee and took a sip. His face was as red as a beetroot. 'If you had to choose between Natalya Rostova and Anna Karenina,' he said, 'who would you rather fuck?'

'Do you mean who's my favourite among Tolstoy's female characters?'

'I mean, who would you take to bed.'

I thought about Colin's question, trying to picture both Anna and Natalya as sexual partners.

'Natalya,' I said, 'towards the end of the book.'

'Why?'

'She's more lovable than Karenina.'

'I think Anna Karenina would be a better fuck,' Colin said.

'How could you possibly know?' I said, for some reason annoyed by Colin's disdain for Natalya. 'You've never read *War and Peace*. What do you know about Natalya?'

'Who's read the entire book? True, I don't really know Natalya Rostova, but I feel Karenina is more my type of woman.'

'Unfaithful? Suicidal?'

Colin thought about it for a few seconds. 'Strong, determined.'

'Natalya is more unpredictable,' I said. 'More fun.'

Colin took a sip of coffee. 'Is Natalya honest? Faithful?'

'Not entirely,' I admitted. 'When it comes to men, she's rather fickle.'

'All Russian women are,' Colin said. He was sweating, pulling on the neck of his black sweater to let some air onto his chest. 'In the end, if you look at it, they are all unfaithful. Anna Karenina, Natalya Rostova—' Colin took another sip of coffee and looked out of the window, giving himself more time to think of the names of other unfaithful Russian characters. 'You know,' he said after a while, 'all of them.'

'Russian women are unfaithful. Is that your insight of the day?'

Colin turned his head both ways, as if checking that nobody could hear us. 'That's what makes them more interesting and challenging. It's their culture. They're always looking for the next thing.'

'That's not true,' I said. 'Look at Pushkin's Tatyana. She was a faithful and devoted wife.'

'Pushkin is Pushkin,' Colin said.

A tall dyev with red boots walked into the café and glanced around, as if looking for a friend. Colin waved at her with a smile. He did that often with female strangers – as far as I could tell, with no results. She returned the smile politely, turned and walked back out to the street.

Colin opened *The Exile* and started to flip the pages. He always went straight to the club reviews to check if there were any new ratings to disagree with.

'Karenina's infidelity is not her main feature,' I said, recalling an article I'd read on Tolstoy's work from a feminist point of view. 'Her decision to abandon her husband is about escaping conventions, about breaking free from the choices society had made for her.'

'Whatever,' Colin said. 'In the end, look at Moscow today. You meet a dyev and you know she's already looking for someone else, better-looking, wealthier. They can't stay put.'

'Neither can we.'

'That's different. We're males. Ours is a biological need. Theirs is a materialistic pursuit. That's the thing, if you scratch the surface, Russian dyevs are incredibly materialistic. All they want is someone to provide for them, buy them expensive clothes, holidays abroad and all that shit. They expect men to open their doors, help them with their coats. They don't believe in equality. Not there yet.'

'That's crap,' I said. 'They're just a bit more traditional.'

'You know why Russian wives are so popular back in the States? Because they're the embodiment of the American dream of the 1960s, taking care of themselves and their husbands, always perfect make-up and hair. Both servile and sensual.'

The snowflakes outside seemed to become smaller.

'Look,' Colin continued, 'even when you take a dyev to a restaurant, she doesn't give a fuck if the food is fine or cow dung, as long as it's expensive.'

'Maybe you meet the wrong dyevs,' I said. 'I know girls who search for romance.'

'It's not romance,' Colin said, finishing his cup of coffee. 'For Russian women, relationships are nothing but a transaction. They always expect something in return. That's why it's easy for them to become prostitutes, because they always feel you owe them something anyway. So they cross the line and ask for money.'

'Four years in Moscow,' I said, 'and you still have such a stereotyped view of Russian women.'

'I'm not doing a PhD on the subject,' Colin said, tapping my red notebook, 'but I've met my share. Believe me, sooner or later dyevs want something from you. That's how they value how much you care, by figuring out how much you spend. Clothes, flowers, restaurant bills, they add up everything in their heads.'

'I've met girls who just wanted to have fun,' I said. 'They didn't expect anything in return.'

'You don't know what's in their heads.'

224

'I certainly don't.'

'Anyway,' Colin said as he stood up. 'I'll leave you with your books, I need to go to a meeting. McCoy tonight?'

'Sure.'

Colin put on his coat, shook my hand and stepped out into the street. Through the glass I watched him walk away under the snow.

40

THEN, AT THE END OF winter, I met Tatyana.

As temperatures rose, the roofs of Moscow began to drop enormous blocks of ice that crashed with force onto the pavement, shattering into a million ice cubes and killing – I was told – about a dozen unfortunate Muscovites every year. To stop this urban massacre, city workers were sent up the buildings to poke at the ice, provoking controlled avalanches over the streets below, after they'd cut off pedestrian traffic with yellow plastic tape. When you saw the yellow tape, you knew spring was around the corner.

'We're meeting the real estate agent by the Chekhov statue,' Colin said, as we walked down Tverskaya. 'Outside the MKhAT theatre.'

It was a bright morning. I was trying to focus on the pavement, avoiding the sludge and the slippery puddles that had frozen during the night. We turned left into Kamergersky. Anticipating the change of season, some restaurants had claimed chunks of the walkway and set up outdoor terraces — with mushroom gas-heaters and blankets draped over the chairs. All the tables were empty.

'I hope it's a nice flat,' Colin said. 'Would be great if I could move in around here.'

We stood beneath Chekhov's statue — Anton Pavlovich, up on a pedestal, looking sad and lonely. I noticed how, as the city defrosted, the remains of sweaty ice sparkled with more intensity, as if trying to resist the sun before melting, emitting thousands of tiny reflections and covering Moscow in glitter.

'It's been a long winter,' I said.

The corner between Tverskaya and Kamergersky was one of my favourite spots in Moscow. Maybe it was the way the small-village feel of Kamergersky — a pedestrian street which you might easily see in Western Europe — met the metropolitan grandeur of Tverskaya. Or perhaps it was the historical imprint of the place, with the central post office covered in Communist symbols on one side, and the Moscow Art Theatre on the other. It was in this very theatre, before and after it moved to its current location, that Chekhov had premiered his main plays: *The Seagull*, *Uncle Vanya*, *Three Sisters* and, just before he died, *The Cherry Orchard*.

The red kiosk on the corner was selling fresh blinis and the smell of fried butter wafted into the street. I suggested we have a couple of blinis while we waited. As we were about to head over, a young woman walked towards us holding a folder in her arms.

'Hello,' she said, in English. 'Tatyana, from Evans.'

Tatyana's pretty face was flushed, from the cold or perhaps because she'd been running late and walking fast. Her eyes were apple green.

We followed Tatyana into a side alley. She stopped in front of a metal door, peeked at some papers in her folder, then tapped in the door code. She climbed the stairs to the first floor, with us behind her. She was wearing a yellow woollen hat, a black coat, tight jeans.

'Cute ass,' Colin said into my ear.

On the landing, Tatyana rang the bell of the apartment and turned to us. 'It's a very nice place,' she said. 'You'll see.'

Tatyana took her hat off and a mass of blonde curly hair unfurled over her shoulders. Our eyes met and she smiled for a brief moment, nervous, naive – clearly unaware of her own beauty. Her smile, which was marked by a small gap between her front teeth, cut through my many layers of skin and bone and muscle, ripping its way into my chest, making my heart pump with violence. Fucking 1917.

The doors opened and we were greeted by an old Russian couple, well-dressed, smiley – obviously expecting us. The old man was even wearing a tie.

We took our shoes off and walked in. The flat was furnished in dark soviet style, not unlike Stepanov's flat. In fact, it was remarkably similar to Stepanov's. The walls were lined with bookshelves. Tapestries hung above the couch. The centre of the living room was occupied by an enormous piano.

The babushka went around the apartment showing us what she thought were its best features. Her husband followed behind without saying a word.

'The piano is well tuned,' she said, tapping three or four random keys. 'The apartment is very quiet because all windows face a backyard and not the pereulok.'

That was a pity, I thought, because it would have been nice to have at least one window overlooking the cafés in Kamergersky.

Colin asked a few questions, out of politeness, I imagined, as I could see he was disappointed. He knocked on the tables, pulled open a few drawers. I noticed a bunch of framed pictures crammed on top of the piano and a family portrait hanging by the entrance. After a few minutes we thanked the old couple, Tatyana told them she would be in contact, and we left the building.

'What the fuck,' Colin said once we were in the street. 'This is their own flat. These people live here.'

Tatyana seemed confused. 'Of course,' she said, 'but they would move out if you rented it.'

'But I'm looking for an empty flat.'

The three of us stopped beneath Chekhov's statue.

'It would be an empty flat if you took it,' Tatyana said, blushing. 'The owners would move out.'

'Out where?'

'I don't know,' Tatyana said, 'maybe to live with their family in the suburbs, or in a dacha, if they have one. It's a common situation, these people are the old intelligentsia who had good connections in the Communist party and occupied the best flats in the centre. With the perestroika they were allowed to privatise their flats but they now live on very small pensions. Life is very expensive in Moscow. They have to move out and live off the rent.'

Colin seemed distressed. 'I would be kicking them out of their own place.'

'They like foreigners as tenants,' Tatyana said. 'They know you pay well and won't stay for ever. If you rent their flat you'll be doing them a favour.'

'I was thinking about something more modern,' Colin said. 'I don't want to move into someone else's apartment.'

Tatyana forced a smile. 'Don't worry,' she said, 'we'll find something. There are good apartments in this area, renovated to Western standards.'

I felt sorry for Tatyana, who'd come all the way to show us the apartment and, I guessed, worked on commission. Her eyes looked teary from the cold.

'This is a very nice area,' I said.

'It is,' Tatyana said. Then, pointing at the MKhAT, 'This is a very famous theatre in Russia. Stanislavsky, Chekhov, you know. See the emblem above the entrance?'

'The bird?' I asked.

'It's a seagull, after Chekhov's play.'

I could hear in the humble way she spoke that Tatyana was not from Moscow.

'I'm also looking for a flat,' I heard myself saying.

Colin looked at me, at first surprised, then grinning.

'You are?' Tatyana asked.

'Yes, my flat is small. I could move somewhere bigger.'

Tatyana smiled. 'Maybe I can also try to find something for you.'

She handed me her card, and we agreed to keep in touch. We said goodbye and shook hands. She then walked away, turned left at Tverskaya, and disappeared in the direction of Okhotny Ryad.

41

I WAITED IN THE MIDDLE of Pushkinskaya, observing how the snow that had covered the streets for months was now melting away, revealing the tarnished skin of the city. Without its white layer, Moscow looked exposed, somewhat uncomfortable, like a dyev the morning after – too much light and no make-up.

I saw Tatyana crossing the street, marching towards the centre of the square. She was wearing the same black coat and yellow hat. A couple of hours after she'd given me her card, I'd sent her a message asking if she wanted to meet for a drink.

I took her to Maki, a new café five minutes away from Pushkinskaya. Decent music, polite waitresses, dim lights – Maki was the closest thing to a modern European café. By now I preferred it to Pyramida. The young clientele was better dressed than the students in Project OGI but not as pretentious as the elitni tusovka of Vogue.

We sat at one of the small tables, checking out the menu. I asked for a bottle of red wine. When the waitress came back with the wine, Tatyana remained undecided, her eyes fixed on the menu as if she were reading a book. She looked at me and blushed.

'The mushroom soup is very good,' I said.

'Great,' she replied with relief, 'I'll have that.'

'What else?'

'I'm not that hungry.'

'Salad, maybe?'

'Davay,' Tatyana said. 'That would be nice.'

I ordered two mushroom soups and two Caesar salads.

At first Tatyana wasn't very talkative but, after a swiftly drunk glass of wine, she became more relaxed. She told me that she came from Novosibirsk and had been living in Moscow for six months. She liked Moscow but she missed her family, especially her babushka, who was the one who had really raised her. It felt good sitting in Café Maki with Tatyana. I imagined everybody around us would be admiring her blonde, curly hair and her eyes, so green and perfect. She was clearly unaware of it, but Tatyana was without doubt the prettiest girl in the café.

'I'm happy that my aunt found me a job in Moscow,' Tatyana said. The aunt lived in a small town two hours away by elektrichka and Tatyana dutifully visited her every weekend. 'Back in Novosibirsk it's impossible to find work that pays decently.'

What she liked best about the capital, Tatyana said as our plates of soup were laid in front of us, was the culture on offer.

'There are so many things going on in Moscow's theatres,' she said. 'The classics, but also very nice new musicals. If I had the money I would go every night.' She smiled, her lips closed, probably conscious of the gap between her front teeth.

As Tatyana was talking about her interests, I took my red notebook out of my backpack and placed it to the right of my soup plate. I took some notes – Novosibirsk, babushka, aunt, theatre.

'What's that?' Tatyana asked.

I told her about my research project, how it was not just about reading books, but also about getting to know what Russians thought about life.

'But I don't have any interesting thoughts about life,' Tatyana protested.

'That's an interesting thought in itself,' I said, scribbling in the notebook.

Tatyana smiled. Her face was red. 'Can I have a look?'

'Sure,' I said, pushing the notebook towards her side of the table.

She turned the notebook round, glanced at it in silence. 'But it's in English.'

'Of course.'

Then she started to read slowly, sliding her finger under the lines, in heavily accented English. She started from the top of the page.

'"When you saw the yellow tape, you knew spring was around the corner."

'What does it mean?'

'Just random thoughts.'

She continued reading.

'"Black coat. Yellow woollen hat. Apple green eyes."' She laughed. 'You are so funny.'

I kept refilling her glass of wine. When the salad arrived, I ordered a second bottle.

Tatyana wanted to know what I thought about Russia, as a foreigner.

When we were done with the salads I suggested we share a plate of blinis with preserved strawberries and mascarpone.

'Davay,' she said.

The blinis arrived and I slid the plate into the middle of the table.

'I didn't know what mascarpone was,' Tatyana said, her mouth still half full. 'But I like it, it's just like thick smetana.'

After dessert, we finished the bottle of wine, I paid the bill and we walked out into the dark street.

'Thanks for dinner,' Tatyana said. 'It was lovely.'

'Let's walk to the metro,' I suggested.

She looked at her watch. 'I think I'm a bit drunk.'

It was colder now and, as we walked in silence back towards Pushkinskaya, I had to repress the urge to put my arm around Tatyana. Reaching the square, we descended into the pere khod but, instead of going all the way to the metro entrance, we climbed the stairs out into the street again, and stood next to Pushkin's statue, where we had met earlier.

I pointed to my block across the street. 'That's where I live.'

'Above McDonald's?'

'On the other side of the block,' I said. 'You know the Scandinavia restaurant?'

'Never heard of it.'

'Would you like to come up for a cup of tea?'

'I showed a flat in that block,' she said. 'A couple of months ago.'

'It's very central. I love it.'

'Wonderful location,' Tatyana said. 'I don't understand why you want to move somewhere else.'

I smiled, said nothing.

'Is it noisy?' she asked.

'Not really. My balconies face the courtyard and I live on the top floor. There is a great view. I'll show you. Let's go up for a cup of tea.'

She stared at me in silence. For a few seconds we stood in the middle of the square. Cars piled at the traffic lights, expelling white fumes into the chilly night air. Muscovites rushed out of the metro, onto the street, cramming into McDonald's, Café Pyramida, the Pushkin cinema. I could see the neon lights of the casino reflected in Tatyana's eyes. Just above us stood Aleksandr Sergeyevich, leaning slightly forward, ready to descend from his pedestal. In the darkness of the night, Pushkin's face revealed a soft smile.

Tatyana looked at her watch, then back into my eyes. She opened her mouth, as if about to say something, then closed it again without uttering a sound. I put my arm around her shoulder, squeezed her body against mine, gave her a kiss.

42

THE RAIN CAUGHT ME by surprise as I walked down from
Mayakovskaya. I increased my pace, hoping to reach my
apartment before the water soaked my clothes. A gust of
wind came out of nowhere, flapping the advertising banners
above Tverskaya with unusual strength. The sky dimmed
to leaden grey, the rain thickened and – though only two
minutes away from home – I had no choice but to take shel-
ter from the storm. I stepped into the Stanislavsky theatre.

The entrance hall of the theatre was empty, aside from
a babushka at the ticket booth. I smiled in her direction.
She grumbled back. Waiting for the rain to clear, I began to
study the posters on the walls. I noticed the babushka glancing my way above her thick glasses, frowning in a menacing
manner – accusing me with her gaze of having entered her
theatre under false pretences.

To dispel her suspicions, I approached the programme on the wall and ran my finger down the list of plays. After all, I could be a genuine theatregoer, interested in the shows the Stanislavsky had on offer. When I peeked back at the babushka I could see she was irritated, impatient, about to ask me to leave. Outside, the rain was battering the pavement with increasing force, forming lakes and flooding the asphalt. Realising that I would have to stay inside the theatre for a while, I approached the booth and asked the cranky babushka for the best pair of tickets available for the evening performance.

That night's show turned out to be a play based on Bulgakov. I placed a thousand-ruble note on the counter and, after checking its validity against the light of a table lamp, the babushka relinquished the tickets and the change, still reluctantly, as if suspicious of my intentions.

When the rain eased off I rushed home. I changed into dry clothes, boiled some pelmenis for lunch and lay on the couch. Tatyana and I had agreed to meet that evening.

A month had passed since we'd met and Tatyana was now spending two or three evenings a week in my flat. After dinner, we would linger at the kitchen table, brewing tea with the samovar, and she would tell me about her day: how the price of real estate was going up, about the difficult clients she had, mostly expats who were looking for perfect apartments but were stingy with their budgets.

Tatyana's angelic beauty — her blonde curls, soft smile, trusting green eyes — stirred something buried deep inside me. Even the gap in her front teeth, the only imperfection in her otherwise faultless face, made her real, provincial, likeable. For some reason, I often found myself picturing Tatyana and myself from an outsider's point of view, as if we were actors in a film. Cooking at home, walking in the street. Every time Tatyana was next to me, I would pose for an imaginary viewer.

I fell asleep on the couch. When I woke up I made some tea, picked up my book of Chekhov's plays, sat by the balcony. It had stopped raining. The sky was now white.

I started to read bits from *Three Sisters*. I went through the first act, pondering Irina's daydreaming of Moscow and the symbolic value the city acquired in the play.

Chekhov had turned Moscow into a symbol of yearning, standing for things left behind and for the unreachable horizon that lies ahead.

After finishing the first act, I looked up from the book and saw the city extending away beneath my balcony, the white sky pierced by soviet constructions and redbrick chimneys. The wet roofs and terraces reflected the brightness of the sky like pieces of broken mirror. I thought how different my Moscow was from Chekhov's Moscow, the city the three sisters dreamed about. And yet, the enormous amalgam of buildings and squares and wide avenues continued to capture the dreams of thousands of people, like Tatyana and myself, who, coming from different places, had been brought together by the city. I wondered whether being in Moscow made us happier.

Tatyana had left her hometown in Siberia – her babushka, her family – to search for a better life in Moscow. Had she dreamed in Novosibirsk about Moscow? Now that she was in the city, with a job and a few friends, now that she had me, was she happier than before?

'We want happiness,' Vershinin says in Anton Pavlovich's play, 'but we are not happy and we cannot be happy.'

Tatyana came over just after six. She hung her faux-leather handbag on the kitchen door handle, kissed me.

'I have something for you,' I said, handing her the pair of theatre tickets.

She grabbed the tickets and, before even looking at them, thanked me with another kiss.

'Tickets to the theatre,' she said, with a broad smile, her eyes shining. 'Great, I haven't seen this play. I only saw the film. An old soviet film, in black and white, very good one.'

'I'm glad you like them,' I said. 'Would you like to eat something before we go or should we just grab a bite afterwards?'

She looked back at the tickets. 'But they are for *today*?'

'The show's in an hour.'

'But you should have warned me,' she said, anxious.

'It's supposed to be a surprise. A change from watching a movie on the couch.'

Tatyana's smile was gone. 'But I didn't know we were going to the theatre.'

'It's the Stanislavsky theatre,' I said, 'just around the corner, a two-minute walk.'

She looked at me, her face red. 'But I have nothing to wear.'

'What do you mean? You look great like this.' She was wearing a black jacket and a black skirt, which I found quite elegant.

'These are not theatre clothes. If you had told me I could have brought a nice dress from my flat.'

'If I had told you then it wouldn't have been a surprise. Don't worry, it's a small theatre, not a fancy opera. You look really good.' To emphasise my words I kissed her again.

She was unconvinced. But, noticing my disappointment at her reaction, she forced a smile. 'At least this is not Novosibirsk,' she said. 'Nobody knows me here. I'll try to look my best.'

Tatyana took her cosmetics bag into the bathroom and locked the door behind her. First I heard the shower, then a hairdryer, which she must have had in her bag because I didn't own one. Then I heard more water, and then silence for at least thirty minutes.

'Are you OK?' I asked through the door. 'We're going to be late.'

When she came out of the bathroom, Tatyana was wearing tons of make-up and a bizarre hairdo, her beautiful curly hair all tied up in a knot on her head.

Truth was, I loved Tatyana best in the mornings, when she'd just woken up and was wearing one of my old T-shirts — the green of her sleepy eyes a miracle every time, her cheeks warm and rosy. Tatyana didn't need make-up. You look so pretty like this, I'd told her a few times. But she insisted that a girl needed to wear make-up all the time to look prilichnaya, decent. By now I had given up.

241

I gazed at her face, unnecessarily caked in powder. 'You look gorgeous,' I said, kissing her on the cheek, careful not to spoil her lipstick.

We made it to the theatre just in time to find our seats. They were in the third row, close to the action. The lights went out and the actors appeared on the stage. I found the play hard to follow. I'd expected a simple plot, a dog that becomes a human, but the Russian was complicated and, as I used my imagination to fill in the gaps in my understanding, the story in my head became darker and darker, chillingly interrupted every time the audience burst out laughing at jokes that I kept missing.

Tatyana was sitting with her back upright, her eyes fixed on the stage, completely absorbed by the action. Even with her hair like this she looked beautiful. She was wearing an overly sweet and pungent perfume which I didn't recognise and which stuck in my throat. I was afraid the perfume could also be smelled by the people around us, even by the actors on the stage. I told myself that I would buy Tatyana a new perfume, something more subtle, when the occasion presented itself.

And so it was, at that precise moment, watching an adaptation of *The Heart of a Dog* at the Stanislavsky theatre, that I realised Tatyana had somehow become my girlfriend. Why would I care about buying her perfume otherwise?

After the play finished we followed the crowd into the street. People gathered on the pavement of Tverskaya, discussing the show. I was flooded by a sense of well-being, thinking about Tatyana, my girlfriend, but also about going to the theatre, which for some reason I regarded as something exceptional — kulturno, intelligentno — something I should have done more often. I knew all the bars and clubs in Moscow, but hardly any theatres. Maybe I could take Tatyana out more often, I told myself, and we could also watch Chekhov plays, which would be easier for me to follow. With these thoughts in my head, we walked into the French Café next door and sat at a small table by the window. My initial plan had been to stop at the kiosks in Pushkinskaya after the play and buy a couple of blinis for dinner, but since Tatyana had made such an effort to look special, I felt the French Café would be more appropriate.

'I'm so happy we came to the theatre,' Tatyana said, holding my hand. 'Such a beautiful show. Thank you, Martin.'

She was radiant.

It was so easy to make her happy. She enjoyed reading books, cooking, watching movies, going to the theatre. All Tatyana wanted from life, she had told me, was good health, friends, family, a man. It was as if, by limiting the things she cared about, Tatyana had distilled life to its essentials. When I was with her, the rest of my existence seemed unnecessarily complicated. Even when I asked her about Russian books, her answers betrayed a simplicity that had to be admired. 'I enjoyed reading *Anna Karenina*,' she told me one day, 'but I didn't like the ending.' That was all Tatyana had to say about Tolstoy's masterpiece, that she didn't like the ending, as if she were talking about the latest Hollywood blockbuster.

Now she was my girlfriend, and that made me her man. A couple of times, when referring to me, she had in fact used those very words, my man, but she hadn't used the usual Russian word for man, muzhchina, but muzhik, which, as had been explained to me, implied a degree of added masculinity and roughness. Tatyana pronounced the word in a natural manner, without irony, moi muzhik, despite the fact that we had only been seeing each other for a few weeks and had never talked about the nature of our relationship.

Yet, despite accepting Tatyana's role in my life, I wondered about the implications of having a girlfriend, about the unwritten set of rules that falls upon two individuals whose existence has thus far been unknown to each other. And, every time the brothers dragged me off for a night out, I faced a series of connected and inevitable truths: that attraction is a fickle and capricious motherfucker; that even the selfless affection of someone who really cares for you can't compare to the liberating excitement of meeting someone new; and that, if I wanted to preserve my feelings for Tatyana, to stop her from becoming a cause of frustration, I had no choice but to keep considering myself a free man.

43

AFTER A LONG AND EXHAUSTING night with the brothers, I spent the morning at home, lying on the couch with a killer hangover, watching DVDs I'd bought on my last Gorbushka run. I had lunch, slept for a couple of hours, had coffee, tried to read a bit.

When Tatyana arrived in the early evening, as well as fresh clothes and cosmetics, she was lugging a bag of groceries. She kissed me hello, changed her clothes, disappeared into the kitchen. Soon, the homely smell of boiled cabbage wafted into the living room.

She was making golubtsy. 'My babushka's recipe,' Tatyana had said when she cooked cabbage rolls for the first time, about a week after we'd met. I'd said that I really liked them and, as a result, we were now eating stuffed cabbage rolls once a week. They were juicy and meaty and had a citrus aftertaste, which came, Tatyana said, from the grated orange zest added to the mince, her babushka's secret.

We sat for dinner. The smell of boiled cabbage somehow matched the new decoration of my kitchen. Two weeks after meeting Tatyana, I had hung a miniature painting on the wood-clad wall, next to the samovar. The painting — which I'd bought in the Old Arbat — depicted a colourful Russian winter scene, with children sledging and throwing snowballs. Above the samovar and the painting, on the kitchen shelf, I had placed lacquered wooden spoons and honey pots I had bought at Izmaylovsky Park. I thought the Russian handicrafts — black, red and gold — gave my kitchen the look of a Siberian izba, rural and traditional. The perfect setting for my evenings with Tatyana.

As we ate the golubtsy, I wondered how to tell Tatyana that I planned to go out again with the brothers on Friday. I didn't want to make a big deal out of it so I was waiting for a way to drop the information into the conversation. Except, we were not having a conversation.

'This is very tasty,' I said.

Tatyana smiled, picking at her cabbage roll without really eating it, saying nothing. She was quieter than usual, visibly worried.

'I might go out tomorrow night with some friends,' I finally said. 'You know, the guys from football.'

'That's good.' Tatyana placed her fork on the plate. 'Martin, can I ask you something?' She was blushing, her pale forehead covered in pinkish stains. 'I need to ask you a favour. But please do not feel obliged to say yes. I know it's a lot to ask, but I think I have no other choice.'

Her voice was trembling.

'What is it?'

'Katya and I had a fight,' she said.

Katya was her flatmate, a friend from Novosibirsk who had come to Moscow a few months before Tatyana. They shared a small flat in the outskirts, at one of the last metro stops on the orange line.

'A fight about what?'

'We're no longer talking to each other,' Tatyana said. 'She's going out with guys all the time and then she brings them home. It's not very nice, you know. Our place is very small, I can hear every time she has sex. They are always different guys. I asked her not to bring guys home and she got angry, told me it was none of my business.'

'I see.'

Tatyana took a sip of juice and wiped her mouth with a paper napkin. 'I told her that if we lived together we had to respect each other.'

'Right.'

'She asked me to move out.'

I set my fork down too. 'In what sense?'

'She said she wants me to leave the apartment immediately. The contract is under her name. I was just paying her my share.'

'But she can't kick you out like that.'

'If she had a boyfriend,' Tatyana said, 'that would be fine by me. But they are all different guys, you know, foreigners or older guys. I no longer feel comfortable at home.'

Tatyana was now staring down at her plate, avoiding my eyes, her blonde curls dangling over her food.

'I'm sure you can sort out things with Katya,' I said. 'You are old friends.' Then, pointing at my empty plate, 'Are there any more?'

'Of course.' Tatyana stood up, took my plate and served me two more cabbage parcels. 'Katya has changed since she came to Moscow,' she said. 'All she thinks about now is going out to clubs and meeting men. She's not the same.'

'Moscow changes people.'

'Why does everything have to be so hard in Moscow?' Tatyana's eyes were moist.

I poured some juice into her glass.

'People are so mean here,' she went on. 'Back in Siberia people are nice to each other, friendly. Here in Moscow, everybody pushes you in the metro, in the street, nobody cares about anybody.'

I forked a piece of cabbage roll. 'Moscow's a jungle.'

'Martin, you know I cannot afford to rent my own apartment. A friend at work said I could stay with her for a couple of weeks until I find something. But she lives with her family and has two small children.'

I stood up, opened the fridge and grabbed a bottle of beer. 'Are you sure you can't sort out things with Katya? Friendships go through rough patches. I'm sure you can both find a way to go on living together.'

'Martin, I don't want to live with her any more.'

I stood leaning on the kitchen bench, took a sip of beer. One cabbage roll remained on my plate.

'I know this is a lot to ask,' Tatyana said, now almost crying, 'but would you mind if I moved in here for a few days a week while I looked for a permanent place to stay?'

'What do you mean a few days a week?'

'I don't want to be a burden,' Tatyana said. 'I know you enjoy being alone, to read your books and go out with your friends. I thought maybe I could just stay here from Monday to Friday, so that I can go to work. It's so convenient from here, only two metro stops. On Fridays I could take the elektrichka after work and spend the weekend at my aunt's.'

'Have you told your aunt about this?'

'Yes. She offered to let me stay with her all the time but, you know, her place is two hours away from Moscow. I can't spend four hours on the train every day.'

'I see.'

'I don't want to interfere with your life and your friends. This is just for a few weeks until I find something more permanent.'

Her lips were trembling. An unexpected warm feeling climbed up from my stomach. I kissed her on the cheek. Tatyana burst into tears.

Suddenly I hated Katya, whom I'd never met, for bringing guys home and hurting Tatyana.

I held Tatyana in my arms. She was breathing heavily. For a few seconds I wanted to tell her, don't worry, you can stay with me as long as you want, also during weekends. Let's live together. Let's give it a serious try. But those were not the words that came out of my mouth.

'A few days a week would be fine,' I said. 'You can stay here from Monday to Friday. No problem.'

Tatyana breathed deeply and I realised how difficult it had been for her to ask. She kissed me, took hold of my face and looked straight into my eyes. 'Are you sure? Martin, I really don't want you to do it if you don't feel good about it. I know we have only known each other for a little while.'

The green of her moist eyes was almost transparent.

'Stop crying,' I said, wiping her cheeks with my fingers. 'Moscow doesn't believe in tears.'

She smiled. 'Martin, I adore you.'

'We can move your stuff here on Sunday.'

'You know I can't afford to pay half the rent you pay, but I can help with a bit and also with the groceries.'

'Don't worry about that.'

I finished the cabbage. Tatyana made tea and we moved to the living room to watch a movie. She fell asleep before the end.

Next morning, after Tatyana had left for work, I opened the balcony door and stepped outside with a cup of coffee. It was sunny, the roofs of Moscow gleaming under a clear sky. I took a deep breath, the warmth of the air taking me by surprise. Summer had arrived.

Sipping my coffee, listening to the clamour of the city, I looked forward to the warm days – going out with the brothers, nights on the restaurant terraces, the party boat – but also, I now realised, to Sunday evenings, to having Tatyana back at home. As far as I could see, I was looking forward to every single day that was coming to me. Standing on the balcony, I felt lightness in my heart, a sense of plenitude. And for a few minutes, gazing at the urban horizon, contemplating the arrival of summer in Moscow, I believed in happiness.

PART FIVE

Liza's Choice

44

IN *NEST OF THE GENTRY*, Turgenev nails the quintessential Tatyanaesque heroine. Liza is young, naive, pure-hearted. She lives with her mother and aunt in a provincial city, enjoying the simple life of the Russian gentry, which involves, Ivan Sergeyevich tells us, a lot of piano-playing, tea-drinking, book-reading, church-going. She's particularly pious, Liza, raised under the influence of her Russian peasant nanny.

Liza finds herself with two suitors. Panshin is a young officer: handsome, entertaining, respectful, charmant. Even if somehow superficial, Panshin possesses plenty of social and artistic skills, and a promising career ahead of him. By any standards, a good catch. To top this off, Panshin enjoys the full approval of Liza's mother.

Liza's other suitor, Lavretsky, is an older landowner: thoughtful, melancholic, married.

Lavretsky, the protagonist of the book, had been living in Paris with his wife, Varvara Pavlovna, and has just returned to Russia on his own after discovering that she had been cheating on him with a Frenchman. In sharp contrast to the very Russian Liza, Ivan Sergeyevich depicts Varvara Pavlovna as a flirtatious socialite, a man-eater, a femme fatale who is shamelessly Europeanised.

Back at home, Lavretsky rediscovers the beauty of the Russian countryside and its people. He starts to work on his neglected properties, making plans to provide for his peasants. As he adapts to his new surroundings, he's impressed by Liza's pure heart. He regrets that her goodness and beauty are to be lost to the superficial Panshin, whom he sees as a charlatan, undeserving of Liza. Gradually, Lavretsky, still hurt from his Paris debacle, develops feelings for Liza. Perhaps, he thinks, he could enjoy a second chance to renew his faith in love. The problem is that, as a married man, he's not in a position to act upon his romantic interest. This is the case until one fine day, flipping through the newspapers he receives from Paris, Lavretsky reads with astonishment that his estranged wife has died. He is now a free man.

Lavretsky tells Liza about the death of his wife and makes his own feelings clear. Meanwhile, Panshin proposes to Liza and she asks for time to think about it.

Now, Liza has a choice.

Russian as she is, Liza finds herself attracted not to the young charming officer, but to the older melancholic widower. Her decision is made on the spur of the moment, when, during a furtive night-time encounter, she lets Lavretsky steal a kiss. This being nineteenth century Russia, the kiss kind of seals their mutual intentions.

Happy ending? Not so fast. Now comes destiny, always capricious and stubborn, returning in the form of Varvara Pavlovna, who unexpectedly shows up in the provincial town, with her fashionable Parisian clothes and refined manners – the announcement of her death having been a mistake born of a baseless rumour. She asks for her husband's forgiveness.

Varvara Pavlovna's return means that Lavretsky is no longer free – death being in those days pretty much the only way out of a marriage. Lavretsky has to give up on Liza, and Liza – whose heart had been set on Lavretsky – is condemned to live without love.

But why had Liza chosen Lavretsky? Even if Varvara Pavlovna had really been dead, anyone could see that Panshin offered a more promising future.

Ivan Sergeyevich doesn't linger on Liza's choice and yet this choice stands at the core of the novel. Because, for some reason, Liza chooses the option that will clearly make her less happy.

Happiness on Earth does not depend on us, Liza says, as she retreats into a state of melancholy.

Liza's choice tells us a great deal about the Mysterious Russian Soul. Liza shows us that toska, a deep spiritual sorrow, is worth pursuing in itself. Beautiful, self-inflicted pain.

Liza's sheer beauty as a character derives from her suffering, her tragic destiny, her Russianness. Even Dostoyevsky, in the Pushkin Speech, mentions Turgenev's Liza as the one female character capable of standing up to Pushkin's Tatyana.

At the end of the story, Liza enters a monastery, embracing a life of sacrifice and privation.

'Happiness was not for me,' she says, explaining her decision. 'Even when I had hopes for happiness, my heart was always heavy.'

45

AS SUMMER HIT MOSCOW, a troop of corpulent babushkas took over the stairs of the metro entrance in Pushkinskaya. They sat every morning on tiny stools, leaning against the wall next to the newspaper stands, selling flowers, jam, honey, salt cucumbers, pickled mushrooms. They kept their flowers, which were tied with rubber bands, inside buckets of water or plastic bottles that had been cut in half. I never bought flowers but I liked the home-made jams, especially strawberry, and so did Tatyana. I would buy one or two jars, and, every night, drinking tea after dinner, Tatyana and I would eat the jam with a shared spoon, straight from the jar.

Tatyana was now spending five nights a week in my flat. I'd emptied three drawers and given her half the hanging space in the wardrobe, but she had more clothes than

I'd imagined — most of which she never wore — so she also kept two bulging suitcases in a corner of the living room.

Most nights we stayed at home but sometimes, on Wednesdays or Thursdays usually, we went out to the theatre or to eat sushi. Every Friday morning, Tatyana took an overnight bag with her and, after work, she went to her aunt's to spend the weekend.

'Sounds like you got yourself a part-time girlfriend,' Colin said when I told him about the arrangement.

In the mornings, after Tatyana was gone, I would take a shower, dress, and go for walks around the centre. I would walk for an hour or so and, when I got tired, I would sit in cafés, reading Russian books, taking notes.

One warm day in July, I was in Coffee Beans, on the leather couch by the window, trying to read yet another chunk of *War and Peace*. I was unable to focus on the task — distracted by a parade of miniskirts and high heels in Tverskaya — when one of the parading dyevs entered the café, bought a cup of coffee, and sat at a small table in front of me. Dark hair, brown eyes. She was wearing a white summer dress with colourful flowers. Out of her handbag she took a book and placed it on her table. She sipped at her coffee — a cappuccino, I noticed, as she licked the foam off her upper lip — opened the book and held it on her lap. Our eyes met a couple of times and she smiled. I smiled back.

Two months earlier I would have initiated a conversation straight away. But now things were different. Even if I had resolved to feel free, an unwelcome change that having a girlfriend had brought to my life was guilt. I felt guilty, not about seeing other girls on the weekend, which was necessary if I wanted to sustain my relationship with Tatyana, but about having to lie. The stories I made up to account for my weekends made me uncomfortable, especially since Tatyana believed every word I said. Her blind trust only made me see her as vulnerable, in need of protection. My protection. As a result, the more I lied to her, the stronger my feelings for her became.

The dyev with the flowery dress stared at me and I felt my entire body heating up. I could no longer keep my eyes on my book. It crossed my mind that, at that moment, it would be best to stand up, leave the café, forget about her. Let it be 1905. I'd done this before so I knew that, if I moved on – if I walked away and tried to fill my mind with different thoughts – in an hour or so I would beat the urge to be with the dyev with the flowery dress.

She went for a second cappuccino and returned to her table.

In my head, I summoned the image of Tatyana and tried to remember how I felt when I'd first laid eyes on her, in Kamergersky. Surely something like this. I knew that what I felt for the dyev in the flowery dress, the ferocious desire crawling up from my stomach, was not a long-lasting feeling. I knew this. I knew this. I knew this. But this knowledge was rational, self-imposed, totally useless.

Next thing I knew, the dyev was talking to me.

'Do you mind keeping an eye on my stuff for a minute?'
she said.

Her voice was deeper than I had imagined.

'Please,' I said, nodding.

After a couple of minutes she came back from the toilet.
She had put on fresh make-up.

'I love the coffee in this place,' I said.

Her smile revealed perfect white teeth. 'What are you
reading?'

'Tolstoy,' I said, holding the book up.

'*War and Peace*, interesno. We were forced to read it in
school, but I never finished it. Such a long book.'

I smiled.

'I prefer modern writers,' she said. 'Do you know Akunin
or Pelevin?'

'I've heard about them. Haven't read anything yet.'

'Vika, by the way.'

'Martin.' I took my book and my empty mug and moved
to her table.

Twenty minutes later we were wandering down
Tverskaya. The air was warm, the pavement full of people
strolling leisurely, in summery clothes. The scent of
coconut oil rising from Vika's tanned shoulders provoked
in me a flash of feeling, a half-memory of salty beaches and
childhood summers. When we reached Kamergersky, we
turned left and passed Chekhov's statue – where I tried
not to think about Tatyana – and walked among tables
and chairs that were now busy with people gathering for
lunch.

Vika asked for my coming-to-Russia story, and, for no particular reason, I decided not to tell her about my research. Instead, I told her that I was in business, that my business partner owned a car dealership in Prospekt Mira.

'And you don't have your own car?' she asked.

'I prefer to walk.'

'What about long distances?'

'Moscow has the best metro system in the world.'

Vika smiled, partly satisfied, but obviously puzzled that I was able to afford but did not own a car. Then she told me she was studying journalism. She wanted to become a foreign correspondent.

Vika was petite but, unlike Tatyana, she walked with determination and self-confidence. At the end of the pereulok we turned left and walked along Bolshaya Dmitrovka, keeping on the shaded side of the street. We then reached the Boulevard and walked down along the central dirt path. I was looking for a place to sit, but all the benches were occupied by young people drinking beer, smoking and kissing. Then I spotted an empty bench in the shade. We walked towards it, and, without saying a word, took a seat. Vika sat on my right and I put my right leg through the space between the seat and the back.

'It's so nice that we met,' she said.

'Sudba,' I said, sliding myself closer to her.

We kissed. I wrapped my hands around her waist, pulled her against me. My entire body was electrified. My hands, which I no longer seemed to control, began to move up and down her body. We went on kissing and I found myself fantasising that Vika was not someone I'd just met but my actual girlfriend. The thought filled me with an unexpected sense of well-being. After a few minutes we took a breather. I was sweaty. Vika was blushing.

'This is so weird,' she said, smiling.

I had four hours before Tatyana came back from work.

'I live nearby,' I heard myself saying. 'Would you like to come to my place for a cup of tea?'

She remained silent for a moment, staring at the ground, which was strewn with the empty shells of sunflower seeds.

'Maybe better if I don't come,' she said.

'I understand.'

'I really like you.'

'I like you too.'

We kissed again.

'Maybe we can meet tonight and go to the cinema?' Vika said with a wide smile, her brown eyes sparkling.

I wanted to say yes. I wanted to take Vika to the cinema. I wanted to kiss her in the darkness and, after the film, I wanted to take her to Café Maki. I wanted us to drink loads of wine, share a plate of blinis with preserved strawberries and mascarpone. And, after that, I wanted her to come to my place for tea.

'I can't tonight,' I said, feeling a squeeze in my chest.

Vika looked confused, disappointed.

'Maybe we could meet over the weekend?' I said.

'Sure, that would be nice.'

We exchanged phone numbers and walked down the

Boulevard, towards the metro. We kissed one more time, said do svidaniya.

As I walked home, I texted Yulya Karma, who I hadn't seen for a while, and asked her if she was free to meet for a quick cup of tea.

46

FOR THREE DAYS I'D been picturing Vika in the flowery dress she wore when we met, so when, on Saturday morning, underneath Pushkin's statue, I was approached by a girl wearing sunglasses and a bright yellow dress, it took me a few seconds to realise it was her.

'You no longer remember how I look?' Vika said, lifting her sunglasses.

'Of course. You look beautiful.'

She laughed and kissed me on the cheek.

It was a sunny morning and Muscovites had taken to the streets en masse. At least ten other couples had agreed to meet by Pushkin at the same time.

'Let's go for a walk,' I said.

We crossed the perekhod, emerged on the other side of Tverskaya, and passed through the terrace of McDonald's, where all the tables were occupied. We reached the Boulevard and strolled down the path, under the trees, as we had done the day we met.

'I remember the first time I went to McDonald's,' Vika said. 'Just after it opened, during the perestroika.'

'You must have been young.'

'I was a little girl. A friend in school had gone and he told us about the Happy Meal. For days and days I asked my mum to take me to McDonald's. Finally, one day, she took me and my cousin. When we arrived, the queue was so long that people were waiting outside the restaurant, all the way to Tverskaya.' Vika pointed back, to the corner of Tverskaya and the Boulevard. 'We had to wait for at least three hours.'

'Three hours for McDonald's?'

'It was the first McDonald's in the Soviet Union, everybody wanted to try it. It was something exotic, from the West. Everything that came from the West was considered superior. Besides, people were used to queues at the time.'

'I've heard,' I said.

'We had to stand in the queue for so long, I was exhausted. And the worst thing was, by the time we arrived at the counter, there were no Happy Meals left.'

'What did you have?'

'A cheeseburger.'

'Liked it?'

'I was so disappointed,' she said. 'All I really wanted was the box with the toy.'

It was always a pleasant walk along the Boulevard, especially in summer, if you ignored the lanes of traffic on either side and the drunks on the benches. We passed other couples, dyevs carrying bouquets of flowers, men holding bottles of Baltika. Vika walked slowly, as if savouring every step, her sandals treading elegantly along an imaginary straight line ahead of her. She took my arm. I let her hold it a minute, then withdrew it.

At the junction of the Boulevard and Malaya Nikitskaya, we crossed the road into a small park that ended in a circular open space with a gravel path and a few benches. Vika wiped the surface of one of the benches with a paper tissue, we sat down.

'That's where they got married,' she said, pointing at the yellowish church across the street.

'Who?'

'Pushkin and Natalya. That's why they made this fountain.'

The benches formed a circle around a fountain, at the centre of which stood a bizarre shrine with a golden dome and thick Greek columns. It looked like a tacky burial monument and, although I'd passed in front of it many times during my walks, I'd never noticed the statues sheltered by the golden dome. Now, as Vika pointed inside, I realised the statue was none other than Aleksandr Sergeyevich himself, standing next his wife, Natalya Nikolaevna.

'It's so romantic,' Vika said. 'Pushkin, Natalya, such a beautiful love story.' She took her sunglasses off and threw them into her handbag. Her lovely eyes were framed by long eyelashes, thick with mascara.

'It is,' I said, 'except, she was a bit of a slut, wasn't she?'

'What do you mean?'

'You know, she was cheating on Pushkin and all that.'

'We don't know that.' Vika inched away from me, seemingly annoyed by my remark.

'Of course,' I said, 'we don't know. But I always assumed that if Aleksandr Sergeyevich challenged D'Anthès to a duel it was because something must have being going on. Why would Pushkin risk his life if his wife was not cheating on him?'

'To defend her honour.'

'So you think D'Anthès and Natalya didn't have a thing?'

'Of course not,' Vika said, fiddling with her glossy hair. 'Natalya loved Pushkin very much.'

'It doesn't mean she couldn't have had a little fling with the French guy.'

I squeezed Vika's arm and laughed, but Vika remained serious.

'If you truly love someone,' Vika said, 'you would not want to be with another person.'

We remained silent for a couple of minutes. A duel, I thought, what a stupid way to die. And yet how beautiful and poetic. Pushkin. Lermontov.

I wrapped my arm around Vika's waist. She closed her eyes and threw her head back, facing the sun. I kissed her. She kissed me back. I could hear the heavy traffic, as our kissing got faster and deeper.

Now my hands were under her dress and I was kissing her neck and shoulders, with the bitter taste of suntan lotion. Abruptly she pushed me away. 'Ne nado,' she said. Then she took a deep breath and laughed. She opened her handbag, took out a small mirror and put on some lipstick. People on other benches paid us no attention.

'Nu, tak,' she said.

'Tak,' I said. 'Let's walk.'

'Davay.'

As I stood up I realised I was all sweaty, my shirt stuck to my back. We walked into Malaya Nikitskaya, then turned right through Spiridonovka and meandered among the quiet streets and alleys of this old part of town. I knew these streets well because they headed towards the back of my building. We walked in silence, my entire body aching with expectation. I put an arm around Vika and slipped a finger under the strap of her dress. Her skin felt soft.

As we turned a corner into one of the smaller pereuloks, we bumped into a Caucasian fruit seller, sitting sleepily on the shaded pavement, next to a large cage brimming with enormous watermelons. I bought one of the smallest melons, which he handed me in a black plastic bag.

We carried on and soon we were at the garden entrance to Scandinavia.

'This is where I live,' I said, casually, as if it was only by chance that we'd arrived at my building. With one hand I was carrying the watermelon, with the other I was pointing at the balconies on the top floor.

'Nice place.'

'Let's go up for a cup of tea,' I said and, not waiting for an answer, I grabbed her hand and led her towards the door of my building.

47

THE OFFICIAL VERSION — AS I first heard it from Lyudmila Aleksandrovna — is that Aleksandr Sergeyevich was going through tough times. On top of financial difficulties, he was bored of aristocratic life in Peter, and, for some reason, pissed off at the tsar. It was at that low moment in his life that his enemies spread a rumour that linked D'Anthès, a French exile and notorious womaniser, to Natalya Nikolaevna, Pushkin's beautiful wife. So Aleksandr Sergeyevich, who was not only the greatest of poets but also an honourable gentleman, challenged D'Anthès to a duel.

Of course, when I first heard the story, I assumed there was more to it, some facts buried in order to avoid a scandal. You can be as Russian and romantic as you want, but you don't go around asking someone to shoot you with a gun for nothing.

In any case, despite attempts by his friends to avert the

271

duel, on the fateful morning of 27 January 1837, Aleksandr Sergeyevich Pushkin met D'Anthès in a forest outside Peter. Pushkin got shot in the stomach and fell, bleeding, on the snow. He was taken back home to Peter, put to bed. After two days of agony, he died. He was thirty-seven.

When I went up to Peter for a weekend I visited Pushkin's last apartment, a museum these days, and was shown around by a very old and very devoted guide. She narrated the story of Pushkin's final days with enormous dedication, interpreting the voices of the different characters, as if telling a fairy tale to a child. I found myself absorbed in the storytelling and, as I listened to the monologue that the guide must have repeated thousands of times, I could picture Aleksandr Sergeyevich vividly, in his flat, but also in the forest, pointing the gun, receiving the shot, falling in the snow, firing a shot that only wounded D'Anthès' arm. By the time the babushka had finished her narration, all the museum visitors were standing around her, next to the exhibit of a gun similar to the ones used by Pushkin and D'Anthès.

As far as I could tell, Russians are divided on Pushkin's wife. Some, like Vika or Lyudmila Aleksandrovna, seemed to believe the official version, the beautiful love story depicted in statues and monuments across the country — such as the golden statue of Aleksandr Sergeyevich and Natalya in the middle of the Old Arbat, at whose feet young Moscow lovers lay bouquets of flowers.

Others think differently. All these years, entire generations of more cynical Russians have blamed Natalya for Pushkin's death.

In the end, we will never know what really happened between Natalya and D'Anthès. Besides, in the eyes of most Russians, causing Pushkin's death is not Natalya's worst sin. Natalya is most loathed for not understanding Pushkin's greatness, for taking him lightly. For that, she cannot be forgiven.

Yet, Pushkin's self-induced death doesn't make much sense. From a historical and artistic perspective he was a successful man. Why did he risk his precious life in a stupid duel? Fuck knows. But whatever his reasons, his early death assured him the kind of glory older people don't attain. It made him an instant legend. And whether D'Anthès was banging Natalya or not is, to a certain extent, irrelevant.

Perhaps, if Aleksandr Sergeyevich was unhappy at the time, he thought that risking his life was worth a shot and that, whatever the outcome of his duel, at least things would no longer be the same.

48

BEING ON THE TOP floor, on summer days my flat was always hot. I had left the balcony doors open and now flies were circling in the middle of the living room. Except they weren't exactly circling. Moscow flies had a peculiar way of moving around — they flew in straight lines, turning in sharp corners, drawing geometrical figures in the air, as if avoiding walls that were invisible to my eyes.

Vika and I lay sweating on the couch. I was observing the flies, trying to remember a passage from Turgenev's *Nest of the Gentry*, where Marfa Timofeevna, the bitter old lady, says something about envying the simple life of flies until she'd heard a fly complaining in a spider's web.

Vika was breathing into my neck, her hair all over my face. She felt unusually warm, her skin sticky. Once naked, her petite body was somewhat softer than I'd expected. Unlike Tatyana's, Vika's thighs were round and fleshy.

I was hit by a sudden urge to leave my flat.

'Let's go and grab some lunch,' I said.

'Now?' She kissed my neck. 'Maybe we can stay here for a little while, eat the watermelon.'

'It's too hot in here,' I said.

The voices from Scandinavia's terrace came over the balcony. I could recognise some of the brothers'. If only Vika would leave now, I thought, I could go down and enjoy a cold beer and a hamburger with the brothers, then come back for some sleep.

I felt dark clouds forming in my head. I stood up and went to the shower. It was that time of year when my building had no central hot water – the profilaktika, they called it, about three weeks every summer during which, I was told, the hot water of entire neighbourhoods was cut so that the pipes could be serviced. It was a collective purifying ritual of sorts that Muscovites seemed to endure without much protest.

The icy water washed away some of my sorrow, brought me back to life.

Back in the living room, I slipped back into my jeans, sat next to Vika. She lay inert and naked on the couch. I placed my hand between her legs – she was freshly shaved, the skin of her pubic area reddish and irritated. She smiled, placed her arms around me, kissed my ear. I concentrated hard on pushing Tatyana's image out of my mind. Vika was a wonderful girl, I told myself, and, for the few seconds I could maintain the fantasy of Tatyana's non-existence, I enjoyed

Vika's company. But as soon as Tatyana forced herself back into my head, my chest tightened and Vika's presence in my flat felt oppressive.

Vika stood up, walked into the bathroom, washed herself. Back in the living room, she let her yellow dress unfold over her head and cover her body. We went down to the street.

'Why don't we just have something to eat here?' Vika said, pointing at the tables of Scandinavia. The waitresses, who knew me by sight, carried trays with grilled burgers, fresh salads, cold beer.

'I feel like walking,' I said. 'Let's go somewhere else.'

We strolled down Tverskaya, turned left at the end and crossed the street into Teatralnaya Ploschad. We sat down at a summer terrace with orange plastic tables, next to the Metropol hotel.

When the waitress brought our food, Vika was talking about her family, something about a brother, or a cousin — in Russian you never knew. I wasn't really following what she was saying. At a nearby table a group of foreign business-men, guests at the Metropol, I figured, were drinking beer and talking loudly, in English. They were accompanied by three young Russian women, who laughed wildly at each of their stupid comments.

I was overcome by a wave of exhaustion. I didn't feel like talking. It was as if all the anticipation, all the hunger, had evaporated in a matter of seconds on my couch. All I wanted now was to be left alone.

I thought about Tatyana, about how she gave me space, even when she was in my flat, about the unobtrusiveness of her presence. Tomorrow evening she'll be back home, I thought.

'Do you have brothers or sisters?' Vika was asking.

I cut open my chicken roll, melted butter flooded my plate.

'I think I'll go home,' I said.

'What do you mean?'

'I'm tired, I need some rest.'

'But you wanted to get out. You can't go home now, with such nice weather. Let's finish eating. Then we can walk towards Aleksandrovsky Sad and have ice cream.'

I ate some chicken in silence. Vika said her salad was very nice.

'I'd rather go home,' I said. 'I'm meeting some friends tonight.'

Vika looked at me, perplexed.

'I can come with you.'

'I need to rest, I'm quite tired from last night.'

She placed her fork facing down on her plate – her face suddenly transformed, her smile gone. Her brown eyes looked somewhat menacing.

'So you want me to go home now? Is that what you are saying?'

'Vika, I'm just saying I need to meet my friends later on and I would like to rest.'

'I can also meet your friends.'

'Not tonight,' I said. 'Another day.'

'Martin, you asked me to meet you today.' Her voice sounded now coarser. 'I want to spend time with you.'

'But we *have* spent time together. We met at eleven, it's four o'clock. That's five whole hours we've spent together.'

'You've been silent for the last hour,' Vika said.

'I need to be alone for a little while, that's all.'

Vika took the sunglasses out of her handbag, placed them on her head as a hairband. Then she grabbed the fork and started picking at her salad.

I tried to finish my chicken as quickly as possible.

'I shouldn't have slept with you,' she said.

'I'm just tired. We'll meet another day.'

'You wanted to fuck me, that's all.'

'Vika, please.'

She now put her sunglasses on. They were far too large, the sunglasses. They made her look like an oversized insect.

'Why don't you want to spend more time with me?' she said, softening her voice again.

I searched for something suitable to say, but at that moment the image of a fly flashed up in my head. Vika, with her giant sunglasses, transformed into an enormous fly.

'We just met,' she continued. 'There is so much we can talk about. I don't know anything about you. On Wednesday when we first met, you were talking all the time, it was so nice. I had a great time. And now you ask me to leave?'

'Those glasses are too big for you,' I said.

'What are you talking about?'

'Vika, I had a great time with you today. But I'm just not in the mood. 'Ia-ne-v-nastroenii,' I said, probably raising my voice above what was appropriate. 'Let's meet another day.'

'Why another day? I'm here now. Let's spend this weekend together.'

'But my friends—'

'I can also meet your friends.'

'Vika.'

'If you don't want to spend time with me, what's the point?'

'The point?'

Vika lowered her voice, looked at her salad. 'The point of us being together.'

I stood up.

'Are you married or something?' she asked, gripping my arm. 'I saw women's stuff in your bathroom. If you are married, just tell me, but you should have told me before. I wouldn't have slept with you.'

'Vika, listen. I need to go now.' I shook her hand off, threw a thousand-ruble note on the table. 'I'll call you.'

'Go to hell.'

49

On Sunday I woke up just before noon. I put the percolator on the stove and two slices of bread in the toaster. I sat at the table, my head throbbing, waiting for the coffee. My mobile had been on the kitchen table all morning. I had six new text messages that had arrived during the night without my noticing. All from Vika.

privet, kak dela, sorry about earlier

why are you ignoring my message?

oh, maybe you are with your friends, have a good time

maybe we can meet tomorrow to talk

if you have time. otherwise another day

I'm thinking about you

I typed a short reply proposing to meet for coffee during the week, pressed send and immediately switched off the phone. After I finished my coffee and toast, I bundled the bedsheets into the washing machine, lay on the couch.

It had been a long night. I stopped drinking at about four in the morning, when I found myself on the basement dance floor in Karma, barely able to keep my eyes open. I said goodbye to Diego, who was slow-dancing with a fat dyev, but I was unable to find the others. I walked upstairs, into the open air, and was surprised to see daylight. I ignored the drivers waiting outside Karma and decided to walk, heading towards Petrovka Ulitsa. In summer I loved to walk home from a night out, crossing empty streets, breathing fresh air, observing how the night retreated and a new day took over the city. It was the only time of day when Moscow didn't feel crowded.

I went back into the kitchen and made another cup of coffee. I hung the bed linen on the balcony. The sun was now hitting the western façade of my building. It would be dry in a couple of hours, I thought, just before Tatyana arrives.

I had a cold shower. Feeling refreshed, I lay back down on the couch, naked, observing the little white dots on my Indian tapestry. If I kept my eyes fixed on one of the dots that surrounded Lord Ganesh, the intricate painting seemed to shift slightly, the elephant head somehow peeking out of the wall. It was a bizarre visual effect I had noticed before, usually when drunk or hungover, and I wondered if that was the intentional purpose of the white dots – dots that otherwise didn't add anything to the image. I closed my eyes, my mind drifted, and, in the sweet moment when my awareness was slipping away but I wasn't yet asleep, a thought flitted across my mind: I missed Tatyana.

I stumbled to the kitchen, switched on my phone and sent Tatyana a text message. *Miss you.*

She replied in a minute: *Me too, love you.*

See you tonight.

At five, feeling a bit better, I decided to go out for some fresh air and to buy stuff for dinner. I walked into Eliseevksy, always comforting with its elegant gilded ceilings, chandeliers and wall paintings. The most beautiful place in the world to buy dried fish and imported biscuits. At the deli counter I got cured salmon, sturgeon, liver blinis, a jar of red caviar and smetana. On the way back I stopped at a booth in the perekhod and bought a film of the type Tatyana liked. The seller at the stand, who recognised me from previous purchases, assured me that the English subtitles worked well.

Pushkinskaya was bursting with life. Muscovites walked in and out of the metro, rushed through the perekhods, sat at the outdoor tables of Café Pyramida. I walked on among the crowd, towards my building, bag of groceries in one hand, movie in the other, feeling light-hearted at the thought of the night ahead – at the thought of Tatyana coming home.

50

STEPANOV WAVES HIS HAND at the waitress and points at his empty coffee mug. 'But I don't understand your problem,' he says, turning back to me. 'You can keep your girlfriend at home from Monday to Friday and enjoy your freedom on weekends.'

I glance around the garden. The morning is grey, threatening rain. A few ravens are pacing on the nearby grass, awaiting our departure to jump on the breakfast leftovers.

'Russian women are forgiving,' Stepanov says. 'They accept that we have lovers on the side.'

The waitress fills our mugs with coffee, then heads off to attend to a table further away, where two white-haired expats are reading copies of the *Moscow Times*.

'Not sure about that,' I say. 'I've met girls who were less trusting than Tatyana.'

'Perhaps spoilt Muscovites,' Stepanov says. 'But real Russian women, from outside Moscow, it's a different story. They understand that men need to chase women, that it's in our nature and we can't do shit about it. They don't take it personally. They know it has nothing to do with feelings.'

I take a sip of coffee.

'Of course there are rules to observe,' Stepanov says, 'but as long as you don't bring other women home, and you're discreet and respectful, you're allowed to sleep around.'

'Like in Chekhov's stories,' I say.

'What do you mean?'

'It's not just that people cheat in Chekhov's stories, adultery is old in literature. It's the factual way Anton Pavlovich tells us his characters cheat. No moral consequences.'

Stepanov adjusts his sunglasses, which today are large and greenish. 'That's my point. In Russia infidelity is something that can be addressed with a bit of discretion and mutual understanding.'

I take a red notebook out of my bag, place it on the table, begin to scribble.

Stepanov leans forward, takes his sunglasses off, places his elbows on both sides of his empty plate. His blue eyes are bloodshot. 'We, Russians, accept cheating as part of life,' he says, speaking slowly now, 'because we accept life as it is. Some things you can't change, you have to live with them.'

I stop writing, look up. 'You mean you just accept your sudba?'

'Exactly. We're fatalistic.'

I drop the pen and take a sip of my coffee.

'Russians are fatalistic,' Stepanov repeats, tilting his head towards my red notebook.

I nod. 'Right.'

Stepanov's eyes stay fixed on my notebook, and it hits me that I'm expected to write down his acute insight into the Russian mentality. I lift the pen and write *Russians = fatalistic*. I circle the word 'fatalistic' so that Stepanov sees it.

Stepanov nods with an approving smile. 'You Westerners are always angry because you want to change everything in life. We Russians are always sad because we know that most things cannot be changed.'

I feel Stepanov has been waiting for the right moment to squeeze this pearl of wisdom into our conversation. I'm about to write it down when I see Colin and Diego approaching our table.

'Sorry we're late,' Diego says. He's wearing a baseball cap, green, white and red, the word 'Mexico' stamped on the front.

'It's fine,' Stepanov says. 'I was sharing with Martin some of the secrets of the Mysterious Russian Soul.'

'Nonsense,' Colin says, taking a seat at the table. 'The Mysterious Russian Soul is—' He doesn't finish his sentence, distracted, glares at a raven that has approached our table begging for food. 'Nothing but a marketing trick,' he finally says, scaring the raven away with a wave of his hand. 'An old slogan to promote a culture of laziness and alcoholism.'

My mind drifts back to the moment when Lyudmila

Aleksandrovna gave me her take on the Mysterious Russian Soul. The expression Russian Soul, as known today, had been coined in the 1840s by Belinsky, the influential literary critic. It was Russia's reaction to German romanticism, an ideal to agglutinate a divided nation, to put Russian idiosyncrasies above those of other European states. Lyudmila Aleksandrovna told me how the expression had been part of the romanticising of Russian peasant life and how, in her view, it had been Fyodor Mikhailovich – good old Dostoyevsky – who had popularised the term later on, making the soul, she said, the depository of human contradictions, of the eternal struggle between God and evil. I had written down her exact words: *In Dostoyevsky the soul is the depository of human contradictions, of the eternal struggle between God and evil.*

Stepanov reclines in his chair. 'I was telling Martin how Russians accept life as it is.'

Colin grabs the copy of *The Exile*. 'Interesting,' he says, referring either to *The Exile* cover – which shows a naked woman holding a hand grenade – or to Stepanov's remark.

'Martin is giving up dyevs,' Stepanov says.

'Again?' Colin says. He's wearing a brownish shirt, the logo of an expensive Italian designer stamped on his chest. 'Is it because of your Siberian dyev?'

'Tatyana,' I say. 'This time I'm really done. I need to take it easier.'

'That's great,' Diego says, taking off his cap and rearranging his long hair. 'I knew this was going to work. She's beautiful.'

'Bullshit,' Colin says. 'You've said that before. How many Tatyanas have you been with?'

'I don't know,' I say, irritated by the question. 'Two. Perhaps three.'

'So,' Colin says, 'this is Tatyana Four?'

In my mobile phone, I realise, she remains Tatyana Evans.

'What's your point?' I say.

Colin grabs my shoulder and looks at me with a half-smile. 'We've been over this, there's no point wasting your time with one single dyev in Moscow.'

'I can't keep meeting new dyevs every week,' I say. 'I'm sick of all the plotting and scheming, of switching my phone off in the evenings, of having to come up with excuses all the time. I want to enjoy cooking at home, watching films, reading books, going to the theatre.'

'You can do all that back in Europe,' Colin says. 'Why waste your Moscow time with books when you can enjoy real life?'

'Maybe I'm not that excited about real life,' I say. 'Look at us. We get pissed, meet dyevs, then what? What's the point of all this?'

'Martin's been reading Chekhov again,' Stepanov says.

Stepanov and Colin laugh. The ravens, which have been silently approaching our table, retreat a couple of metres, wings fluttering.

Colin leans over the table. 'Martin,' he says, 'fucking around is a great way to be happy.' He glances over the terrace, then he drops his hand on my shoulder and looks into my eyes. 'There is nothing sinful about fucking around.'

'I just want a simpler life.' I point at the copy of *The Exile*. 'Maybe I'm getting too old for all this.'

Colin moves *The Exile* away from me, as if my finger-pointing were desecrating a holy text.

Diego is hiding behind one of Starlite's laminated menus. 'Martin is right,' he says. 'If he is happy with Tatyana, why should he meet other dyevs?'

'So what,' Colin says, 'now you are giving up sex?'

The white-haired expats are looking at us from the other table.

'If you stop sleeping around,' Stepanov says, 'your life will lose all its excitement.'

'Excitement,' I say. 'Is that what we're after?'

Stepanov shrugs his shoulders. 'What's wrong with excitement?'

'Isn't there anything more durable?' I say. 'More mean-ingful?'

'Man, you need to stop reading Russian books,' Colin says. 'Excitement keeps you alive. It's not the sex, it's the chase. That's the fun part of life. Do you know what the main difference between young and old men is?'

I lean back in the chair. 'Age?'

'Older men have given up on the chase,' Colin says. 'Once you stop looking for sexual partners, that's death, man. Life becomes this dull, boring experience.'

'Maybe a dull life is not such a bad thing,' I say. 'Maybe a dull life allows you to appreciate the beauty of it all.'

'You'll always have time for a quieter life down the road,' Colin says. 'When you leave Russia.'

'Maybe I don't need to leave Russia. I could stick around here. Make more money, buy a dacha. Grow vegetables, read, write. Live in touch with nature, like Tolstoy. Be happy.'

'Tolstoy wasn't happy,' Stepanov says. 'He was tormented. And he fucked his maids and peasants all the time.'

'You know what I mean,' I say.

'Nobody is happy all of the time,' Colin says, as the first drops of rain pepper our table. 'Life is like a big ocean of boredom and then you bump into little islands of happiness. Total happiness doesn't exist. Imagine that you marry your dyev, move to a dacha in Siberia and build yourself a quiet life. You'll be going deeper into the ocean, with no happy islands in sight. Man, stop fucking with your head and enjoy what Moscow has to offer.'

'So when does it stop?' I say.

Colin raises his arms. 'Stop what?'

'The chase,' I say. 'The fucking around.'

'Your dick will tell you when,' Colin says. 'He'll know when you're done.'

51

First I see a pair of black leather boots. Spiny high heels, shiny leather. I've never seen her wear that kind of footwear before. I'm at the bar, ordering a round of drinks for the brothers. She's on the dance floor. Not even sure it's her. Not just the boots. The way she dances, elbows in the air, breasts pushed out.

It's been a while since I last came to the Boarhouse. We used to come often during my first year, usually on Wednesdays, to enjoy the Countdown, back then the best happy hour deal in town. But today is Saturday, there's no happy hour and we shouldn't be at the Boarhouse.

These days the place is trashy. For some reason it's maintained its two fuckies in *The Exile*. The Boarhouse remains a popular place among white-haired expats, those who don't care about trendy clubs or are too old and too ugly to make it through face control. But earlier in the night we were at the Bavarian Brewery, drinking large jugs of beer with a bunch of expat football buddies and someone had suggested we go for drinks at the Boarhouse. And here we are. Wasted.

I pay for the drinks, ship them back to the brothers. I'm holding my shot of vodka in one hand, bottle of beer in the other. I drain the vodka at once, leave the empty glass on the table, take a sip of beer to wash it down. With the bottle of beer in my hand, I stumble out of the bar area and thread my way between the people, towards the dance floor.

Up close the boots look more plastic than leather. She's wearing heavy make-up, bright red lipstick, thick eyeliner, her face more aggressive and hostile than I remember. Lost in the dancing, she doesn't notice me. Deep inside, I still hope it's not her. She's dancing in a group of four, with another dyev and two older guys, clearly expats. They seem to be coupled up. Her girlfriend dances next to a tall guy with glasses, late forties. She – now I'm sure it's her – is dancing with the older man, fifty-something, fat and bald, wearing a white short-sleeved shirt, sweaty around the armpits.

Old disco hits from the 1980s blast through the loud-speakers. Dyevs in the club seem to love the music and are dancing with their arms up in the air, twisting their bodies in inelegant ways.

I tap her shoulder. She turns round, looks at me for a couple of seconds and smiles.

'Privet, Martin, kak dela?' She doesn't seem surprised to see me.

'Privet, Lena. I wasn't sure it was you.'

'It's me.'

Her breasts are pushed up, look enormous. I've never seen Lena wear anything like this before. I can almost see her nipples. I notice that she's not wearing her golden chain with the cross.

Here she is. Lena. My long-disappeared Lena.

I find myself thinking of the days we spent together, just after my arrival, when I had plenty of energy and Moscow was a white canvas. The Propaganda era. I picture Lena lying on her kommunalka bed. Or sitting on the floor of my balcony, her legs dangling through the bars, gazing over the city.

'It's been a long time,' I say.

She nods.

'Oh Bozhe, Lenushka, you look so different.' My eyes can't help going from her face to her breasts and down to her mini-miniskirt.

'Thanks for the compliment.'

'I sent you so many messages,' I say. 'You never called me back.'

She stops dancing, steps aside. 'Call you? What for?'

'To talk, to see each other. I thought a lot about you. Lena, I've missed you.'

Behind Lena, the two older expats are looking at me, impatient. Lena steps back as if to go back to dance.

'Would you like a drink?' I ask.

'No thanks, I'm OK.'

'I didn't know you came here.'

'I've come a few times,' she says. 'I like the music.'

I can hardly hear her, I step closer. She's wearing the same perfume she wore back then, and, as I inhale as much of the sweet aroma as I can, I feel a shudder through my body, and now I'm seeing Lena in Propaganda, the first night we met, when she was the most beautiful dyev in the club and I whispered a few Pushkin verses in her ear.

'Where are you working now?' I say. 'I went to the restaurant. They told me you don't work there any more.'

'I quit work. I'm taking a break now.' She comes closer. 'Listen, I can't talk right now.'

Her girlfriend comes over, talks in her ear.

'I really need to go,' Lena says. 'It was nice seeing you.'

She turns round but I grab her arm and pull her aside.

'I've been wanting to see you for ages. Lena, you look great. I've missed you so much.'

'Martin, you are drunk.'

'I really miss you, Lena. I miss what we had.'

'What *did* we have?' She shakes me off. 'You only wanted me for sex.'

'That's not true, Lenushka.'

'Martin, I need to go now, let's talk another day.'

'What are you doing later tonight?'

Lena puts her hand to her neck, as if to grab the necklace she is not wearing. 'Martin, you are drunk. Go back to your friends.'

The old fat expat comes to me. 'Listen, man,' he says, 'tonight these two ladies are with us. Move on and look for another one.' He is American.

'Don't worry,' I say, 'she's just an old friend.'

293

'Tonight she's *our* friend.'

'Whatever.' I turn to Lena. 'See you later. Don't leave without saying goodbye.'

I go back to the brothers, who have gathered in a corner next to the entrance.

'I see you're relaxing your policy,' Colin says.

'What do you mean?'

Colin smiles and points his bottle of beer at the dance floor. 'I just saw you over there,' he says, 'trying to pick up a whore.'

I look back at the dance floor, where Lena is dancing. The shiny boots. The push-up bra. The miniskirt. The make-up. I should have realised sooner. Of course Lena can't possibly like the fat American. Of course Lena has not come to the Boarhouse for the music.

I leave my beer on the floor, rush outside the club to get some fresh air. I sit on the kerb. Maybe everything is a misunderstanding. Sure, there are plenty of prostitutes at the Boarhouse. It's a trashy place and that's why we don't like it. But not Lena, I tell myself, not my Lenushka. I need to talk to her, clarify things. I need to hear her tell me what's going on. I need to go back into the club. I try to get up on my feet but I realise I'm too drunk, I can hardly stand.

The image of the fat American flashes in my head, the hollow feeling in my stomach grows. I feel a spasm, as if I were about to cry, but I hold back my tears and, instead of crying, I puke. Beer. Pieces of mashed Bavarian sausage.

I feel a bit better. I breathe deeply, find some chewing gum, go back into the club.

The air is steamy. I find Lena next to the bar, drinking a cocktail with her girlfriend and the two old guys.

I approach her. 'I need to talk to you,' I say.

'You are drunk, Martin.'

'I'm OK, Lena, I just don't know what's going on. Let's go out for just five minutes.'

The fat American guy now steps in between Lena and me, puts his hand on my chest. 'Back off, asshole.'

'Be cool, man,' I say. 'I only want to talk to her.'

Then he pushes me and, pissed as I am, I fall to the floor, which is dirty and wet. I get to my knees, and I feel I'm about to puke again. I breathe deeply, trying to gather my thoughts, and then someone grabs me and pulls me up. It's Diego.

I see the American guy smiling, now putting an arm around Lena, and I find myself punching him with all my strength, except that what I hit is not his face as I had intended, but his neck. It doesn't feel like a clean punch, not that I really know how a clean punch feels. Somebody pushes me. A soft slap lands on the back of my head. Now Stepanov steps in, shouting in Russian. Diego is holding me and I'm confused. I never get into fights.

Next thing I know I'm outside the club, sitting on the pavement, next to what I suspect is my own vomit. Colin sits on my other side with a bottle of water.

'Drink some cold water, man.'

I feel pain in my hand and in my knees. For a few seconds I don't remember Lena or the guy or how I ended up here and during these seconds I'm puzzled but unhurt. Then the image comes back into my head, the shiny boots, the red lipstick, the push-up bra, the American man with sweat patches under his armpits, and it hurts like hell and, with embarrassment, I notice tears in my eyes.

'Where is she?' I say.

'Who?'

'Lena. Where is she? I need to talk to her,' I say, trying hard to hold back my tears in front of Colin.

'They're all gone, man.'

'Where to?'

'Fuck knows. We've all been kicked out. Congratulations, our first time. Now we know what it takes to get kicked out of a trashy club in Moscow.'

'Where did they go?' I ask.

'Forget about them,' Colin says. 'Come on, throw up a bit more before you get in a car. We need to get you home.'

52

I WAKE UP AROUND NOON. I open the balcony door, step outside. I glance at the grey roofs and the grey sky, trying to gather my memories of the night and, as soon as a coherent sequence of events forms in my head, I feel my lungs shrink. Back inside, the flat feels small, claustrophobic, as if during the night the ceiling has lowered and the walls have moved closer to each other. I need to get out. I shower quickly, dress, rush down the stairs and out onto the street.

I turn the corner into the Boulevard, my pace faster than usual, my mind bombarded with images of the Boarhouse: the boots, the cleavage, the miniskirt, the fat American. My right hand is swollen, my entire body aches. As I instinctively turn left at Bolshaya Nikitskaya, I start to recall the Amsterdam moment, now three years ago, when I found out about Katya's affair. I remember how the entire university knew by then, everybody except me, and how the thought of Katya with her law professor sparked a physical ache, a painful emptiness in my chest, not unlike what I now feel thinking of Lena and her Boarhouse companion.

At the end of the street I turn right and walk until I reach the Russian State Library, still known as Biblioteka Imeni Lenina, with its enormous neoclassical columns, and I approach Dostoyevsky's statue, a mournful Fyodor Mikhailovich facing the street, far from the entrance, his back to the library like a punished schoolboy. The soul is the depository of human contradictions, of the eternal struggle between God and evil, he says to me, and I walk towards Okhotny Ryad and then Red Square, following the tourists – the guests of the capital, as they are called in metro announcements. As I cross the cobblestones of Red Square, which, it being a Sunday, is crowded, I find some comfort in seeing myself surrounded by other people. The fact that all these strangers don't know about Lena, that they go on with their business as if nothing had happened, enjoying their morning stroll through the heart of Moscow – unperturbed by the thoughts in my head – makes me feel somehow lighter, less oppressed. I pass by the fairy-tale towers of St Basil's Cathedral, which always strikes me as smaller and less impressive than in postcards and books, and I see tourists taking pictures of each other, dyevs from the provinces posing like models, one hand on the hip, the other behind the head, walking away from the camera to fit the entire cathedral and the Kremlin into one single frame. I walk past, knowing from my own experience that it's impossible to take a good photo of Red Square, that the ploschad is too three-dimensional to be captured in a single image and that, whatever the chosen angle, the person in the picture will look small and insignificant.

I cross the bridges, over the dark waters, onto the southern bank, then wander into Pyatnitskaya Ulitsa, which feels like ancient Moscow, with its low buildings and pastel-coloured façades.

Around the metro station there is an explosion of life, Muscovites emerging from the subterranean stairways like disciplined ants, couples holding hands, a stand selling honey and soap, a babushka selling flowers, and for the first time I feel like buying flowers, a nice bouquet for Tatyana, I think, that will make her happy. I approach the babushka, and choose the biggest bouquet. Yellow roses. Twenty-five yellow roses, the babushka says.

I walk towards the river, retracing my steps, and I feel awkward with the flowers, wondering if I should carry the bouquet upright in front of me or if it's fine to clasp it by the stems with the flowers pointing at the ground, and people are looking at me, the muzhik who's bringing flowers to his woman, and, in the midst of my pain, the idea provokes – I think – a smile on my face.

It then occurs to me that I didn't buy the flowers for Tatyana. For a split second my mind replaces the image of Tatyana receiving the yellow roses with that of Lena. I'm aware that I cannot give the flowers to Lena, that it's Tatyana who will be coming home tonight after the weekend at her aunt's, and I wonder if I want Lena because I know she won't be there, and, maybe, if Tatyana were the one who had disappeared from my life, I would feel the same about her.

I cross the bridges back onto the northern bank, turn left and follow the southern wall of the Kremlin towards the cathedral of Christ the Saviour. I walk on the left pavement, by the river. I know Christ the Saviour is gigantic, an enormous building, and yet, as I look up at the distant golden dome under the lead-coloured sky, I'm surprised to see that it looks small and boxy, lacking the elongated elegance of European cathedrals, as if a small Russian country church had been artificially magnified and placed in the centre of Moscow.

There is a sad story about Christ the Saviour. When Sergey first told me about it, I was surprised to learn that it is in fact a brand new construction. Now, as I walk towards the cathedral with the yellow roses in my hand, I wonder where Sergey is, and I think of Ira and wonder if they got back together, and I regret having lost touch with them, because they were my real Russian friends, and back then, when we met, life was simpler and Moscow was such a great place.

Christ the Saviour was initially built to thank God for Napoleon's defeat in 1812, Sergey had told me after a dinner in his apartment with Ira and Sergey's mum, as he showed me a series of black and white photographs he had taken of the building. A couple of tsars worked on it but the whole construction wasn't finished until the 1860s, when it stood as the largest Orthodox cathedral ever made. The cathedral was erected by the Moskva river, its golden dome within sight of the Kremlin. But the soviets, who dropped the capitalisation of the word God and wrote bog instead of Bog, had other plans for the site. In 1931, under Stalin's orders, the cathedral was dynamited and reduced to rubble.

I walk along the naberezhnaya and cross under the Bol-shoy Kammeny Bridge, and on my left across the river I see the House on the Embankment, with its giant Mercedes-Benz logo, and I'm thinking that Tatyana can give me calm and security, but she can't reach as deep into me as Lena. Lena hurts. And I wonder if perhaps it's precisely the pain I'm attracted to, and pain is what people search for when they say they want love. Pain is what keeps us awake, what makes us feel alive. We need pain as a reference point, to recognise and measure happiness. Why, otherwise, would we choose to chase only those who can hurt us?

The depository of human contradictions, of the eternal struggle between God and evil.

After the cathedral was destroyed, Sergey said, a grandi-ose project started to take shape, the construction of the Palace of the Soviets, which, Stalin hoped, would be the tallest building in the world. According to plans, the palace was to be crowned by a giant statue of Lenin, his arm raised to the sky, pointing at the horizon towards a better future. Construction of the palace began in the mid-1930s – the riverbank was dug, the foundations were laid for what was to be a monument to the workers' paradise.

I know I can't stop thinking about Lena because she's no longer within my reach. I want the Lena of my first days in Moscow – not Boarhouse Lena, but Propaganda Lena – and suddenly it occurs to me that maybe back then she was

301

already a whore. I want a Lena who no longer exists. I want a Lena who perhaps never existed.

The Palace of the Soviets was not meant to be. When Russia was attacked, this time by Hitler, construction had to stop. It never resumed. There were technical problems, the site kept flooding, and superstitious Muscovites believed it was a divine punishment for having destroyed the cathedral in the first place. For many years, the site of what was intended to be the tallest building in the world, the ultimate monument to the working class, was nothing more than an empty construction site, a monument to abandoned dreams.

It was in the late 1950s, under Khrushchev, that the site was turned into an immense swimming pool, the biggest open-air pool in the world. Muscovites loved the swimming pool, especially in summer months, Sergey had told me, and now I wish the site had remained a pool – a man-made lake, perfectly round, as I had seen in photos – in which I could take a dip and refresh my body, relieve my headache, purify my soul, but I'm heading not towards a public swimming pool but an enormous cathedral with a golden dome, because, after the perestroika, the mayor of Moscow and the Patriarch of all Russians decided to rebuild Christ the Saviour exactly as it had been before the soviet demolition.

The cathedral was newly completed when I arrived in town, so, as I walk towards the golden dome with my bouquet of yellow roses I think, we have this in common, we're both newcomers to Moscow, Christ the Saviour and me, and it's a bizarre name, and I'd never thought much about Christ, whom I'd always considered a mythological figure, at least until I read Bulgakov and saw Yeshua pleading with Pontius Pilate for his life and then it occurred to me that maybe Christ had been, after all, a real man.

As I arrive at the esplanade in front of Christ the Saviour I feel ridiculous. Who the fuck am I kidding with such a big bouquet of flowers. The twenty-five yellow roses feel heavy and treacherous.

I turn towards the river and throw the bouquet of flowers into the air, over the balustrade, with all the strength and anger I can muster, and I try to project them far into the river, but the bouquet spins clumsily, loses one rose in the air, and drops into the water, making a pitiful splash, like an injured bird. The water is black and the yellow roses floating on the Moskva river make me think of death.

PART SIX

Sonya's Faith

53

WHILE OLYA, MASHA AND Irina, Chekhov's three sisters, spend their idle existence hoping for things to get better, Sonya Marmeladova holds no such illusions. Forced into prostitution as a teenager, living in misery at the very bottom of Peter society, she knows her life is, and will always be, nothing but shit.

In Dostoyevsky's *Crime and Punishment*, Sonya stands as a powerful symbol of universal suffering. With Christian resignation, she has accepted that her existence will be a long road of martyrdom. If she expects any reward, an end to her suffering, it's not something that will come in this life. For Sonya, it's not a choice between happiness and meaning – it's all sudba, God's will. Put on Earth to suffer for others, she leaves it up to her creator to judge after death.

With Sonya, Fyodor Mikhailovich created the antithesis of

Raskolnikov. Although she is — like Raskolnikov — a sinner, her sins do serve a purpose and, in the end, hurt no one but herself. Sonya sostradaet, co-suffers. She's a whore because she needs to feed her family. She endures pain for the sake of others. It's part of the cross she bears — the burden of humanity. Yet, Sonya — the whore, the social outcast — is, from a moral point of view, the purest and most honest character in the novel.

We find out, early in the story, that Sonya's occupation is not a temporary thing; she holds a yellow ticket, which makes her an official prostitute. She has crossed a threshold of sin and social stigma with no return. Unlike the three sisters, who can still dream about a better future — if only they could go back to Moscow — for Sonya, becoming a whore is not something that can be undone.

For Sonya Marmeladova there is no Moscow to go back to.

Still, she finds purpose in life. When Sonya meets Raskolnikov, soon after he has committed his crime, she becomes his maternal whore, the figure who will nurse him and wrestle him onto the path of salvation. In a famous scene, Sonya opens her New Testament and reads aloud to Raskolnikov. What she reads is the story of Lazarus, from the Gospel of John. Lazarus's resurrection, four days after his death, is proof of Christ's divinity. In a similar manner, Sonya aims to resurrect Raskolnikov's soul, which, in her eyes, has been dead ever since his crime.

When Raskolnikov, who's now losing it with the psychological burden of his crime, confesses the murders to Sonya, the first thing she says is, you've done this to yourself. For her, Raskolnikov's crime is not a question of man's law and order. It amounts to spiritual suicide.

Sonya will be able to forgive Raskolnikov though, because all men are equal before God — and God forgives.

Knowing that redemption must start with repentance, Sonya asks Raskolnikov to confess his crime to the authorities. Carrying her New Testament, she pesters Raskolnikov with ideas about God and forgiveness. Raskolnikov challenges her religious convictions and goes as far as questioning the very existence of God. Sonya does not consider it necessary to argue. All she says: I believe in God. Sonya's faith is unshakeable, the source of her strength.

And so, Raskolnikov, whose soul can no longer bear the anguish of his guilt, finally decides to give himself up. Sonya hands him her small wooden cross, the cross that she had been wearing all along, the cross of Christ, the Saviour. On the way to the police station, where he is to confess his crime, Raskolnikov follows Sonya's advice and stops at the Hay Market, where — in the pivotal scene of the novel — he kisses the ground and asks the world for forgiveness.

Facing a final test, Raskolnikov finds out at the police station that he could easily get away with the murders. But, thanks to Sonya's spiritual guidance, he knows that, even if he is never caught by men, in the eyes of God he will not get away with his crime. Raskolnikov has understood that in order to be saved he needs to pay: he must endure his punishment. He must carry the cross.

In the epilogue, we see Raskolnikov a year and a half later, serving his sentence in a prison in Siberia. Sonya has moved to the city nearby and visits him often. It's only in Siberia that Raskolnikov's spiritual resurrection can take place, in the vastness of nature, under God, far from the infested streets of the city.

For Dostoyevsky, our existence is a lifelong struggle. In a life with no bright future, Sonya embraces spirituality as a way to cope with suffering. Without that blind acceptance of her own destiny, without her unwavering faith – without the existence of God, really – Sonya's life would have no meaning whatsoever.

54

'WHERE WOULD YOU LIKE to be in five years?' I asked.

It was a warm summer day and Tatyana and I were strolling along the shaded alleys of Novodevichy cemetery. We had spent the morning visiting the adjacent convent, an impressive citadel with ancient churches that Tatyana had been wanting to see. Now we were wandering among trees and tombstones – map in hand – searching for the VIPs of recent Russian history.

'Five years,' Tatyana said. 'What do you mean?'

'Like, if you could choose your dream life, your perfect job, the best city to live in, everything. Where would you like to be?'

'Why five years?'

'Just because.'

'What's happening in five years?' Tatyana was wearing

bright red lipstick and a silvery top that sparkled every time we crossed a sunny patch.

'Forget about the five years,' I said as we stepped onto a gravel path. 'That's not the point. What I'm asking is where do you want to be in the future? What do you want to do with your life?'

'That's a serious question,' she said. 'If we keep going in circles, in five years we might be stuck in Novodevichy, still looking for Chekhov's grave.' She laughed and took hold of my arm. A fresh breeze shook the trees above our heads, releasing a snowfall of white blossom.

'In five years I'll be almost thirty,' Tatyana said. 'I want to have children before I'm thirty.'

'What about work?'

'I don't care about work. That's less important.'

'Why so?'

'Family is the most important thing,' she said, brushing the little flowers off her shoulders. 'A woman cannot be a woman without children.'

'But professionally,' I said, 'would you continue to work in real estate or would you rather do something else?'

'I don't know. I don't care, really. You know work is not the most important thing for me. I'm not a man.'

I picked some petals from Tatyana's curls, then brushed my hand over my own hair. 'Women also care about work,' I said.

We walked in silence for a couple of minutes, then came across a large memorial of someone who must have been a famous soviet pilot, an aviation pioneer perhaps, a life-size statue of the man resting his hand on an aeroplane propeller. A group of older Russians – tourists from the provinces, I guessed – were taking pictures of each other in front of the memorial.

'But imagine you have it all,' I said to Tatyana. 'A beautiful family and a great man who would take care of you. What would you do?'

'Well,' Tatyana said with a smile, 'if I have a great man to take care of me I won't have to work. I'll stay at home and raise my children. I work now because I need the money. I don't want a career. I'm not a modern Western woman. You know that.'

'You don't have to be modern or Western, some women just want to have an interesting career. We are in the twenty-first century, you can have both: a job *and* a family.'

'I'm Russian,' she said as we moved towards a sunnier alley lined with little chapels. 'I don't believe in this equality thing between men and women. We are not equal, you and me, we want different things in life. I don't want to be like a man any more than you want to be like a woman.'

'Would you like to live abroad?'

'Do you want to take me abroad? Martin, what is this? Are you going to propose? Here, in a cemetery?' She turned to me and bent her knee ceremoniously, bowing her head, one hand up in the air, the other lifting an imaginary long skirt. She was laughing.

'Stop it. I'm just curious, we've never talked about this.' I glanced down at our map, trying to figure out if perhaps the pilot was on it and could help us find our way to Chekhov.

Tatyana gripped my arm. 'Let's just walk around,' she said, removing the map from my hand and sliding it into her handbag. 'We'll find it.'

We strode in silence among the sea of graves. Rulers, generals, scientists, poets, writers, composers, actors, painters – an elitni crowd like no other, an impressive number of world-famous personalities who had undoubtedly made great contributions to humanity. Yet it occurred to me that, considering the scale of the cemetery, the big names were but a chosen few. The majority of the Novodevichy graves were occupied by people whose lives had not justified a mark on the visitors' map. Lives that were already being forgotten.

'I'd like to live in Russia,' Tatyana said.

We had stopped by a cluster of headstones with elaborate wrought-iron fences that formed garden-like plots. I wondered if it was all right to sit on the enclosed stone benches and picnic tables or if they were reserved for the relatives of the dead.

'Look around,' Tatyana said, sweeping her arm over the rows of graves. 'So much greatness. Why would I want to live anywhere else? Russia is the best country in the world. Of course I'd love to travel and see other places. But, to live, I'll always prefer Russia. This is my home, my rodina, where my friends and family live. I love the food. Everybody speaks Russian.'

'In Moscow? Would you like to live always in Moscow?'

'Martin, why are you asking me all these things?'

'I don't know,' I said, resuming our stroll. 'Just wondering.'

'I wouldn't mind going back to Novosibirsk. Live closer to

my family. Or somewhere else in Siberia, in Altai for example. Everything is much cheaper over there. You can buy property for next to nothing if you compare to Moscow prices. It's very beautiful, there are lakes and mountains and the air is so fresh. A better place to raise children. And people are much friendlier than in Moscow.'

The crunching sound of our shoes on the gravel made me think of fresh snow and, for a fleeting moment, I missed the feeling of winter. 'Moscow has its advantages,' I said.

'Of course. Moscow is the cultural capital of the world. We don't have that many theatres and museums in Siberia. I could always come to visit every now and then.'

'What about the weather?' I said. 'Winters must be harsh in Siberia.'

'As my grandma says, there is no such thing as bad weather, only bad clothes.' Tatyana stopped and took a deep breath. For a moment her bright gaze was lost above the graves. A tiny white flower remained trapped in her curls, just beneath her ear. 'You know what?' she said finally. 'If I lived in Siberia, I would not care about the weather.'

55

It was Friday afternoon and the entire city was fleeing to the dacha for the weekend. Dachnikis moved around the crowded platform of Kursky Vokzal, lugging overloaded plastic bags, beer crates, sacks of coal, birdcages, potted plants, metal buckets, grills, toolkits.

Tatyana introduced me to Marina, who had dyed black hair and a sickly Goth-looking face, and Anton, Marina's boyfriend, a tall lad with cropped blond hair and a crushing handshake. Anton was carrying a crate of Baltika. I was told that the third couple would join us at the dacha on Saturday morning.

As the train arrived, Marina and Tatyana pushed themselves through the crowd, leaped into the wagon and claimed four seats facing each other. The elektrichka began to move and Anton opened four bottles of warm beer. It was hot inside the train and through the open windows I could hear the deafening metallic noise of the wheels grinding on the rails. Within a few minutes everybody on the train was drinking and eating – the entire wagon smelled of smoked sausage, dried fish and pickled cabbage.

Tatyana had insisted that we spend the weekend at a dacha with her two girlfriends from work and their muzhiks. To overcome my initial resistance, Tatyana had argued that it was very important to her that I meet her friends, that she'd been accused of having an imaginary boyfriend.

The elektrichka advanced through the outskirts of Moscow, snaking through large suburbs of identical buildings and industrial zones, until the landscape became greener.

Every few minutes, someone would show up at the wagon door and, screaming above the noise, would address the crowd as respected passengers, thereafter touting a bewildering array of merchandise: out-of-date women's magazines, sets of knives, dried fish, ice cream, potato peelers, pens, pads.

Anton kept opening bottles of beer and, by the time we arrived at our destination, two hours later, we were done with what I'd thought were the drinks for the entire weekend. At the station's produkty magazin we bought more beer, four bottles of Moldovan wine, three bottles of vodka and two bags of ice. Then, for only forty rubles, a zhiguli drove us down dirt roads, following Marina's directions, until, after twenty minutes, we arrived at the dacha.

Wooden walls, flaking paintwork, tin roof: a classic soviet dacha. The garden was overgrown but charming, scattered with flowers and vegetables. On one side of the plot, next to the fence, grew an enormous cherry tree. Marina insisted that Tatyana and I take the master bedroom, which was on the first floor, at the top of steep wooden stairs.

While the girls opened the windows and dusted the house, Anton and I went to the nearby forest to gather soil and twigs for the outdoor toilet. Back in the dacha, Anton grabbed two bottles of beer from a tub of ice and handed one to me. We sat on plastic chairs in the garden.

I took long sips of chilled beer, listened to the birds and to the chatter of people in neighbouring dachas. I could hear the girls in the kitchen chopping vegetables, Tatyana's laughter rising above the sound of the knife hitting the wood. She was unusually chatty, full of energy, clearly enjoying herself. Soon – overwhelmed by the aromas of fresh dill and chopped cucumbers that hung in the air – I began to feel little currents of beer-induced joy sparking in my brain.

'This is the life,' Anton said.

From a nearby dacha I heard the voice of an old lady teaching a boy to unearth potatoes. For some reason, per-haps because of the old lady's didactic tone, it made me think of Lyudmila Aleksandrovna. If this was the kind of soviet life she longed for – a simple life, without the stress of modern Moscow – I could understand why Lyudmila Aleksandrovna was in a permanent state of nostalgia. Perhaps, it now occurred to me, she was right and the soviet system provided everything that people needed to enjoy life, the essential things, without the infinite choices that made our capitalist existence stressful and complicated.

Tatyana and Marina set the outside table with candles. For dinner we had cucumber and tomato salad with dill, boiled potatoes with butter and dill, sliced kolbasa, cheese and black bread. There was an additional bowl of freshly cut dill on the table. We had wine, but agreed not to open the vodka. After dinner we moved inside to avoid the mosquitoes and had tea with jam. We played a few rounds of a card game they taught me, and Tatyana and I lost, but she kept smiling. We opened another bottle of cheap Moldovan wine. Tatyana told a couple of anekdots – the narration interrupted by her own laughter – and I realised that it was the first time I'd seen her really drunk. We went to bed soon after midnight.

'Thanks for coming to the dacha,' Tatyana said, kissing me goodnight.

'I'm glad we came,' I said, just before falling asleep.

The next morning Tatyana and I woke up early and decided to go to the forest for a walk. My head was aching from all the beer and wine. We walked down the creaking stairs, trying not to make too much noise, and stepped into the fresh air and the smell of wet grass. Following a dirt road, we wandered through the village. Most dachas were closed up, but a couple of neighbours were taking advantage of the morning chill to work on their gardens. We crossed a small meadow and reached a thick line of trees.

Inside the forest, the air was cooler and moist and, as we walked, I started to forget about my headache.

'So nice here,' I said.

I kissed Tatyana. She wasn't wearing any make-up and her

319

beautiful hair was all messy. Holding hands, we followed a path under the trees. I was a bit disappointed that the ground was scattered with beer cans, vodka bottles and plastic bags. Tatyana pointed at different trees and told me their names in Russian, but to me they all looked the same. After five minutes the forest ended abruptly. The trees had been cleared, we were facing a construction site.

'Look,' I said, 'they're building new dachas.'

'These are not dachas,' Tatyana said. 'They are cottages. For New Russians. They are big and ugly.'

For a few seconds I pictured Tatyana and myself in one of these cottages, taking up gardening, having friends over for beers and shashliks.

We retraced our steps back into the forest.

'Maybe we can pick mushrooms,' I suggested.

Tatyana laughed. 'It's not the season, stupid.'

We stopped by a tree and kissed. I grabbed her ass and moved up to her breasts. She closed her eyes. We hadn't had sex in a few days. We kissed with increased intensity and, to my surprise, she unzipped her jeans and pulled them down, together with her underwear.

'I adore you,' she whispered in my ear.

She was now wearing a T-shirt but naked from the waist down. She dropped to her knees and unbuttoned my jeans. I grabbed her mass of blonde curls and looked around, worried someone would see us. Only trees and rubbish. When I was hard, she pulled me to the ground.

'Hold on,' I said. I was now sitting with my back against the tree.

'Don't worry, it's safe. I've just had my period.'

Then, she positioned herself on top of me, her apple green eyes bursting with life.

When we returned to the dacha, Marina was making tea in the kitchen.

'Where have you been, love birds?' she said.

Tatyana blushed.

We all sat at the outdoor wooden table with steaming cups of tea, pecking at a plate of bread and cheese. Above the cherry tree, the sky was blue and clear and immense.

It wasn't a lake, really, but a large pond with stagnant water. By the shore, the ashes of old campfires were surrounded by broken glass and rubbish. I hid my disappointment, but couldn't help comparing the muddy waterhole to the lake I'd pictured in my mind, something like the beautiful lake Pavel and Marina visited with their friends in lesson six of *Russian As We Speak It*.

The better spots around the shore had been taken by other dachnikis, so we had to set our blankets on a sandy slope a few metres from the water. We all changed into swimming clothes. There were six of us now. Diana had arrived earlier in the morning with her boyfriend, coincidentally also called Anton. Tall, freckled, ginger-haired, Diana was wearing a red bikini a size too small.

After swimming we lay in the sun drinking beer with bread and kolbasa. I put my head on Tatyana's lap and closed my eyes, letting the sun warm my face. Tatyana stroked my hair and I found myself thinking of Lena, when she came to watch me play football in Kazakova and we lay in the sun. I wondered where Lena might be now, and why she hadn't answered any of my messages after our encounter at the Boarhouse. I finished my beer. With the sun warming my skin and the sound of Russian chatter in the background, I fell asleep.

Back at the dacha, the Antons started to prepare the mangal to cook the shashliks. I went into the kitchen and offered to help the girls with the salads.

'Go help the men with the meat,' Tatyana ordered, mock-threatening me with a large knife.

Dinner. Vodka. Toasts. We were sitting around the table, eating grilled meat, which I found delicious, and I wasn't sure if Diana was looking at me or if it was just the vodka clouding my head. I was haunted by the image of her red bikini. She was now wearing a white skirt and a white shirt – the milkiness of which accentuated her fiery red hair. I felt Tatyana squeezing my hand. Tatyana was listening attentively to one of the Antons, who was sharing his secret recipe for the shashlik marinade. I didn't know if Tatyana was squeezing my hand because she'd noticed my attention drifting towards Diana or if she meant it as a spontaneous act of affection. I tried to focus on what Anton was saying, something about yoghurt and herbs, but I was missing most of it – he was speaking in drunken chubak slang, and I wasn't used to Russian spoken by men.

We drank and drank, until I couldn't keep my eyes open.

My brain shut down, my stomach lurched. I stood up, staggered down to the toilet hut, closed the door behind me and vomited. I made an effort to keep it a silent puke, which I managed to place entirely into the shitting hole, and then I threw a few twigs and a bit of soil on it, as I had been instructed. When I came back to the table I felt better.

I forced myself to drink water, and then Marina made tea, but I was too wasted to put anything other than water down my throat. I needed to lie down.

'I think I'm going to bed,' I said as I got up from the table.

Tatyana stood up, looked at me, laughed. 'Let's go, my little drunkard.'

I couldn't sleep. I wanted to let it all out — vodka, wine, shashlik, salad — but I didn't have the strength to crawl out of bed and go all the way to the toilet. I closed my eyes and tried to focus on soothing thoughts but what I saw was the lake and Diana in the red bikini and the table strewn with food and vodka and the cherry tree, and it was only when I heard Lyudmila Aleksandrovna shouting that I was a superfluous man that I realised I was dreaming. I forced my consciousness to abandon the drunken dream and return to the room, where the air was now steamy. I was sweating. Tatyana was fast asleep, breathing rhythmically. I tried to keep my eyes open for a while. I threw one of my legs out of the bed, to the floor, but, after a couple of minutes, I felt I was about to be sick again and decided not to risk it any longer. I tumbled down the stairs, holding the walls, trying not to make too much noise, but the floorboards creaked all the same. As I crossed the garden towards the toilet, wearing nothing but my underwear, my stomach lurched once more, and I managed to reach the hut just in time. I knelt down over the hole, which smelled of fresh shit, and vomited at length.

Feeling better, I spat in the hole, wiped my mouth with toilet paper and stepped into the fresh air. As I was about to go back inside the dacha, I saw Diana sitting on the grass.

'What are you doing here?' I asked.

She was wearing the white shirt but her legs were now uncovered, extended in front of her. 'Couldn't sleep.'

'And the others?'

'Everybody's sleeping,' she said. 'You OK?'

'I've been better.' I sat next to her, keeping my breath away from her face. The ground felt wet.

Diana drew in her long legs and embraced them, her head now resting on her knees. 'You shouldn't try to drink as much as Russian men.'

'Do you know any stars?' I asked.

'Over there.' She pointed above the cherry tree. 'I think that's the Great Bear.'

I moved closer to her and with my eyes followed the direction in which she was pointing. I tried to swallow as much saliva as possible to kill the smell of puke on my breath.

'That must be Orion,' I said, pointing to the sky.

'Where?'

'There. I think.' I grabbed her arm and directed it towards a place in the sky where Orion may or may not have been. When I dropped my arm I held her hand.

'Here, zagorod, you forget about everything,' she said,

clutching my hand. 'It's like a different life. Moscow feels so far away.'

A dog was barking in another dacha. I put my arm around Diana and she leaned her head on my shoulder. I swallowed more saliva. We remained in silence for a minute or so, our hands clasped. Then I kissed her. She kissed me back. We kissed for a couple of minutes. I could hardly breathe. I pushed her back on the ground, my left hand under her shirt. She rolled away and, just when I thought she was about to get up and leave, she took her shirt off. She was wearing no bra.

'Let's go to the forest,' I said.

'Ne nado. Everybody's sleeping.' Then she rolled her knickers down her long legs.

All lights were off at the dacha. I took off my own underwear.

I lay next to her, kissing her neck, holding her breasts, breathing heavily but realising in a panic that I wasn't ready. I tried to calm down, focused on her elongated body, on her pretty freckled face. I rubbed my groin against her thighs for a minute or so but, to my horror, my body was not reacting.

Diana put her hand between my legs. 'Relax,' she said.

'I really want you,' I whispered, embarrassed.

'I want you too.'

We kissed, and she tried for a while, but down there nothing worked.

'Sorry,' I said. 'I drank too much.'

'Don't worry. Let's go to sleep.'

*

Back in bed, Tatyana remained in the same position I'd left her, face up. Her breathing was heavier now, with a hint of a snore.

My head was flooded with dark, impenetrable thoughts that vanished as soon as they appeared, leaving traces of bitterness. A black hole was growing inside me.

Tatyana remained peaceful in her sleep.

I kissed her.

She rolled over and dropped an arm over my chest. Her body exuded warmth and moisture.

'I love you,' I whispered.

Tatyana didn't react. She was sleeping.

56

THE LATE-AUGUST MORNING was fresh and lovely. I was sitting on the terrace of Coffee Mania, reading *The Master and Margarita*. I felt cheerful as I nibbled my slice of Napoleon cake and sipped my coffee, glancing occasionally at the square and the trees and the façade of the Tchaikovsky conservatory.

Ever since Tatyana had moved into my flat for most of the week, I felt as if my body had more energy to face my Moscow days. This new vitality didn't come so much from the novelty of sharing my flat with Tatyana, I thought, as from the fact that, coincidentally, I was sleeping better at night.

Besides, things had changed since the draining weekend by the lake. In the days that had followed our trip to the dacha, I'd felt a gradual but definite change in my mental state—an unexpected re-set of my inner self. The thought of meeting a new girl — which had in the past motivated a large number of my daily actions — now made me feel exhausted. I couldn't face the prospect of taking someone to Pyramida or Café Maki for the first time, of having to deal with all the misplaced expectations. After almost three years in Moscow, I realised, I couldn't be bothered to meet more Russian women.

I finished my coffee, raised my empty cup to order another one.

These days, when Tatyana visited her aunt for the weekend, I would usually stay home in the evenings, enjoying the novelty of waking up fresh the next day. Cooking, walking, reading. These activities, which at present occupied the greater part of my day, felt somewhat meaningful. Even on the rare occasions when I'd gone clubbing, it had been mostly to catch up with the brothers. The time had come for me to do other things. Perhaps, I thought as I looked around the square, I could start writing my thesis. After all, I had collected enough material. My red notebooks were brimming with observations.

The waitress brought my second cup of coffee with a smile. Unable to concentrate on *The Master and Margarita*, which I was reading in Russian for the first time, I closed the book. I looked at good old Tchaikovsky, who was sitting outside the conservatory, in the middle of the square, his right arm over a lectern, his left hand half raised, as if asking people in the street for silence. The muted notes of *Swan Lake* tried to emerge from a remote corner of my memory, carrying the forgotten sadness of another time, of another life, of Amsterdam.

I glanced back at the book. The cover featured a black and white sketch of Margarita flying on a broomstick. I started to picture myself as Bulgakov's Master. I'd gone through a similar mental exercise in the early days of Yulya Karma, but now I was considering the book from a different angle. I was wondering why, among all the women in Moscow, it was Margarita the Master was obsessed with. What was it that made Margarita irreplaceable?

If you thought about it, it was a matter of chance that they'd met in the first place, Margarita and the Master, when she was carrying a bouquet of yellow flowers. I began to think of how most relationships are based on a random encounter, a set of small interlinked events that lead to the fateful meeting. It was Margarita that the Master had met, but it could have been any other woman. Then, once things get complicated, with the Devil coming to Moscow and all, the Master could have decided to move on, to forget Margarita. He doesn't. The way Tatyana doesn't forget Onegin. Or Karenina doesn't forget Vronsky. Or Liza doesn't forget Lavretsky. Moving on is the easy way out, the path that's never chosen, at least not in books. For some reason, in most novels, once you've made a romantic choice, even if it's a random choice, you stick to it. And you accept all the suffering that comes with it. This is, after all, a fundamental premise in classic literature: a lover is irreplaceable.

And yet, this kind of love, the maddening attraction we read about in books, is nothing but a literary device, I thought, an author's trick to endow characters with strong motivations. In real life feelings are more malleable —

suffering is optional. If things go wrong, you can move on and search for someone else.

Take Dushechka, in Chekhov's story, who's happy as long as she has *someone* to love, to worry about, regardless of who the recipient of her affection is. Maybe Dushechka's kind of love, a strong feeling whose object is replaceable, is the real kind of love.

I thought about Tatyana. If she were taken from me by a Devil-like figure, or if she decided to leave me for someone else, should I suffer and fight for her? Couldn't I just move on to the next girl?

All this was new to me. Had I understood these things earlier, before Moscow, I wouldn't have had to go through the pain Katya had inflicted on me. Now, when I looked back at my time in Amsterdam, I wondered why I hadn't just moved on, like Dushechka. Why had I decided to suffer, as if I were a character in a novel?

After Katya came Lena and after Lena came Tatyana. In the end, in an unplanned manner, I had replaced the object of my affection. But what I felt now was not an endless capacity for love — as Tolstoy had said of Dushechka — but rather a comfortable degree of nonchalance. Like the Master with Margarita, my relationship with Tatyana had also evolved from a casual encounter: the moment she showed up at Kamergersky to show Colin an apartment. Our being together had been determined by a series of random actions without much individual meaning in themselves — random actions that, put together, marked the direction of my life.

This bothered me. Maybe Colin was right and the one thing

to do was to forget about relationships and fuck around. But then, if we accept this readiness to replace a lover, to care about nothing, life itself dissipates into Chekhovian lightness. With nothing to care about, how do we go about looking for happiness?

Perhaps the antidote to this weightlessness is to endow life with a forced sense of gravity. Choose to care about things. Choose to consider our relationships as a matter of life or death.

Once, when Lena had been crying in my flat – I no longer remember the reason – I asked her why she always made such a big drama about everything. Why couldn't we just have a happy relationship, without the tears and the shouting? 'If we don't suffer for it,' Lena had told me, 'how do we know our love is real?'

Buried in their mysterious soul, I thought, there is something that makes Russians avoid superficial joy and choose to pursue deeper, sadder feelings – something that makes them chase the resonance and aesthetic value of melancholy. Liza's choice. And, perhaps, they got it right.

I looked across the square at the statue of Tchaikovsky, thinking that I needed to care about Tatyana as if I were the protagonist of a Russian novel: without doubts. I must decide to be with her, I thought, and blindly take all the shit that comes with my decision. To relieve myself of the burden of choice, I now realised, I needed to believe in destiny. And accept pain. Like a Russian.

57

I HAD BEEN WANDERING around the centre for an hour. The morning heat was so unbearable that I decided to take refuge at the subterranean shopping centre in Okhotny Ryad. In the Internet café, I bought a cup of coffee and sat in front of a computer, enjoying the cooled air. I read a few international papers online, then responded to emails from family and old friends.

As I was walking out of the café, I received a text from Tatyana suggesting that we meet for lunch at Ris i Ryba, a sushi restaurant in the Dom na Naberezhnoy, the House on the Embankment. Sure, I texted back. I wandered among the shops, trying on clothes but buying nothing, and, when it was almost noon, I came up to the street.

There was nowhere to hide from the sun. I walked past the fountain with the horses, where a bunch of children were

332

messing around with the water, covering some nozzles in unison to increase the water pressure and catch distracted pedestrians by surprise. They seemed to be having a good time. I dragged my feet through the park, under the blasting sun, and reached the end of Aleksandrovsky Sad – my shirt, drenched in sweat, stuck to my back.

On the other side of the asphalted esplanade, across the river, stood the Dom na Naberezhnoy, crowned with its enormous Mercedes-Benz logo against the blue sky. The encircled three-pointed star was not entirely aligned with the façade of the building and, every time I walked by, I wondered if perhaps the logo was meant to rotate around a central axis that no longer worked. As I walked over the bridge towards the building, it occurred to me that, maybe, at sunset, the Mercedes-Benz shadow would reach across the river, towards the walls of the Kremlin, a reminder to Russian rulers of their country's defeat in its twentieth-century crusade against capitalism. The giant logo had probably been installed in the mid-1990s, when Russia, naively in love with the West, had embraced everything foreign with enthusiasm. I wondered if the country felt betrayed and, in my head, I imagined Russia as a woman writing a love letter – Tatyana's letter to Onegin – to an unresponsive and arrogant West who had arrived after the collapse of the Soviet Union, not so much to help with the reconstruction, but to oversee the country's capitulation and collect the spoils of the Cold War.

I entered the building through one of the southern entrances next to the Udarnik cinema, passed the okhrannik and went through a metal detector which I suspected hadn't worked for years. I took the lift to the first floor.

The doors opened and I stepped into the fresh, artificially cooled air. Soothing lounge music played in the background. The waiter, probably Kazakh or Uzbek – most waiters in Japanese restaurants were of Central Asian origin – was dressed in black trousers and a black shirt with a white collar. He led me along the central aisle, passing by the open kitchen and sushi belt, to a small table by the huge floor to ceiling window. I found the smell of boiled rice comforting. The window overlooked the road, the park, the river. I ordered green tea and waited for Tatyana.

Built in the early 1930s as a residence for the soviet nomenklatura, the Dom na Naberezhnoy had also hosted distinguished academics, war heroes and pretty much everybody who had been elitni back then. Other than ample apartments and the sushi restaurant, the residential complex boasted a cinema, a clinic, shops, a stolovaya, common spaces. But what made it a legendary building in Moscow was not just the social standing of its former inhabitants, but the fact that many of them had vanished during their stay. I had been told that the building contained an elaborate system of secret passages connected to the luxurious flats and that, at the peak of Stalin's repression, these corridors were used by the secret services to spy on the building's notorious inhabitants and snatch them in the middle of the night.

Tatyana arrived a few minutes after me and was escorted

to my table by the same waiter. She was wearing a white top with a scooped neckline, almost see-through. I could see the lacework of her bra. Her face was flushed from the heat, her eyes greener than ever, her blonde curls untied and airy. I served her tea and we ordered two lunch menus — mine with salmon sushi, hers with chicken teriyaki.

I asked Tatyana if she had ever shown any apartments in the Dom na Neberezhnoy.

'I showed a three-room apartment a few months ago,' she said. 'So expensive. This is one of the most exclusive buildings in Moscow. The views are very beautiful, you can see the churches inside the Kremlin.'

'Beautiful indeed,' I said, glancing out of the window.

'Most available flats are now rented by foreigners though. Russians don't want to live here.'

'Why's that?'

Tatyana tried to take a sip of tea, but it was too hot. She placed the cup back on the table. 'Because of the ghosts.'

'Ghosts?'

'You know, the spirits of dead people. The building is haunted.'

'Of course,' I said. 'Ghosts.'

'The building's residents were killed here during Stalin,' Tatyana said. 'Their spirits remain in the building.'

'And people believe in these things?'

'I wouldn't want to live in this building,' she said. 'Just in case.' She tried to smile, but I could see something was bothering her.

The waiter brought us bowls of miso soup. I held mine

with two hands and looked out the window. I could see the traffic thickening, cars crawling across the bridge with their windows open, then the river, dark and silent. The glass was thick and I could not hear the traffic or feel the heat. Like watching a silent movie.

'We need to talk,' Tatyana said.

This was unusual. Tatyana and I never needed to talk, at least not the kind of talk that needed to be announced. It had crossed my mind, walking in the heat on my way to Ris i Ryba, that she might want to discuss something in particular. Why hadn't she suggested lunch before she left for work that morning? In fact, I had felt a slight distancing in the last few days, a small drop in the temperature of our relationship, as if she were holding something against me. Nothing dramatic, just the tone of her voice or the way she wouldn't follow up on a conversation I initiated.

Perhaps Tatyana was about to suggest moving into my apartment on weekends as well, fully taking over what was once my separate life. I wasn't sure I was ready to give it up. I took a sip of miso soup and I prepared myself to defend the nature of our arrangement, to repel any threats to the status quo.

Tatyana left her bowl of soup on the table and held my hand. Her hand was warm from the soup.

'Martin, I'm temporarily,' she said, with a shaky voice, then stopped and looked at me, waiting for a reaction.

'In what sense?'

'You heard me.'

'I don't think I understood.'

Tatyana tried to smile. 'You did.'

'I didn't,' I said, a bit irritated. 'Temporarily what?'

At that moment the waiter brought our plates of salmon roll and chicken and two small bowls of seaweed salad. I took a pair of wooden chopsticks from their paper wrapping, split them and offered them to Tatyana. She accepted them with two hands, somewhat ceremoniously.

'I'm pregnant,' she said. In case I still didn't understand, she added, 'With a baby in my belly.'

That's when I really learned the difference between vremennaya, with a v, temporarily, and beremennaya, with a b, pregnant.

I saw that the line of cars was now stuck on the bridge, inching towards the centre, their exhaust pipes expelling smoke into the hot Moscow air. Old soviet cars, Ladas and Volgas, and new German cars owned by rich Russians. I could now recognise luxury models, at least those sold at Stepanov's dealership.

'How do you know?' I said, turning to Tatyana.

'Women know these things.'

'Have you been to a doctor?'

Tatyana's lips were shiny, the sunlight reflected on her lip-gloss. 'I took a test. I'm probably five or six weeks pregnant.'

'And you are sure it's mine?'

'Why do you even have to ask? You know you're the only man in my life.'

Giving myself time to think, I gazed at the river, focusing my eyes on the closest of the fountains. The water was pumped high into the air, with strength, and, in the cloud of falling drizzle, I could discern the timid shades of a rainbow.

Gradually, Tatyana's words started to become a reality, the concept of her pregnancy growing in my head, like a balloon inflating and occupying all the corners of my mind. But I wasn't exactly thinking about the life-shattering implications of the news, or pondering our options. For some reason, I found my mind preoccupied with Tatyana's teeth, the one imperfection on her face. It occurred to me that perhaps I should take Tatyana to the international medical centre and have her front teeth fixed.

When I looked back, Tatyana's face was red.

I held her hand. 'Everything will be OK,' I said.

She smiled.

Sunlight illuminated her from behind, a halo of bright light forming around her loose golden hair. She looked prettier than ever.

I kissed Tatyana across the table.

'Who have you told about this?' I asked.

'Nobody, I only found out this weekend. My breasts hurt a bit, and I was late, so I bought the test.'

'I thought we had been careful,' I said.

'Most of the time. These things happen. It must have been at the dacha, in the forest. Remember?'

'But you said it was safe.'

'Martin, I'm a grown woman. I want to have the baby.'

'We didn't plan this,' I said.

'You can't plan everything in life.'

A long-ago memory from a rainy day was now casting a shadow over my thoughts. 'Sudba,' I said.

'Yes.' Tatyana smiled. 'It's destiny.'

The food remained on the table, untouched. The waiter came to ask if everything was OK.

'Everything's good,' I said. Then, turning to Tatyana, I repeated, 'Everything's good.'

I looked at my sushi roll, poked at it with my chopsticks, unable to eat. When I looked up, Tatyana was having a go at her chicken.

58

SATURDAY MORNING, THE RAIN is streaming down the old windows of my Amsterdam flat. At the dining table, under the dim light of a shaky floor lamp, Katya and I are having breakfast. Moscow is, at this point, nothing but a remote possibility. We finish our omelette, discuss our plans for the weekend and, over a second cup of tea, Katya says, 'Martin, I'm pregnant.'

I remember the moment clearly because, later on, after she'd left me, I went back to it often, and the memory of that morning had a particular way of making me miserable. Katya is wearing a green Adidas T-shirt she used to borrow from me. We've placed a brick under the windowpane to lift the heavy wooden frame a little and let a fresh breeze into the flat. A few raindrops drip onto the carpet, but Katya says it's OK, leave the window open for a while. We're listening to Tchaikovsky's *Swan Lake*, a CD from Katya's small, classical-oriented music collection. She has just refilled our mugs with boiling water, not bothering to replace the used tea bags.

It's funny how the same episode of one's own life, viewed from different moments in time, acquires a different significance. Later on, after she'd left, I saw that morning, and Katya's pregnancy, not as a storm threatening to wreck my existence, but as a missed opportunity to start a new life.

But when she makes the announcement all I know is that Katya and I are not going to stay together much longer. Even if we haven't worked out the details of our separation – or indeed spoken about it – we're both aware that our cohabitation is a convenient and temporary arrangement, that, sooner or later, Amsterdam will come to an end. As far as I understand, we're both fine with this.

'This was not planned,' I say, once I've realised the gravity of the situation.

'So what?' Katya says. 'We can go ahead with it. I was planning to have children some day. It's as good a moment as any.' She's sitting upright, holding the cup of tea with two hands, her long black hair cascading over the green T-shirt. Her tone is neutral, her voice and body language unchanged from our previous conversation.

'But we hadn't planned this,' I insist.

'You can't plan everything in life,' she says. 'It's destiny.'

In the beginning, when Katya had just moved into my flat, she had mentioned a couple of times the possibility of a long-term relationship, even hinting at marriage. But I hadn't shown much enthusiasm for the idea and she'd never raised the issue again. Until that rainy Saturday morning.

'You can choose your own destiny,' I reply. I stand up, overcome by an urge to clear breakfast leftovers from the table. 'There are so many things I want to do.'

'It's not the end of your life,' she says. 'You can be a father and still do things.'

'It's not the same.'

'What's different?' she says. 'It'll be me taking care of the baby.'

'I'm too young.'

'Too young for what? You are twenty-four, a perfect age to start your own family.'

'Maybe in Minsk,' I say. 'Not in Europe.'

We talk about it all day. To me, her refusal to acknowledge that we have a choice doesn't seem the result of a moral dilemma. Uninitiated in the Russian notion of destiny, my feeling is that she just can't be bothered.

On Monday, I accompany Katya to a private clinic, where the medical procedure is explained to us. The best method, we're told, consists of forcing a miscarriage with a load of hormone pills. Katya seems relieved that the procedure doesn't require surgery.

Then, the night before taking the pills, Katya asks me if I'm sure I don't want to have the baby. Except she doesn't say *the* baby – she says *our* baby. At first, this irritates me. Hadn't we already taken a decision? But then I realise that, for Katya, asking me one last time is more of an obligation than genuine doubt.

'I'm sure,' I say, trying to make things easier for her.

In the end Katya spends two days in bed with cramps,

vomiting and crying. She drinks vodka. It hurts to see her like that — and I wish I could share some of her physical pain so that I'd stop feeling like the perpetrator of an unjust punishment. I stay next to her, trying to cheer her up, and, when everything's over and she's feeling better, I take her to an expensive Indonesian restaurant we'd always wanted to try, down on the main street. That night, over dinner, we don't talk much. A week later the whole issue is, as far as I can tell, forgotten. She never mentions it again.

A few months later, Katya is gone and I can't stop thinking about that Saturday morning. Unable to go back, I'm on a plane to Moscow.

59

About a hundred soldiers had been killed. At first, the news said the helicopter had crashed after a technical failure. Then, as the hours passed, the story started to change and, by Wednesday night, two days after the crash, they were no longer talking about an accident – it was a terroristicheskiy akt.

Tatyana and I were eating take-out pizza on the couch as we watched the news. The heavy transport helicopter, they were now saying, had been hit by surface-to-air missiles while carrying more than a hundred and forty Russian soldiers. The fatal missile had hit one of the engines as the helicopter was approaching a Russian military base near Grozny. The helicopter had then fallen onto the minefield that surrounded the base and, as a result, some of the survivors who had tried to escape had been blown up by the mines.

'Oh Bozhe,' Tatyana said. God. She was almost in tears.

An expert was saying that, according to investigators, the doors of the helicopter had jammed after the crash and the soldiers had been trapped inside the burning wreckage. Only the crew and about thirty soldiers, who had managed to escape through a small hatch, had survived the attack. The news anchor was referring to the incident as the 'new Kursk', in reference to the sinking of the nuclear submarine two years earlier, in August 2000, during my first summer in Moscow. The Russian president, they said, had declared a day of mourning.

Suddenly, in the middle of the news bulletin, which I was watching attentively, Tatyana wiped her hands, took the remote control from my side of the coffee table and flicked through the channels, stopping at Kanal Kultura, which was showing Russian ballet. This was unusual. Tatyana rarely touched the remote control.

'I want to know what happened,' I protested.

'We know what happened,' she said. 'I can't watch it any more.'

I could see in her face that she was deeply disturbed by the news. We had just been talking about the possibility of moving to Siberia, perhaps soon after the arrival of the baby. Maybe she felt the pain of those mothers who were mourning at that very moment across Russia.

'Let's watch something else,' she said. 'Please.'

As we watched a bunch of ballerinas hopping across the stage to the sound of what I guessed was Tchaikovsky, I wondered how many people in Moscow had switched channels, or looked away from the horrifying images of the helicopter burning with its human cargo inside. Although now that I think of it, so many years after that evening – I'm no longer sure if I saw the grainy images of the burning helicopter with Tatyana, or if I saw them later on, when I checked old footage on the Internet, trying to understand what had been going on in Chechnya during my time in Moscow.

60

THE METRO SPEEDS THROUGH the tunnels, crowded, rock-
ing passengers from side to side. The windows are open, the
noise deafening. It feels as if the wagon is about to derail,
hit a wall. Then the train brakes with ferocity, an invisible
force pushing passengers towards the front, and stops at
once. Across the carriage, a woman is sitting on the bench,
holding a little boy who stands between her knees. They
are everywhere. Not only in the metro. In the streets, in
shops, in restaurants. Children of all ages. Even during
my morning walks, I see children's playgrounds I hadn't
noticed before, with sandpits, swings and slides – hidden in
the courtyards of central Moscow.

As the train starts to move again, I grab the handrail. The
metro clanks through the tunnels. Everybody is silent, reading books or magazines or gazing at the floor, minding their

own business. It's only a few weeks since Tatyana told me about the baby and I hardly recognise myself.

In the days after Ris i Ryba I'd started to notice how my mind felt unexpectedly clearer, unclouded. Things I'd long held to be essential no longer seemed important. The thorn of Lena, for instance, which had been lodged inside my chest ever since the Boarhouse, disappeared at once; the pain of Lena turned into *a memory* of the pain. As if the person who had been crying outside the Boarhouse hadn't been me, but rather a fictional character in a book I'd read.

I hadn't told the brothers about Tatyana's pregnancy. Not yet. They would feel betrayed, I thought. Especially Colin. Only the week before, he had called me again, on Thursday night, trying to drag me to Propaganda. 'For old times' sake,' he'd said. I told him I wasn't feeling good, maybe next week. I didn't really mean it, and he knew it. I could feel his disappointment. But what the fuck, I'd wasted so many nights in Propaganda.

As the metro speeds up, I let go of the rail and I try to keep my balance, testing how long I can go without grabbing it again. I wonder if this mental transformation, the radical change of priorities in my life, is mostly a biological response to parenthood, an animal reaction over which I have little or no control.

The metro brakes to cross the bridge. Now I can hear the wheels toc toc tap on the rails, in beautiful rhythm. Tatyana is right, I think, it was all meant to happen. Her pregnancy fills me with tranquillity. So what if her love is purer than mine. With her I can live a virtuous existence, stop being superfluous. Everything is easier, I think, when choice is replaced by destiny. It feels as if, after rushing through life, my soul is slowing down.

I've been thinking about Siberia, the setting for a simpler life, where I could perhaps find the remnants of the real Russia. By starting a family with Tatyana, I think, I'm consciously stepping into the language-book universe of *Russian As We Speak It* — embracing not just the cultural and linguistic immersion, but also the simplification of my daily existence. One day, our lives will be nothing but a succession of daily routines, like the lives of Pavel and Marina: the post office, the supermarket, the restaurant, the park, the lake.

I glance around at the other passengers. Babushkas, old men, students, the mother with her child. They all look serious, grim. And so do I, I realise, spotting my reflection in the window. My face looks aged, my eyes sunken. My nose and mouth are connected by two deep shadows. Just then it occurs to me that, despite my new-found tranquillity, I too look sad and self-absorbed. As long as I don't open my mouth, I think, other passengers will be unable to see that I'm not Russian. Like them, I'm wearing dark clothes. My entire wardrobe is now brown or black, the result of almost three years in Moscow. During this gradual, unconscious transformation of my appearance, my body language and my facial expression must have become more sombre too. With this thought running through my mind, I try to force a smile, a Western smile, from my previous life, a simple social gesture meant to demonstrate friendly feelings towards my fellow passengers in the metro. But my experimental smile, which I direct at the woman and boy across the wagon, must have come out somewhat forced and absurd, even threatening, I realise, because the woman instinctively grabs her child tighter and looks away. I stop smiling. After all, what the fuck should I smile for. I don't need to prove anything to anyone.

I get off at Universitet. It's been a while since I last visited the campus. The academic year has just started and I can feel the buzz and excitement in the young students rushing around.

'Ready to work again?' Lyudmila Aleksandrovna says when she sees me. Nothing has changed in her office – except the kettle, a newer cordless model.

I raise my right hand to my forehead, saluting as a soviet pioneer. 'Always ready,' I say. Then I tell her about the books I've been reading and she says my Russian has improved. She seems happy to see me. I can't wait to finally start writing my PhD.

That night, back at home, I feel things falling into place. The beginning of a new life. I'm looking forward to winter, to the first snow of the season, to taking care of Tatyana as she gets bigger.

After dinner and a bit of TV, I sit on the couch, reading *The Seagull*. Tatyana lies with her head on my lap.

'I'm so tired these days,' she says, her eyes closed, her hand on her belly.

Then she falls asleep as I hold Chekhov's book in one hand and stroke her curls with the other.

61

LENA EMERGED FROM THE metro and marched across the square towards me. She was wearing a grey skirt and a grey jacket that stretched tight across her breasts. She looked elegant, refined, as if she were going to work in an office. Beneath Pushkin's statue, we kissed on the cheek. She suggested we go for a walk. We crossed through the perekhod, emerged on the other side of Tverskaya and strolled along the Boulevard. It was a fresh autumn morning, the path was carpeted with dry brown leaves.

She asked about my research at the university, about the brothers. I learned she was going to a new yoga centre now. She had finally found an instructor who was strict but inspiring.

We turned right at Malaya Bronnaya, kept on the sunny side of the street. It seemed to me that Lena walked with

351

more confidence than before, with a hint of arrogance in her gait, more aware perhaps of the impact she had on men. I was waiting for the right moment to tell her about Tatyana and the baby.

Weeks after our encounter at the Boarhouse, Lena had finally answered one of my messages and agreed to see me. I felt a strong need to end Lena's chapter in my life before I could move on to the next. But now that Lena was next to me, I didn't know where to start. I was enjoying her presence, always so physically intense, and all the memories that it triggered.

We reached Patriarshiye Prudy. The trees in the square were golden brown. We circled the pond, our feet crunching on dead leaves. The sun sparkled on the water. We passed the playground, full of children, then sat down on a bench facing the pond. Beneath the silvery surface, the water was dark and muddy. We stared at it in silence.

I wanted to tell Lena how it felt to know that I was going to become a father. I wanted to tell Lena how I had matured, how the person she used to know no longer existed. I wanted to tell Lena how I had learned to accept my destiny.

'Lena,' I said, 'you are a prostitute.'

She looked at me, her expression calm and peaceful. Then she bit her lower lip. 'What do you mean?'

'When I saw you last time,' I said. 'At the Boarhouse. With those guys.'

'I'm not a prostitute.' Her voice was soft.

A few metres away, a boy and a girl were feeding pieces of bread to a flock of excited ducks.

'How long have you been doing this?' I asked.

She shifted on the bench, as if hesitating between answering my question or standing up and walking away. 'Why do you care?' she said, staring at the pond. 'I'm a free person, Martin. I see whoever I want.'

'Were you sleeping around when we were together?'

'Is that why you wanted to see me?' she said. 'Bozhe moi.'

'Were you?' I insisted. 'Were you seeing other guys back then?'

'Of course not,' she said, her tone restrained. 'Martin, I was in love with you. I'm still in love with you. I don't think my feelings for you will ever change.'

'Since when?'

'Since when do I love you?'

'Since when do you sleep with men for money?'

Lena was shaking her head, her eyes now fixed on a clump of brown leaves floating next to the shore.

'Martin, do you know when I fell for you, when I first realised that one day you would hurt me?'

'When we met in Propaganda and I whispered those lines from Pushkin in your ear?'

'No, Martin. It wasn't Pushkin. It was when I saw you the next day, when I caught you playing with plastic bricks in Dyetsky Mir. The night we met I thought you were interesting, but not dangerous. But the next day, when I saw you in the toyshop playing with those bricks, so lost, like a child, I knew instantly that you had me, and that sooner or later you would cause me pain.'

We remained in silence, staring at the pond. I didn't know what to say.

'Lena, you are a prostitute.'

'I am not a prostitute. Sometimes, when I need money, I sleep with men. But it's not my job.' She turned to me, shrugged her shoulders.

'You could work in a restaurant, like you did before.'

'That's not real money. You get nothing as a waitress in Moscow. I want to leave Russia, live abroad. I'm thinking about moving to London. How can I save enough if I earn five hundred dollars a month?'

'But Lena, there are many ways of earning money. You don't need to do this.'

'I do it for my own future. What difference does it make to you? You never wanted me. I will always love you, Martin, but you never took me seriously. Besides, this is not for ever. I just want to save enough money to start a new life. I'm not doing any harm to anyone.'

'You are harming yourself,' I said.

She looked at me, shaking her head again. 'But, Martin, you sleep with plenty of women.'

'It's not the same,' I said. 'I don't do it for money.'

'You sleep with girls you're not in love with. Your sleeping around is no better than my sleeping around. It just happens that I need money and you don't.'

'It's more complicated than that,' I said.

'It's not. It's simple. You go to a club, pick up a girl and sleep with her. I go to a club, pick up a guy and sleep with him. We are the same, you and me. The only difference is that he might give me some cash, but that's a very small difference. The rest of the night is the same for you and for me.'

'It's not the same.'

'Would I be a better person in your eyes if I slept with many guys just like that, for the sake of it?'

'I don't know,' I said. 'Yes.'

'I don't think so. At least I have a reason. I want to leave Russia, start a new life. Here I have no future. But, you, Martin, why do you do it? Why do you go around sleeping with women?'

I said nothing.

The kids by the pond ran out of bread. The ducks lost interest and swam away.

'I didn't sleep with anyone when we were together,' Lena said. 'I was so stupid. I thought you were serious about me. It was you who slept with other women.'

I didn't know what Lena wanted to hear. I moved closer and took her hand.

Her eyes were fixed on the pond. 'My friend who moved to London,' she said after a few seconds, 'she is dancing in a club. It's very well paid. She asked her boss if I could work with her. I can move in a few weeks and stay in her flat while I save enough to rent my own place.'

'A strip club? Is that what you want to do?'

'What I want is to leave Moscow. I'll dance in a club if that's what it takes, until I get something else. It's a great opportunity. My friend is treated with respect. It's very civilised over there, not like Russia. Being a dancer in London is like a normal job. Customers don't even touch you. All I'll have to do is dance and show my tits. And I can earn a few hundred dollars a night.'

'Pounds.'

'Money.'

I put my arm around her. She leaned her head on my shoulder. For a couple of minutes, we sat in silence.

'Remember when you took me to the Chinese tearoom?' I said. 'The small underground place in Kitay-gorod.'

'Of course. The day after we met.'

'We were lying there among the cushions for hours, just drinking tea and listening to sitar music. It was dark.'

'I remember,' she said.

'You told me there's no place in the world like Moscow, that Moscow has a special energy. You were right, Lena. Moscow *is* the best place on Earth. Why would you want to leave? Believe me, compared to Moscow, London is a dead city. Moscow is alive, changing fast, full of opportunities.'

'Not for me,' she said. 'You like Moscow because you are an expat and you know you'll leave one day. For you, this is nothing but a fun phase in your life. For people like me, there is no future in this city. I've had enough of it. There is nothing, no one, holding me back.'

She stared at the water. 'You Westerners are so full of prejudices,' she said, 'so hypocritical. You all go around saying you're so open-minded and tolerant but then you can't accept other people's choices when they don't follow your own views of the world.'

'If you stayed in Moscow,' I said, 'you could finish your

degree. Become a teacher, or find a well-paid job in a Western firm.'

'Martin, I can't even meet a decent man in Moscow. There are too many beautiful women around. Here I'm just an average girl. Like when we met. Why would you want to be with me when there are so many beautiful girls you can be with?'

'Lena, you are very beautiful.'

'Not enough. In Moscow men don't appreciate women. There are too many of us.'

'There are plenty of women in London as well.'

'Western women are fat and ugly,' she said. 'That's why Western men love Russian girls. I'm sure I can find a man in London who'll take good care of me. I don't plan to be a dancer for ever.'

A young man passed by, pushing a boy on a bicycle. I wanted to tell Lena about Tatyana and the baby. About the joy of starting afresh. Get it off my chest, show her that my life had changed and I was now a better man.

But when I looked at her, Lena was crying.

I said nothing.

She stood up, pulled her skirt down, readjusted her jacket.

We started to walk slowly out of the square, in silence, towards Mayakovskaya. When we reached the entrance of the metro I put my arms around her, pulled her body with all my strength against my chest. We hugged in silence for two or three minutes. People pushed past around us. I felt her tears on my neck.

'Lena, you won't be happier if you leave Moscow.'

'You don't understand,' she said, smiling, wiping her tears with her hand. 'There is so much more to life than being happy.'

I tried to kiss her but she had turned away.

The last time I ever saw her she was walking down the stairs, swallowed by the metro, lost among the crowd.

62

IN NOVELS, CHARACTERS ARE often presented with a critical dilemma, the resolution of which will tell us something about their moral composition. These dilemmas – and the choices the characters make – constitute pivotal moments in literature. Pushkin's Tatyana decides to stick with her husband. Tolstoy's Karenina decides not to. Dostoyevsky's Raskolnikov decides to murder the old pawnbroker. Turgenev's Liza decides to link her fate to that of Lavretsky.

These characters are given a clear choice, act upon it, live with the consequences. Yet, to exploit their full dramatic potential, life-shattering choices in literature must be relevant, visibly so – and the transcendental nature of the ensuing consequences must be recognisable.

In real life, things don't work like that.

*

That morning I could have bought a pair of tickets for a play at the MKhAT, or perhaps the Stanislavsky, or any of the theatres scattered across central Moscow. Or, maybe, after finishing my sandwich and coffee in Kamergersky, I could have returned home by a different street – through Bolshaya Dmitrovka, as was my habit. Or even, after I'd passed the ticket kiosk and thought about treating Tatyana to a musical, I could have bought tickets for another day – say Thursday, instead of Wednesday. Thing is, these were all random, unimportant decisions. Choices that involved no moral considerations.

'Two tickets for Wednesday's show,' I say. 'Centre stalls, please.'

The front and sides of the kiosk are completely covered with posters and calendars, Sellotaped to the inside of the glass. Through a tiny front window, a young man whose face I don't see grabs the money and hands me the pair of tickets. I walk home, thinking about Tatyana's smile when she finds the tickets on the kitchen table. In my head she's thanking me, kissing me, and I can visualise the entire night out – Tatyana spends time in the bathroom doing her make-up, then slips into a fancy tight dress, perhaps her black one with tiny faux-diamonds around the neck. We take a cab on Tverskaya, cross the city southwards. Her high heels sink into the theatre's soft carpet. She says something about the wonderful seats we have, so close to the stage. Then she sits upright, concentrating on the musical, her curls tied up in a loose knot, or perhaps dangling over her shoulders, her perfume mixing with that of the other women in the audience.

We enjoy the songs and the dancing and the joyful atmosphere. Then we take a cab home.

I think often about that cab we never took, the ride home that was not meant to be. That's the thing with real life. Unlike literary characters, our future is mostly shaped by small, trivial choices – seemingly insignificant, but deceptively fateful.

63

'I SWEAR TO GOD, WE desire death more than you want life.'

The handsome bearded man was sitting on the floor, his legs crossed, wearing a black winter jacket and a black beanie. He stared into the camera. 'We've come to Russia's capital to stop the war, or to die in the name of God.' His voice was serene. His dark complexion and Caucasian accent called to mind a Moscow taxi driver. The TV titles said he was the leader.

By now, the siege had been ongoing for almost a full day. The live broadcast from outside the theatre, which had begun around midnight, had been showing military trucks arriving at the scene and Russian soldiers sealing off the perimeter. It was a grey October day and you could see the frozen rain dashing across the screen, falling on the police vans and the ambulances.

The entire world was now following the stream of news from Moscow. It was known that the night before, a group of armed Chechen militants had stormed the Dubrovka theatre, interrupting the performance of *Nord Ost*, a popular musical. About nine hundred people, staff, cast and audience, were being held hostage. Mixed into the live coverage, footage relating to previous tragedies flashed up on the screen – the hospital hostages in Budyonnovsk, the bombed buildings in Pechatniki, the explosion in Pushkinskaya.

Then a new clip: this time the bearded man was clad in military fatigues. He sat on a stool inside the theatre, surrounded by armed men and women with their faces covered. 'Either the president orders the immediate retreat of Russian troops from Chechnya,' he said, 'or the theatre will be blown up with all the hostages inside.'

I often wonder what would have been my first reaction to the news had I seen it live on TV, from my couch. Surely I would have been disturbed by the scale of the drama, by the thought of the impending tragedy. Sooner or later, though, I would no doubt have switched channels, turned off the TV, put my mind elsewhere.

But these images I only saw later, after everything was over. While the bearded man appeared on screen for the first time, Tatyana and I were inside the theatre, sitting in the stalls, eleventh row, guarded by a group of women in black hijabs wearing belts of explosives strapped to their bodies.

I have a blurred recollection of those first hours. When I look back, I see a succession of images that never follow the same order, as if they were stored in different and remote corners of my mind and could only be gathered with great effort. Besides, the memories of those eternal hours have melted into the nightmares of the nights that followed. The masked men wore military fatigues, but I never saw their faces – not in my memories, not on the screen. Never in my dreams.

I do recall the moment when the armed men first walked onto the stage, shouting, shoving the actors around. Perhaps I remember this with clarity because for a few seconds I thought it was all part of the show – and so, those seconds ended up being the last before my world shifted. Then I saw the terror on the faces of the child actors who had just been singing onstage and were now being herded towards the stalls.

Tatyana kept grabbing her belly. She was breathing rapidly. I held her hand and whispered into her ear. For a short while, she seemed to calm down. But halfway through the first night, something snapped inside her and she began to mutter hysterically, about missing work, how she had an appointment in the morning to show an apartment in the centre. 'I hope we get out before eight,' she said, her eyes staring straight past me into the red velvet seats.

The women in hijabs were ranged along the side aisles, facing the audience, holding their pistols up. Most hostages were calm, as though ready to endure whatever came their way. The orchestra pit was used as a toilet. People took turns, and a silent queue formed along the first row. Two rows in front of us, an old man spent hours clutching an immense bouquet of flowers, as if expecting the show to resume so that he could hand it to one of the actors during the final curtain call. The scene reminded me of the times when the metro stops abruptly for no reason and passengers, trapped underground, remain serious and composed, waiting for movement to resume; except that, inside the besieged theatre, everybody looked ridiculous and out of place, especially the older women in their formal dresses and complicated hairdos – their best perfume mixing with the stench of shit and piss that wafted from the orchestra pit.

Then came the long hours in which I was neither asleep nor awake. My mind was caught in a feverish state of expectation, drifting in and out of uneasy dreams – every little sound triggered a violent reaction in my head, bringing me back to the reality of the theatre. At some point I heard a muffled shot coming from the direction of the lobby. It's starting now, someone mumbled, but then everything went quiet again. Tatyana slept for hours, or at least lay down in silence, her head on my lap.

It's only when you meet the possibility of your own death that you fully comprehend the banality of the mental processes that kept you going for so long. Suddenly, I could no longer see the horizon and, as a hungry hole of nothingness swelled ahead of me, I couldn't help but think about the fragility of our existence. In the face of extinction, simply being alive became, in itself, meaningful.

You were wrong: I wanted life more than you desired death.

Then, on Friday night, after two days of angst and exhaustion, I woke up gasping for air – my heart racing, the red velvet seats spinning endlessly. My eyelids felt heavy. For a split second I saw Tatyana stretched on the floor, among the rows of seats, her head turned away. Before I could reach out my hand to touch her, an irresistible force sucked at my consciousness and dragged me back down into a pool of blackness.

When I woke again I was a different person. Paralysed by a blinding headache, I squinted around, disoriented, searching for Tatyana. It took me a few moments to realise that I was no longer in the theatre. Two men in white gowns were standing nearby, their eyes fixed on a small TV that hung on the wall. A hospital room, I realised, and, before I was able to speak, I was told we were celebrating. The news coverage had just announced that all nine hundred hostages had been freed, unharmed. All the terrorists had been killed. In preparation for their assault, the Russian special forces had pumped a powerful sleeping gas into the theatre, knocking everybody out. A seamless operation, we were told. Now, on the TV screen in my hospital room, I saw family members celebrating outside the Dubrovka theatre, as messages flew in from around the world to congratulate the Russian leadership on their success. The grainy images on the screen showed the armed men and the women in black hijabs scattered among the theatre seats and on the carpeted floors. Their eyes and mouths were wide open, their foreheads adorned with perfect bullet holes.

64

SADNESS. MELANCHOLY. LONGING. Depression. The Russian word toska is rich in meaning. In his annotated translation of *Evgeny Onegin*, Nabokov warns us that 'no single English word renders all the shades of toska'.

'At its deepest and most painful,' Vladimir Vladimirovich writes, 'it is a sensation of great spiritual anguish, often without any specific cause. At less morbid levels it is a dull ache of the soul, a longing with nothing to long for, a sick pining, a vague restlessness, mental throes, yearning . . .'

Recently I've been thinking about toska. About the way our brain detaches itself from whatever is out there, and glides towards a permanent state of longing. I've been thinking that our feelings of euphoria, accomplishment, satisfaction – they are all transient sensations, ephemeral states of mind. The only lasting human feeling is toska, the 'dull ache of the soul'.

Even tragic events that cause unbearable pain become, with time, nothing more than sad memories. Because time goes on, eroding both our joy and our suffering, mercilessly and relentlessly depriving us of the cause of our anguish. Things that we believe serious, meaningful, very important, there will come a time when they will be forgotten or will seem unimportant.

65

I LEFT RUSSIA AT THE end of 2002. Back in Europe I surrounded myself with new friends, started the process of putting those years behind me. Yet hardly a day passes when I do not think about my time in Moscow.

I think about Lena, of course – but also about Polina and Yulya and Vika, and the others who lay on my couch. The fleeting moments of shared intimacy, which back then I chased so eagerly, are becoming little more than an amalgam of broken thoughts in my head.

I close my eyes and I see the snow settling gently on the rooftops of Moscow. I remember how, on winter nights when the brothers came to my place, we made a heap of snow on the balcony to chill bottles of beer and vodka. Then I see the snow melt, and spring and summer and autumn fall over the city with all the fullness and perfection of the seasons in a children's book.

When I think about Tatyana I often picture our first night, after dinner in Café Maki. She's standing beneath Pushkin's statue, before we kissed for the first time. It's dark and her eyes are gleaming, full of hope but, at least in my memory, also coloured by a tinge of sadness. As if she already knew.

Then I think about that other life, the life I would be living if Tatyana and I had not gone to the theatre on the night of 23 October 2002. That life advances in its own parallel universe, unlived by me, not meant to be – dissolved in the hours that followed the rescue operation, as it became clear that some hostages would never wake up, that they had been killed by the gas pumped into the theatre. Eager to preserve military secrecy, the special forces refused to reveal the composition of the gas; doctors at the scene, not knowing what they were treating, were unable to help. Today, a memorial plaque on the wall of the theatre bears a hundred and thirty names.

66

IN METRO SYSTEMS AROUND the world, a screen above the platform shows the time left until the arrival of the next train. Five minutes. Four minutes. Three minutes. Two minutes. One minute. Then the countdown stops and you feel the breeze and you hear the rattling of a new train approaching through the tunnel.

Not in Moscow.

In Moscow's metro, the electronic counter above the platform shows the time that has passed since the departure of the last train. With unnecessary precision, the seconds keep adding up, one by one, informing you not about the train to come, but about the one you've missed, the train that would be carrying you, if only you had arrived earlier. But that train is for ever gone. You don't know when the next one will arrive.

A NOTE ABOUT THE AUTHOR

Guillermo Erades was born in Málaga, Spain, and has
lived in Leeds, Amsterdam, Luxembourg, Moscow,
Berlin, Baghdad, and Brussels, where he is currently
based. *Back to Moscow* is his first novel.